"Are you sure you should be leaving your bed?" Portia asked. "The wound has closed over but you still have a lump on your forehead."

With a swift motion, Frederick had captured her wrist in a light grip. "Is it bad enough to tempt you to kiss it better?"

Portia sternly told herself to move away. His touch was light enough that she could easily break his hold. But it was sending tongues of flames up her arm and over her shivering skin.

"Certainly not," she breathed, her voice oddly husky.

"Even if I tell you that it still aches like the very devil?"

"Perhaps I should call for the doctor."

"I would prefer a kiss."

The flames spread to curl in the secret depths of her stomach. Oh, yes. A kiss. A simple, delicious kiss.

It was what she had desired from the moment she had walked into the room and saw him lying on the bed like some fallen angel. He gave a light tug on her wrist, steadily pulling her closer to his sinfully tempting lips. Then, before she could pull back, his hands had shifted to capture her face, his lips softening as they swept over hers with slow, drugging kisses.

Sweet, blissful heat flowed through her body as she instinctively parted her lips and allowed his tongue to explore ever deeper. Oh . . . God. Nothing in all her six and twenty years had ever felt like this . . .

Books by Deborah Raleigh

SOME LIKE IT WICKED

SOME LIKE IT SINFUL

SOME LIKE IT BRAZEN

BEDDING THE BARON

Published by Kensington Publishing Corporation

Bedding The Baron

DEBORAH RALEIGH

ZEBRA BOOKS
Kensington Publishing Corp.
www.kensingtonbooks.com

ZEBRA BOOKS are published by

Kensington Publishing Corp.
850 Third Avenue
New York, NY 10022

All Kensington titles, imprints, and distributed lines are available at special quantity discounts for bulk purchases for sales promotion, premiums, fund-raising, educational, or institutional use.

Special book excerpts or customized printings can also be created to fit specific needs. For details, write or phone the office of the Kensington Special Sales Manager: Attn. Special Sales Department. Kensington Publishing Corp., 850 Third Avenue, New York, NY 10022. Phone: 1-800-221-2647.

Zebra and the Z logo Reg. U.S. Pat. & TM Off.

ISBN-13: 978-0-8217-8044-2
ISBN-10: 0-8217-8044-1

First Printing: March 2008
10 9 8 7 6 5 4 3 2 1

Printed in the United States of America

Chapter One

The townhouse tucked in Lombard Street was a perfectly respectable brick structure, with a perfectly respectable garden, in a perfectly respectable neighborhood.

It was remarkable only for the fact that it managed to meld so easily into its surroundings as to be nearly invisible.

The owner, Mr. Dunnington, was equally successful in blending into his surroundings.

Even his most intimate acquaintances would admit they knew little of the gentleman. Nothing beyond the fact that he had once been a tutor who had come into a small inheritance and after buying the townhouse had converted it into an exclusive school for boys of superior, if not precisely legitimate, birth.

Bastards, some would call them, but with enough money from their fathers to ensure that they received a proper education and the ability to establish decent careers.

Beyond his obvious skill at teaching, Mr. Dunnington, however, remained an intriguing mystery.

Of course, there was no one who could have suspected just how mysterious he would prove to be.
Certainly not the three gentlemen currently seated in
the library of the townhouse.

At a glance, the gentlemen held little in common.
Well, nothing beyond the fact that all three were the
sort to cause a riot among the most fastidious of women.

Raoul Charlebois leaned negligently against the
mahogany desk and was perhaps the most captivating
of the three.

It was more than his pale, golden beauty or the perfection of his lean body. There was simply something
in the grace of his movements and the compelling
emotions that played over his classic features with a
mesmerizing ease. There was no surprise that he was
currently London's most celebrated actor.

Ian Breckford, in contrast, was a dark, smoldering
gentleman who managed to succeed in everything he
attempted. He was the best swordsman, he held the
fastest record of traveling from Dover to London on
horseback, he had made a fortune at the gambling
tables, and women throughout London referred to
him as Casanova.

He was a genuine hedonist who was admired and
envied by every gentleman in London.

Fredrick Smith was neither as fair as Raoul, nor as
dark as Ian. His hair was a pale honey with an annoying tendency to curl over his ears and at the nape of
his neck. His features were delicately carved and had
been the bane of his existence when he had been a
lad. What boy wanted to look like a cherubic angel?
Thankfully, age had managed to add a layer of unmistakable masculinity to the wide brow, the angular
cheekbones, and the thin line of nose. Nothing, how-

ever, could alter the eyes that were an odd grey that could shift from silver to the deepest charcoal depending upon his mood.

His body was also thinner, although he spent enough time in his workshops to develop the sort of hard muscles that were nicely displayed by the current fashion of skintight breeches and tailored jackets.

Not that he entirely approved of all the latest styles, he wryly acknowledged. There was nothing pleasant about the black slippers that he had hastily purchased for the funeral. They not only pinched his toes, but he feared the laces were beginning to cut off the bloodstream to his feet. Had he known that this appointment was going to take the better part of the day, he would have worn his comfortable boots.

It had been nearly an hour since the small, annoyingly fussy solicitor had excused himself from the room, but the shocked silence remained as thick as the moment the will had been read.

Seated near the crackling fire that battled the late January chill, Fredrick sipped on the fine brandy that he had possessed the foresight to bring.

He had expected the day to be difficult. Mr. Dunnington had been more than a teacher to him and his two companions. He had been a father, a mentor, and the cornerstone of their lives. Even after they had left this townhouse to seek their fortunes in the world, they had never lost contact with the man who had given them something none of them had ever expected to discover.

A family.

A rare and precious commodity for a bastard.

To know that he had gone from this world forever

left a gaping wound in Fredrick's heart that would not soon heal.

There was a loud pop from the fireplace as one of the logs shifted. It was enough to jerk the three gentlemen from their broodings and with a muffled oath Raoul rose to his feet and paced toward the bow window.

"I'll be damned," he muttered.

"That seems to sum it up nicely," Fredrick said dryly.

Ian made a sound deep in his throat. "The old man was always a bit batty and we all thought he must harbor some mystery in his past, but this . . ." He gave a shake of his head, the handsome face for once devoid of its wicked smile. "Bloody hell."

Raoul leaned against the frame of the window and folded his arms over his chest. His movements were not the smooth, almost profound movements he usually employed. Raoul Charlebois was an actor who considered the whole world his stage. It was only when he was with Fredrick and Ian that he allowed himself to lower his guard.

"It does all seem highly unlikely."

"Unlikely? It is a great deal more than that." Ian surged to his feet, a restless energy crackling around his lean body. "It is one thing to possess a hidden lover or even an addiction to the gaming hells. Good God, even an occasional trip to the opium dens would have been less shocking. Who the devil could have suspected he was a brilliant extortionist?"

Fredrick remained seated, his mind methodically working through the stunning revelations that had shaken all of them. When they had been requested to attend the meeting with Dunnington's solicitor, they had all presumed that the old man had left them some small memento, a reminder of the past they had shared. Certainly none of them expected to be told that they were each to receive a legacy of twenty thousand pounds. Or that the money they were each to receive had been bilked from their respective fathers over the course of near twenty years.

Absently, he reached beneath his jacket and pulled out a small notebook and nub of pencil he always kept handy. He was a man who understood that any problem could be solved once it was sorted into manageable details. No doubt it was the result of his career as an engineer.

Or perhaps he became an engineer because he possessed an obsession with details. Fate was a strange thing.

And getting stranger by the moment, he ruefully acknowledged as he began to jot down notes.

Across the room, Ian paced to pour himself a glass of Fredrick's brandy. "What I want to know is how? It is one thing to manage to learn of a scandal. Hell, I do not doubt that I could be blackmailed under the right circumstances. But to have extorted each of our fathers out of twenty thousand pounds . . . Christ, it is nothing short of remarkable."

Raoul narrowed his gaze as he brooded on his friend's words. "True enough. Not that our dear, beloved fathers led blameless lives. We three are proof of that. Still, what sort of dark sin would they be willing to pay such a sum to keep hidden?"

"They must be sins worthy of the devil." Ian gave a short, bitter laugh. "Hell, it almost makes me hopeful. I assumed that my father must have been forced at gunpoint to actually impregnate my mother, the cold bastard. Now I discover he has another sin or two up his sleeve. Perhaps he is mortal after all."

"I think you have something there," Fredrick murmured, scratching on his pad. "Whatever secrets our fathers are hiding must be of great importance. At least to them."

"What the blazes are you doing, Fredrick?" Without warning Ian was across the room and standing next to Fredrick's chair. "Making one of your damnable lists?"

Fredrick shrugged. "It always helps me to sort things out to see them written in logical order."

"Let me see." Ian plucked the notebook from his hands.

Raoul stepped forward, his handsome features hardening with a flare of annoyance. "Ian . . ."

"Let it be, Raoul," Fredrick said softly. He understood Ian. Behind his sardonic wit and restless need to forever be proving himself, he was a gentleman who felt deeply. The death of Dunnington, followed by this disturbing legacy, had left him unsettled, and battling the desire to strike out.

"Item one," Ian read from Fredrick's notebook. "Dunnington leaves a legacy of twenty thousand pounds to three of his students. Why only three?"

"*Mon Dieu.*" Raoul sucked in a sharp breath, his eyes narrowing as he studied Fredrick. "As usual, you have managed to hit on the pertinent point, Fredrick. Dunnington must have had twenty or more boys here over the years. Why would he choose us three?"

Fredrick reached for his brandy and took a sip. "We were the first three he brought in. Maybe it was no random coincidence," he said slowly. "Perhaps Dunnington already had the information on our fathers before opening the school and when it came time to acquire his first pupils, where better to search than three powerful gentlemen who were clearly willing to go to any length to keep their secrets?"

Ian gave a lift of his brows. "So you suggest that Dunnington had managed to stumble across some intriguing information and he used that to fund his school for bastards?"

"Yes," Fredrick agreed.

Ian mulled the notion for a moment. "Do you know . . . I think it more likely that he started the school *because* of us. He was a sentimental old fool. It would be just like him to have caught sight of us or even just heard about us when he was a tutor at the various households. If he became determined to help us in some way, he could have set about discovering information about our fathers. After he had us settled, it would have been a natural thing to continue his efforts to assist other boys in need."

There was a short silence before Raoul at last gave a low chuckle. "Egad, Ian. Did you actually make use of the organ located in your skull rather than your breeches?"

Ian smiled with dry humor. "Not nearly as rewarding, I fear."

Fredrick smiled at the affable teasing. The three men were closer than brothers could ever be. They had more than the ties of blood, after all. They had the shared shame and burden of knowing they were unwanted. Not only by their families, but by society who considered them as outcasts.

Their lives would be a constant struggle to make a place for themselves in the world. Thank God they had each other.

"I think it is a reasonable hypothesis." Fredrick

reached to reclaim his notebook. "Let us say that Dunnington decided he wished to help us and managed to uncover the sort of information a gentleman would not wish bandied about."

Raoul nodded. "Not a difficult task for a tutor. They are in an odd position within the household. Not precisely servants, and yet, not a member of the family. They seem to disappear between the upper and lower stairs. It would be a simple matter for them to overhear any number of conversations, or to catch sight of clandestine meetings."

Ian returned to his quick, impatient pacing. "Well, whatever information he managed to uncover it had to be more serious than possessing a bastard. None of us were actually denied by our fathers."

"Just unwanted," Fredrick muttered.

"Hear, hear," Ian muttered, lifting his glass in a mocking toast.

"Unwanted by our fathers, perhaps, but Dunnington appears to have wanted us. Quite desperately," Raoul murmured, his perfect features softening as he recalled the man who had altered all of their lives. "After all, he could have walked away with sixty thousand pounds and lived a life of considerable luxury if he wanted."

Fredrick smiled as he recalled the image of the thin, somber gentleman who was always tidily attired with his hair carefully combed to hide the encroaching baldness. At a glance he appeared the sort of staid fusspot that young boys detested. Beneath his stoic demeanor, however, he possessed an extraordinary intelligence and a rare ability to inspire the most reluctant student. Even young Fredrick, who had been a shy lad with the tendency to retreat from others.

It had been Dunnington who had recognized Fredrick's gift for anything mechanical. Indeed, he spent a small fortune on providing Fredrick with a variety of materials so that the young boy could build and tinker to his heart's content. The long-suffering man had even occasionally attempted to make use of the strange (and by and large useless) inventions, including a water clock that had leaked so often that it had ruined the floorboards.

"I am not certain that Dunnington could ever have been satisfied unless he was educating some reluctant lad. He devoted his life to teaching," Fredrick said. "However, I do not doubt he was happier to be in charge of his own school as opposed to being at the whim of an employer."

Ian halted at the fireplace and stared down at the flames with a brooding expression. "More the fool him. He should have taken the money and devoted his days to debauching his way through society."

"Not all of us consider debauching a rewarding career," Fredrick pointed out.

"Certainly not you." Ian turned to regard Fredrick with a narrowed gaze. "How you can bear to spend your days in that cramped workroom with all those bits and pieces of machinery . . . it is enough to give a gentleman the hives."

Fredrick smiled. His workroom was no longer cramped. Indeed, he now owned several large buildings throughout London and employed near fifty people. Not bad for a gentleman who had started with nothing more than dreams.

"Those bits and pieces have made me a tidy fortune."

"Bah." Ian turned his attention toward the silent

Raoul. "At least Charlebois understands the pleasures to be found in debauchery. Eh, old friend?"

Raoul shrugged, as usual far more reserved about discussing the women who warmed his bed. Odd considering most actors conducted their affairs with the same flamboyance as they lived their lives.

"It does offer its share of amusement," Raoul murmured. "Although I must confess that anything can become tedious over time."

Ian gave a lift of his brows. "Ah. Then the rumors must be true that you have ended your torrid affair with the beautiful Mirabelle."

"All affairs must end."

"Of course they must," Ian readily agreed. "Variety, as they say, is the spice of life."

Fredrick gave a shake of his head. He was not a prude, but he had never understood his friends' incessant need to be forever seducing women. He had enjoyed discreet affairs, of course. And he had always chosen women who possessed intelligence and charm and could offer more than just a quick tumble. But on the whole he had preferred to concentrate on building his business. Deep within, he had always known that *she* was out there. That one special woman who would alter his life forever.

Romantic drivel, Ian would call it. Fredrick, however, had never doubted her existence.

"Variety may be the spice of life, but it is also the source of any number of nasty maladies," he muttered.

Ian gave a short laugh. "Good God, I despair of you, Fredrick, I truly do."

Fredrick smiled, not at all offended. Ian was forever chiding him for his dull dreams and lack of stylish dash. But his teasing was always born of affection. Dear God, how different it would have been for Fredrick had he been left in the care of his foster mother and forced to attend a traditional school (always assuming the woman would have allowed him to attend school at all). His shy nature and odd fascinations would certainly have been the source of malicious mocking, if not downright brutality. Dunnington had truly saved his life when he had brought him to this small townhouse.

"Because I do not keep a harem of women at my disposal?" he asked softly.

"Because you were born to be shackled to some harridan who will run roughshod over you until you are badgered into the grave," Ian retorted.

"No, Ian." Raoul regarded Fredrick with a shrewd, piercing gaze. Fredrick found himself resisting the urge to squirm beneath that steady regard. Raoul had an uncanny knack of seeing far beneath the surface of a person. Almost as if he could read their very soul. It was no doubt what made him such a good actor. "Our Fredrick is destined for quite another fate."

"And what is that?" Ian demanded.

"Fredrick happens to be one of those rare and fortunate gentlemen who are destined for true love."

"Bah. It still includes a wife and a pack of squawking brats, poor blighter," Ian groused.

Fredrick rose to his feet, not nearly so flippant about discussing the future as his friends. He was superstitious enough to leave fate (or whatever one wanted to call it) well enough alone.

"As fascinating as I find your profound predictions, I believe we would be better served to devote our attention to our more pressing matter," he said firmly.

Raoul reached out to give Fredrick's shoulder a

brief squeeze, as if sympathizing with Fredrick's reluctance to discuss his very private dreams.

"No doubt you are right, old friend, but at the moment all we are doing is speculating with no real means of knowing the actual truth. Dunnington might or might not have extorted our respective fathers to rescue us and begin this school. There is simply no way of knowing for certain."

Ian grimaced. "Dunnington managed to take his secrets to the grave."

Fredrick paused as he was struck by a sudden thought. "Yes, odd that."

"What?" Ian demanded.

It was Fredrick's turn to do a bit of pacing. "Why did he not reveal the truth when we reached our majority?" he demanded. "God knows we could each have used such a fortune at that time."

They exchanged knowing glances as they recalled the lean years when each of them had been forced to struggle to carve a place in a world that was determined to offer them nothing.

"Holy hell," Ian rasped. "When I think of the years I spent dodging the collectors and living in flea ridden rooms . . ."

"Oh, come, you know Dunnington," Raoul drawled. "He would have told you that a man's character is formed by his suffering, not by his successes. He wanted us to learn to survive by our wits. It is what he preached on a daily basis."

Ian's expression revealed precisely what he thought of such a philosophy, but Fredrick was more concerned with what must have been going through Dunnington's mind.

"That is no doubt part of the reason," he agreed.

"Dunnington did possess a strange obsession with teaching a man to stand on his own two feet. Still, I think . . ."

Silence descended in the room as Fredrick struggled to put his thoughts into words.

"Well, do not leave us in suspense, Fredrick," Ian at last prompted.

Fredrick gave a lift of his hands. "Just consider the fact that if Dunnington had given us our legacies, he would have been forced to explain how he came by them."

"You are off the mark if you believe that Dunnington would have been too ashamed to confess the truth of his . . . unique methods of gaining the necessary capital to begin this school," Raoul swiftly countered. "For all his fanciful notions of teaching, he was at heart a practical man who would take full responsibility for his choices."

"Yes, I agree with you," Fredrick said. "I was thinking more along the lines of protecting us."

Ian frowned. "Protect us? From what?"

Fredrick moved to stare out the window. There was nothing much to see on the quiet street. A maid shivering against the frigid breeze as she polished the doorknob across the way, a coal wagon clattering over the rough cobblestone road, a young boy and his nanny taking a walk through the garden. It was all quite commonplace, something to be seen out the window of a hundred homes in London.

But this view would always be special, Fredrick acknowledged as a fresh wave of pain rolled through him. It was special because this was home.

"If Dunnington were still alive we would not rest

until we had forced him to tell us the truth of what secrets he learned of our fathers."

"Bloody right." Ian refilled his glass with brandy. "We have the right to know what nasty sins our fathers have been committing."

"Perhaps we have the right, but maybe not the will," Raoul said softly. "Is that what you are implying, Fredrick?"

"Yes."

Ian gave a loud snort. "In English, please."

Raoul absently reached to pluck the brandy from Ian's hand. The actor had just celebrated his thirtieth birthday, which made him a year older than Ian and two years older than Fredrick. He took his role of the elder brother quite seriously.

"Dunnington would realize that we would have instinctively demanded that he tell us the sordid secrets that he kept. Curiosity is human nature, after all. But he might have felt that the past was better left undisturbed."

"If he felt that way, then why reveal where the money came from to begin with?" Fredrick muttered. "There was no need to reveal that our fathers were ever involved."

Raoul heaved a deep sigh. "Because it gave us the option of deciding whether we desired the truth badly enough to go in search of it."

"Yes." Fredrick shoved his fingers through his hair. Gads, but he was tired. He had been in Portsmouth when he had received word of Dunnington's death, and he had traveled without halt to arrive in time for the funeral. Since then he had been overwhelmed with one endless task after another. When this was all said and done he intended to reacquaint himself with his very large, very comfortable bed. "It is one thing to simply be told of the past, and quite another to have to go to the effort of returning to our families and seeking it."

"Dunnington has ensured that the truth comes with a price," Raoul whispered softly.

Ian firmly took back his glass of brandy and downed it in one swallow. "What you are saying is that he has left us holding Pandora's Box."

Pandora's Box. Yes, that was a perfect description, Fredrick acknowledged.

The sensible choice would, of course, be to keep the lid firmly closed. After all, none of them had any true relationship with their fathers. And certainly whatever secrets their fathers might be harboring could have nothing to do with them.

More importantly, they had each forged lives that gave them satisfaction in their own way. Only a fool would risk such fragile peace to stir up the past.

A silence descended that was broken only by the crackle of the burning logs as the three gentlemen became lost in their own thoughts. At last Raoul gave a sharp shake of his head.

"It would appear that if we had any sense at all we would take our money, invest it wisely, and forget where it came from."

Ian gave a short laugh. "And when have we ever been wise?"

Fredrick had to admit his friend did have a point. Raoul devoted his life to playing roles upon the stage. Ian lived by the fickle fate of Lady Luck. And even Fredrick took enormous risks with each new patent he invested in.

"I do not suppose it is possible for any of us to know

that there is some secret out there and not try to get to the bottom of it," Fredrick admitted with a resigned sigh. "It is like having a splinter stuck in your finger that you try to ignore. Eventually you have to pluck it out or it becomes infected."

"An unpleasant, if apt description." Raoul gave a short, bitter laugh. "*Mon Dieu,* we are idiots."

"And it would seem that Dunnington has at last had his final revenge for all those frogs we hid in his bed," Fredrick said wryly.

Ian held up his empty glass. "To Dunnington, damn his soul."

Fredrick and Raoul exchanged a wry glance. "To Dunnington," they agreed in unison.

Chapter Two

The violent spring storm hit without warning. One moment Fredrick was tooling his handsome cabriolet through the narrow country lanes, and the next the leaden skies had unleashed a torrent of rain that had him drenched to the bone. Even more aggravating, it turned the road to a muddy bog that threatened the footing of his matching greys.

Cursing the unpredictable weather as well as his own stupidity in ever leaving the comfort of his townhouse, Fredrick slowed his brisk pace to a mere crawl.

It had been years since he had traveled through this God-forsaken countryside, but he dimly recalled a coaching inn not too far in the distance.

When he left London, he had hoped to make it as far as Winchester before settling for the night, but he was not about to risk his horses on the treacherous path. Besides which, he already felt like a drowned rat. The sooner he had any sort of roof over his head the better.

Fredrick shivered as he was hit by a gust of chilled air. Dash it all, he had known that this was a bad notion before he ever left London. Why else would he have found a dozen insignificant reasons to postpone his search for his father's secret?

He was content with his life. He had his career, wonderful friends, and the financial security to live in elegant comfort.

Surely only a fool would deliberately dredge up painful childhood memories simply to discover some deep, dark secret in his father's past?

Oh yes, he was an addle-brained idiot. But a part of him had known the moment he learned of his inheritance that he would have to return to the past. The strange and bizarre legacy held the one thing he could never, ever resist.

A puzzle.

For better or worse (no doubt worse), he was plagued with an obsession to discover the answer to any riddle. It did not matter if it were the inner workings of a steam powered engine or the disappearance of his favorite stick pin, he had to satisfy his insatiable curiosity.

And so here he was, soaked through and through, endangering the beautiful greys that he had purchased from Tattersall's for an enormous sum only last week, and searching for a tiny inn that was no doubt flea-infested, all for the sake of his damnably inquisitive nature.

Perhaps curiosity truly was a sin.

Shivering and cursing his stupidity, Fredrick traveled another two miles before he at last spotted the secluded inn that sported a large sign proclaiming it the Queen's Arms. He turned into the yard, thankful to note that the stables appeared well-tended. His horses at least would pass a comfortable night. Which was perhaps more than he could hope for himself.

Pulling to a halt, he leaped from the carriage just as a gnarled old groom limped from the back of the inn to take the horses in hand. He grimaced as the mud splattered over his highly polished boots.

Dammit, did no one understand the importance of proper drainage?

"Would ye like them stabled, sir, or are ye just passing through?" the groom demanded, his lean, leathered face set in stoic lines and his shrewd brown eyes narrowed against the rain.

"I will be staying the night if there is room."

"Aye, there be room." The groom gave a jerk of his head toward the distant building already shrouded by fog. "Just take yerself to the inn and be sure to ask for the buttered rum. The best in the county."

"In a moment. First I intend to see that my pair is properly settled for the night."

The groom scratched his chin as he regarded Fredrick with a faint smile. "One of them sort, are ye?"

Fredrick gave a choked laugh, fairly certain that he had just been insulted. "What sort would that be?"

The brown eyes twinkled as the groom turned about and began to lead the carriage toward the stables. "Come along, sir. Me bones ain't as young as they used to be and they have an inclination to bark in the rain."

Bark? Did bones bark? Perhaps the poor sod was a bit touched in the upper works.

Waiting until they had entered the surprisingly clean stables, Fredrick watched with a close eye as the elderly man unhitched the greys and led them toward the nearby stalls.

"Rub them down and make sure I did not manage to injure them," he commanded.

The groom gave a low snort as he busied himself with tending the horses. Fredrick continued to keep a careful watch on his slow, methodical motions until he was certain that his horses were in competent hands. Only then did he turn his attention to his surroundings.

Ignoring the unpleasant manner in which his damp clothes were clinging to his body, Fredrick slowly strolled around the shadowed stables, impressed by the highly polished tack and neat rows of ointment that were arranged in precise order upon a shelf.

Plucking one of the ceramic pots off the shelf, Fredrick sniffed deeply of the ointment, attempting to determine the various ingredients. As usual, his thoughts instinctively turned to business. He had an acquaintance in London who had recently made a fortune by patenting a new cough syrup. Perhaps the same could be done for such an ointment as this.

Oh, it was true enough that many grooms created their own mixtures, but the past few years had taught him that it was a simple matter to convince the aristocracy that something they were forced to pay a small fortune for must be vastly superior to something they could have for a few pence.

"I believe you might have neglected to poke yer nose in the far stall. That's where I hide me dastardly secrets."

Fredrick turned his head to discover the elder man regarding him with his arms folded across his chest.

"You have an intriguing assortment of ointments," he said mildly. "Do you make them yourself?"

"Aye. Me own recipes. Nothing short of miracles they

are when it comes to fixing what might ail an animal," he admitted with obvious pride. "Not a neighbor in the county who don't come to me when they are having horse troubles. Including the nobs."

"Do you have these recipes written down?"

The brown eyes narrowed in suspicion. "Do I look like a turnip-top? I keep me knowledge up here." He tapped his forehead with a gnarled finger. "Where it can't be stolen."

Fredrick slowly smiled. If he desired to produce the ointments then he needed to be assured that the recipes were secret.

"Hmmm."

"What?"

"Perhaps we will have an opportunity to discuss these ointments at a later date."

The groom gave a sharp laugh. "Ye ain't near pretty enough to be talking me out of secrets, sir. Not even if I were as drunk as a louse."

Drunk as a *louse*? The old man was truly an unusual old screw, but thankfully Fredrick happened to appreciate the more interesting characters that crossed his path.

"I was thinking more in terms of a business proposition."

"Business, eh?"

"I would need to know much more of your ointments, of course, but if they are as good as you claim then I believe there might be profit in them for both of us."

A considering expression settled on the lined countenance. "Mayhaps," he at last conceded.

Knowing better than to pressure a cantankerous

groom when he had work to do, Fredrick offered his most charming smile.

"You seem to have everything in order. I think I shall seek the warmth of the inn."

Without warning the groom stepped forward, a queer smile upon his lips. "What's yer name?"

"Smith. Fredrick Smith."

The smile widened. "Well, Mr. Smith, I happen to like ye, so let me offer ye a bit of warning. Mrs. Walker runs a tidy establishment that is as clean and well run as any ye can find, but she won't be pleased if she discovers ye rutting about as if ye are searching for fleas."

Fredrick grimaced, relieved he would only be stuck at the inn for one night. He had no taste for bitter, shrill-tongued women.

"A bit of a tartar, is she?"

"Tartar?" The servant chuckled softly. "Nay, just a woman who knows her own business and don't care for people interfering in it."

"What of her husband? Does he have no influence over his wife?"

"Portia has been a widow these past five years. Any woman on her own tends to become a bit . . . bossy. Just mind yer manners and ye will be fine."

"I will keep that in mind," Fredrick promised dryly. "Can you see to my bags?"

"Aye. I'll have them in afore the cat can lick its ear."

Whatever the blazes that might mean, Fredrick acknowledged wryly, stepping out of the stables and into the rain that continued its relentless downpour.

Ignoring the mud that splattered his boots, Fredrick hurried across the yard, only absently noting the weathered stones and slate roof of the ancient inn before he was dashing through the front door and entering a long foyer. He gave his coat a shake to rid it of the worst of the clinging rain and took a step forward.

A step was all he managed before a low, yet commanding voice floated through the air.

"Halt right there."

Fredrick gave a lift of his brows as he watched a slender woman march toward him with a determined step. At first the shadows that cloaked the vestibule made it impossible for him to make out more than the fact that the figure marching toward him was most definitely that of the female persuasion, and that she was a delicate little creature.

It was not until she was halting near the muted light that filtered through the window that Fredrick sucked in a stunned breath.

Good God, this was no aging, bitter tartar.

She was . . . what?

Beautiful, of course.

No, stunning, he absently corrected.

Her thick hair held the dark gloss of ebony and was parted in the middle to be knotted at the nape of her neck. The severe style was a perfect frame for the pure oval of her face and emphasized the smooth porcelain of her skin. Her brows echoed the darkness of her hair as did the tangled lace of lashes that encircled the most startling blue eyes he had ever encountered. Cobalt, he at last decided. A perfect, clear cobalt that could make a man fall to his knees and plead for mercy.

With an effort, he forced himself to continue with his survey, silently deciding her thin, aquiline nose and lush lips (the color of summer roses) were just as perfect as the rest of her.

Well, she would be perfect if not for the appalling

brown gown that was a size too large for her slender curves and buttoned nearly to her pretty chin. Fredrick decided that whatever modiste had been responsible for the hideous gown should be drawn and quartered.

Attempting to disguise this woman's luminous beauty was as unforgivable as defiling Michelangelo's Mona Lisa.

It was the dangerous narrowing of those magnificent eyes that at last jerked Fredrick out of his strange fog of fascination to realize he was staring at her like a bird-wit. With an effort he gathered his composure and attempted to appear as if he had not just been rattled to the very tips of his toes.

"Forgive me, did you say something?" he asked with a smile he had discovered could charm the most fastidious of women.

Most, but not all, he swiftly learned as her gaze skimmed dismissively over his once elegant attire and the beautiful features hardened to an aloof disdain.

"Your boots, sir," she said, her voice low and startling cultured. The sort of culture that came from an expensive governess.

Far from offended by the woman's cold response to his arrival, Fredrick found his fascination deepening. The woman was clearly the dreaded Mrs. Portia Walker, but what the devil was she doing here? She should have been cutting a swath through London's most elite society. She should have earls and dukes panting at her heels.

To be buried here . . . well, it was no less than a sin.

A tingle of anticipation trickled down his spine. The woman was a puzzle.

One that he was suddenly anxious to pursue.

"You object to Hessians?" he demanded mildly. "I assure you that they are quite the latest fashion among civilized society."

Her lips thinned, revealing her obvious distaste.

For him in particular, or did she dislike gentlemen in general?

Had her deceased husband been a brute?

It would explain why she had never traveled to London.

"This may be no more than a quaint, provincial inn, but we do have standards. One of them being that my guests do not track mud throughout the place." She gave a lift of her slender hand and a young lad with bad skin and a shock of red hair dashed to her side. "You will remove them and Tolly will see that they are polished and returned to you."

Deliberately Fredrick assumed a haughty expression that would provoke the most mild-tempered woman. Mrs. Walker was clearly a woman who ran roughshod over others. How could he possibly resist tweaking that lovely nose?

"My dear, a gentleman does not lightly allow a stranger to polish his boots," he drawled. "This boy might very well scuff them, or worse, leave a grease spot."

"Nay, sir," the lad protested, his pale eyes protruding at the implication he would create such a hideous fate. "I am always right careful. I would never—"

"That is enough, Tolly," the raven-haired beauty interrupted, her voice exuding the smooth command of a seasoned general. "If our guest does not trust his precious boots to your care then perhaps he would be happier to stay at another inn. One that does not concern itself with mud on the floor."

"Or perhaps one that has the good sense to properly drain their yard so a gentleman need not concern himself with ruining a perfectly good pair of boots," he pointed out with a taunting smile.

She refused to rise to the bait as she gave an indifferent shrug. "As you say. The Fox and Grape is just another ten miles down the road."

Fredrick smothered a small chuckle. Gads, but she was magnificent as she stood there regarding him with that aloof arrogance. This was a woman who would hold her own against the devil himself.

A familiar heat spread through his body as he briefly speculated on whether she would be as commanding in his bed. Such a notion held unlimited possibilities. All of which were enough to make him hard and aching.

"It is a wonder you have any business if you are always so eager to send your guests on their way without so much a cup of your famous buttered rum," he said, futilely commanding his body to behave.

"Most of my guests understand that my rules are made to ensure their comfort and the comfort of others."

"Very well, then." Taking a seat on the nearby bench he motioned for the nervous Tolly to deal with his boots, his gaze never leaving Mrs. Walker's lovely countenance. "I suppose I have no one to blame but myself. Your groom did warn me that you were a bit of a tartar, although he failed to mention you were such a beautiful tartar."

She did not so much as blink. "Do you wish a chamber for the night?"

Fredrick hastily grabbed the edge of the bench as

the boy threatened to launch him onto the floor with his forceful tugs on his boots.

"That was my hope. Unless, of course, you have any other rules that I am currently abusing?"

"Not at the moment."

"Good. Then I do indeed wish a chamber for the night and a hot bath as soon as reasonably possible."

"Of course." Waiting until Tolly had painfully rid Fredrick of his boots, she offered a meaningless smile. "If you will follow me?"

Fredrick swallowed a groan as she turned on her heel and left the foyer with a gentle sway of her hips.

"Oh yes," he muttered beneath his breath as he hurried to trail after her. "Yes, I will."

Portia Walker had no fear that she appeared anything but cool and utterly serene as she made her way up the narrow flight of stairs. Her composure had been forged in the fires of hell, and there was nothing on this earth that could possible rattle her now.

Inwardly, however . . . well, that was an entirely different matter.

Never in her six and twenty years had she been so vibrantly aware of a man. From the moment she had entered the foyer to see him standing beside the door she had felt as if she had been struck by lightning.

A ridiculous notion.

It was not as if he were any way out of the ordinary, she tried to tell herself, knowing even as the thought crossed her mind that she was lying.

Granted the man was not the massive, intimidating sort that could fill a room with his presence. Instead he was only of medium height with the sleek muscles of a thoroughbred. But that face.

Dear God, it surely did not belong on a mere mortal.

It was not just handsome. That was too mundane a word. The delicately carved features, the shimmering grey eyes, and the lush lips were painfully beautiful. As if he were a creature of smoke and mist that might disappear at any moment.

And his hair . . . his thick curls were not just a predictable blond or brown, but a rich, aged gold with streaks of amber.

He was clearly created for the specific task of breaking poor women's hearts.

Still, she was never susceptible to gentlemen. Especially not those disgusting, loathsome toads from London.

So why then was her back prickling with awareness as he moved to follow her far too closely? And why was her heart pounding against her chest with such force that it was a wonder the entire inn could not hear its frantic beat?

She was merely tired, she attempted to soothe her troubled heart. With the sudden storm her small inn was filled to the rafters. It was only because most of her guests could not afford her most elegant suite that she even had space for the obnoxious London fop.

A pity really. She would have loved to have turned him away at the door. Any fool who spent such an obvious fortune on something so ridiculous as his clothing deserved a good soaking. As it was, she could only hope his boots were smudged and scuffed beyond repair.

Yes. With all the extra work it was little wonder that her weary brain was imagining all sorts of nonsense.

That absolutely, positively had to be it.

At last reaching the rooms at the end of the long wing, Portia pulled her heavy ring of keys from her pocket and unlocked the door.

Stepping over the threshold, she cast a swift, critical glance about the bedchamber, careful to note that the windows framed by the blue velvet curtains had been recently washed and that the heavy mahogany furnishings glowed with a high polish.

She moved aside to allow her guest to enter the room, an unconscious hint of pride squaring her shoulders.

"Our rooms are not as large as some inns," she said. "But the bedding is clean and the linens freshly washed. Through the far door you will find a small parlor that looks onto the woods."

That smile that could charm the birds from the trees curved his mouth.

"Ah, a very nice port in the storm."

"Indeed." She shoved a key into his hands. Regardless of the reasons for her odd reaction to this man, she was anxious to be away from the room. The flutters in the pit of her stomach and the sensation that she could not quite catch her breath were not at all comfortable. "Here you are. If you have need of a servant you need only pull the bell rope."

"And if I have need of you?"

She assumed her most distant expression. The one that could wither the pretensions of the most hardened rake.

"One of the servants will be up to light your fire and to bring your bath." Her voice was coated with a thick layer of ice. "I assume you have luggage?"

The damnable man dared to give a low chuckle, as if he were actually amused by her obvious set-down.

"Your groom promised to attend to it," he assured her.

"Good." She abruptly turned toward the door, not caring if it appeared she was in full retreat. The chamber suddenly seemed far too small. "If that will be all . . ."

"What of dinner?"

With an effort she forced herself to pause, although she refused to turn around. "The cook has prepared shepherd's pie. I will have it served in your private parlor."

"Actually, I would prefer to eat in the public rooms," he announced, being deliberately contrary. "There is nothing quite so refreshing as rubbing elbows with the natives on occasion."

"Condescending ass," she muttered beneath her breath.

"Excuse me, did you say something?"

"Enjoy your stay," she managed to choke out before heading firmly out the door and down the hall.

Chapter Three

Halting her hasty flight at the bottom of the stairs, Portia took several deep breaths. She was behaving like a nitwit.

So, the man . . . disturbed her. What did it matter?

He was just another guest in a long line of guests who had passed through her inn. After tonight he would fade from her mind and be forgotten.

Yes, there was nothing at all to trouble her.

Sucking in yet another breath, Portia took a moment to allow her gaze to drift over the dark paneling and open timbered ceiling of the wide lobby. She had inherited the inn upon the death of her elderly husband, Thomas Walker. It had been a profitable establishment from the time its doors had opened near a hundred years before, and even more profitable since her husband had possessed the good sense to add an extra wing to accommodate the numerous carriages headed to Winchester.

It had been Portia, however, who had made the Queen's Arms famous throughout the district. With her husband dead, and the entire staff depending upon her to keep the inn afloat, she had no choice but rely upon her female instincts. Without her husband's gregarious charm or years of experience, she had decided that she would use what few skills she did possess. And that was how to run an efficient household, and to ensure that her guests were made to feel as content as if they were at home.

Within a few months she had hired a cook who was nothing less than an artist in the kitchen. Her fare was simple, but mouthwateringly delicious, and carriages would readily travel miles out of their way to enjoy her creations. She had also hired on two extra maids to assist in keeping the rooms scrupulously clean.

Her inn might never be the largest, or the most elegant, but it had the reputation of always offering the best service for a reasonable cost. A combination that had kept business brisk.

And more importantly, it had offered Portia an independence she would never have dreamed possible. For the first time, she was in complete control of her life and she would not trade the wondrous knowledge for all the Crown jewels.

Feeling her odd tension slowly begin to fade, Portia smoothed her hands down the skirt of her plain gown and turned toward the back of the inn. The tap room was already filled with both locals and the guests who would be remaining for the night. She needed to make sure that Mrs. Cornell would have plenty of food.

Portia turned into the side passage used by the servants, nearly running down the short, plump maid who was rushing forward with a large stack of freshly laundered towels.

"Oh, forgive me, mum," the girl breathed, her brown curls bouncing about her round face.

"Molly." Portia halted the maid before she could rush away. The servants had learned that while Portia was always fair and willingly paid the highest wages, she demanded nothing short of perfection in their work.

"Aye, mum?"

"When Quinn comes in from the stables, would you have him take a bath to the blue chambers and see that a fire is lit?"

The girl blinked in confusion. "But that is my job."

"Not for this particular guest," she said, her voice hard. "And please inform the other maids that if our latest guest rings his bell no one is to attend him but Quinn or myself."

Understanding dawned in the brown eyes. "Ah, a London gent, is he?"

Portia had never made a secret of her disdain for the worthless dandies that occasionally dribbled their way from London. Nor her determination to protect her maids from their lecherous advances. Beneath her roof such men swiftly learned that the females who crossed their paths were not there for their entertainment. Not unless they desired to be tossed out on their arrogant noses.

"The very worst sort," she said. "Hopefully he will be on his way as soon as the sun rises. Until then I intend to protect my own."

"Is he handsome?"

Portia frowned as the memory of elegant features and smoke grey eyes sent a rush of heat through the pit of her stomach.

Drat it all. Was she coming down with a fever?

"What does that matter?" she demanded.

Molly heaved a sigh. "It is just so rare to have a real gentleman in these parts."

The brief warmth fled as a familiar chill spread through her body. Good Lord. Molly was no wide-eyed innocent and yet she continued to flutter and flirt whenever a nobleman crossed the threshold.

As if they were somehow superior to the more common male.

Portia knew the truth.

"Let me assure you that supposed gentlemen are vain, pompous peacocks who consider nothing and no one beyond their own pleasures."

The brown eyes twinkled. "Aye, but is he handsome?"

Portia rolled her eyes. "Yes, Molly, he is obscenely handsome. Now return to your work and stay away from the blue chambers."

Continuing down the hall, Portia gave a rueful shake of her head. Had there ever been a twenty-year-old girl who did not have her head stuffed with foolish fantasies of handsome princes come to sweep them off to their fairy tale castle?

Even she had harbored such dreams. At least until her prince had arrived and promptly turned into a worthless toad.

She shoved her foolish thoughts aside as she stepped into the kitchen, her expert eye skimming over the long wooden tables loaded with freshly baked bread, peeled vegetables, bundles of dried herbs, and baskets of strawberries.

The kitchen had been recently remodeled to incorporate the latest inventions, but the delicious scents that wafted through the air were a product of good old-fashioned talent.

A rather smug smile touched her lips. It had been a stroke of genius to lure the older woman to the inn. It did not even matter that she was forced to pay nearly two hundred pounds a year to keep her. Her profits had nearly doubled since the woman's arrival.

"Good evening, Mrs. Cornell," she said as she crossed to where the silver-haired woman rolled out a lump of dough. "Is everything in order?"

The thin woman with a pinched face continued with her task. "The pies are in the oven as well as lovely stuffed mushrooms in cream sauce. I am just working on the strawberry tarts."

"It all smells delicious."

"I heard as we have another guest."

Portia grimaced. "Yes."

"Shall I have a tray fixed?"

"No, he wishes to eat in the public rooms."

"Does he now? That is right decent of him."

"The man would not know decency if it bit him on the arse," she muttered before she could halt the words.

The cook glanced up in surprise. "Has he done something to offend you?"

"Not at all. I think I must be tired," she admitted. "I will be in my rooms if you have need of me."

"Aye."

Assured that the inn would not tumble into oblivion, at least not within the next hour, Portia made her way back through the inn and climbed the stairs to the upper floor. With a stern effort she kept herself from glancing toward the door that led to the blue chambers, and moved to the end of the hall. She pulled her keys from her pocket and unlocked the door that led to the narrow stairs to the attic.

After the death of Thomas, Portia had sold their pretty cottage and used the money to keep the inn from plunging into disaster. Over the past two years, business had been good enough to finance a separate home, but Portia was in no hurry to quit her snug chambers. Not only was it convenient to be on hand to deal with the problems that occurred on a daily basis, but the tidy nest egg she was managing to acquire gave her a sense of security.

Never, ever again would she be alone and penniless.

She was a woman who had made her way in the world and no one could take that away from her.

Freshly scrubbed and attired in dry clothing, Fredrick realized that he was starving. With a last glance in the mirror to check that his cravat was precisely knotted and his curls tamed, he left the room.

He closed the door behind him, his heart giving a sudden leap as he watched Mrs. Walker marching down the hallway.

For some unfathomable reason, he had been unable to thrust the thought of the woman from his mind. Strange, considering he was a man who never allowed himself to be distracted. How could he have possibly made such a success of his business if he could not concentrate fully on his goals?

On this evening, however, it did not matter how often he sternly turned his thoughts to his upcoming confrontation with his father, his mind refused to cooperate. Instead of plotting out a strategy, he had brooded upon the perfection of a sweet Madonna countenance and tender curves hidden beneath layers of ugly wool.

Mrs. Walker was not the first woman he had ever desired, but she was by far the most intriguing.

That aloof disdain. The air of unshakable command. The delicious femininity disguised beneath a layer of ice.

It was a challenge that no man could resist. Especially a man who preferred to earn his rewards rather than having them handed to him on a silver platter.

Unfortunately, his first attempt to discover the means of slipping beneath her fierce composure had accomplished nothing. Rather than the maid he had been expecting to tend to his needs, it was the surly Quinn who had brought up his bath and stoked the fire. The elderly man had made it clear that he had no intention of gossiping about his employer, at least nothing beyond confirming to Fredrick that the woman held men in contempt, and most particularly those from London.

It seemed, however, that his luck was just about to take a turn for the better, he told himself as he deliberately moved to block the narrow corridor.

With a scowl Mrs. Walker came to a reluctant halt, her expression revealing she was not nearly so pleased as himself with the stroke of fortune.

"Ah, Mrs. Walker."

He slowly smiled, his gaze dipping down to discover she had changed her gown to one of a pale grey. Unfortunately, it was even less flattering than the brown monstrosity. The woman might be an extraordinary businesswoman, but her taste in clothing could leave a man limp at a hundred paces. Which was no doubt the object of the hideous gowns.

Thankfully, it took a great deal more to make Fredrick limp. Instead his cock hardened as lurid images of stripping off the thick wool to discover the satin beneath danced through his head.

"Good evening, sir."

"There was no need to escort me to dinner. Not that I am complaining, mind you. I appreciate any opportunity to be in the company of a beautiful woman. Still, it does seem we should at least be properly introduced before we proceed any further." He performed his most elegant bow. "Fredrick Smith at your service. And you, I presume, must be Mrs. Walker, the proprietress of this fine establishment?"

The blue eyes glittered with an artic chill. "I am. And as proprietress I have a number of duties awaiting my attention. So if you will kindly move aside?"

"I will just as soon as you answer a simple question for me."

"What question?"

Fredrick took a step forward, startled to discover that beneath the scent of starch and wax was a lovely hint of roses.

A startling new piece to add to the puzzle of Mrs. Walker.

"To my knowledge we have never encountered one another before today. So precisely why have you taken me in such great dislike?"

The cool dignity never faltered. "You are mistaken, Mr. Smith. I do not like or dislike you. You are merely a guest at my inn who will soon be on your way."

Fredrick swallowed a hasty laugh. Either she did not know much about men, or else the men she had dealt with were spineless creatures. Otherwise she would have known better than to blatantly toss down the gauntlet.

"Perhaps not so soon," he said before he could even consider the words.

The frost briefly flickered. "What do you mean?"

Fredrick slowly smiled. Why not stay at the inn? It was less than twenty miles to his father's estate. Close enough to conduct his investigation, but not so close as to cause his father alarm. This was as good a place to remain as any.

Indeed, it was far better than most.

What other place in all of England could include an exquisite widow just ripe for the plucking?

"I intend to remain in this area for the next few days, and, as you pointed out, your inn is clean, and if your food is as good as the smells coming from the kitchen, I shall be perfectly satisfied." He gave a challenging lift of one golden brow. "That is, unless you have some objection?"

Less than half a beat passed before she tilted her chin to a militant angle.

"Certainly not. We can always use the business."

"Then we shall have plenty of opportunity to discover precisely what you find so offensive about my presence," he murmured smoothly.

"Oh, I doubt you will be staying that long, Mr. Smith."

Ah, she was good, he acknowledged with a flare of anticipation. It had been a very long time since he had crossed swords with a woman with such swift wits.

"Perhaps it is only fair to warn you, poppet, that while I may not be the smartest, or wealthiest, or even the most talented of gentlemen, I am without a doubt exceedingly patient. When I set myself a task I do not waver until it is completed."

The blue eyes hardened to chips of sapphire. "Let me return the favor, Mr. Smith . . ."

"Fredrick," he interrupted smoothly.

"Mr. Smith," she retorted, her voice dripping with ice. "I am not one of your frivolous London socialites. I have struggled and sacrificed more than you can imagine to reach my current position. Never again will I ever be forced or bullied or coerced against my will. If you become a bother I will have you escorted from my property."

Fredrick felt his chest squeeze at the stoic dignity etched into every inch of her tiny body. Christ, what had she suffered to give her such a deep distrust for men?

Had it been the heavy hand of oppression, or had she suffered physical abuse?

The thought sent a startling fury through his heart. To think anyone could harm such a tiny and fragile creature . . . well, if he knew where to find the bastard, or bastards, he would rip them apart limb by limb.

Suddenly the fierce desire to have her in his bed, her slender legs wrapped about his waist, was over-shadowed by a need to melt that frigid wariness she wore as a shield to protect her vulnerable heart. He wanted to see a genuine smile touch those lush, per-fect lips. He wanted her to discover that for all the rakes, and lechers, and tyrants in the world, there were also decent men. Men who could offer more than pain and oppression.

"You have my solemn word, Mrs. Walker, that I have never bullied or forced a woman in my entire life. There is nothing I would find more repulsive," he said.

"Then tend to your business, Mr. Smith, and do not waste either of our time with foolish games."

With a rustle of starch and wool she pushed her way past his stiff body, heading toward the stairs with those firm steps that looked as if she were marching into battle.

Fredrick turned to watch her retreat, his expression thoughtful.

Tend to your business, Mr. Smith . . .

"Mrs. Walker, you just became my business," he murmured softly.

Clever enough to realize a front assault would only drive the lovely Mrs. Walker deeper behind her barriers, Fredrick enjoyed his surprisingly delicious dinner among the various guests and went bed early.

The next morning he was on his way before most of the inn was stirring. Despite his fascination with the widow, he had other duties that awaited his attention.

A pity, he acknowledged as he rode up the tree-lined drive to his father's estate. He would much rather be charming a delicious woman than enduring the awkward discomfort of his father, Lord Graystone.

A wry smile touched his lips at the thought of the stranger who had managed to father him.

Throughout the years it had always baffled Fredrick why his father had insisted that he visit this estate at least one month during the summer. Not only were Lady Graystone and Fredrick's half-brother, Simon, always notably staying in London, but Graystone himself seemed as anxious as a cat on coals in his presence.

Certainly, there had been no efforts at creating a genuine relationship. In truth, Fredrick had spent more time with the servants, often seeing his father briefly at dinner before the man once again disappeared.

In time, Fredrick had come to realize that his father must be embarrassed by his illegitimate brat. After all, when he had indulged in his affair with Fredrick's mother, he had been an obscure younger son with few responsibilities. It was not until after the death of his older brother that Graystone had suddenly been thrust into the role of head of the family and forced to marry a wealthy merchant's daughter to salvage the estate from ruin.

From that moment, Graystone had shouldered his duties with a grim determination. Which had convinced Fredrick that he was just another duty that had to be endured, a shameful duty his father would rather sweep beneath the rug if only it were possible.

Once Fredrick had reached his majority, he had brought an end to the forced visits. It was obvious to him that his father wanted to be done with his duty, so Fredrick had made it simple for him.

Until now.

A bittersweet sense of familiarity struck Fredrick as he passed through the open gates and caught sight of the redbrick mansion.

Built in the late 1600s with a classical portico and soaring columns, the house had been returned to its former glory during his father's reign. Even the grounds had been reclaimed from nature and now spread beneath the pale sunlight with a manicured perfection.

It was not the largest or the best known estate in the area, but Oak Manor held an ancient charm that would never be dimmed by time.

For once Fredrick did not ride directly to the stables. On this day he was no more than a guest at the manor, and, properly halting before the wide oak doors, he waited for a groom to dash forward to take the reins of his horse before he climbed the worn steps.

He had barely reached the entrance when the doors were pulled open and a tall, thin butler with ginger hair now liberally sprinkled with grey regarded him with a dignified expression.

"May I be of service, sir?"

Fredrick's lips twitched as he regarded the man who had taught him to play chess and cheat at cards.

"Hello, Morgan. I see that ugly mug has not changed over the years."

The servant briefly stiffened, then with a sudden hitch of breath he took a step forward. "Good heavens . . . Mr. Smith?"

Fredrick offered a small bow. "For my sins."

A sudden pleasure warmed the pale blue eyes. "It is very good to see you, sir. Please, come in and I will inform the master you have arrived."

Fredrick smiled fondly as he followed the butler through the small foyer. Despite Morgan's stiff manner, he had a soft heart and a cunning wit. He also had a startling ability to keep a young, fretful lad entertained and out of most mischief.

Fredrick would never forget Morgan's kindness over the years.

His smile abruptly faded as they entered the Staircase Gallery. Not from the heavy, ornately scrolled chairs that lined the long hall, or the open timbered ceiling. No, it was the framed portraits of his half-brother, Simon, that were hung with splendid prominence along the paneled walls that stole his momentary sense of homecoming.

With loving devotion, the passing years had been captured upon canvas, revealing the alterations in Simon as he had grown from a chubby, blond-haired boy into a rotund man with a florid face and peevish expression.

He looked more like a butcher than a nobleman, Fredrick thought as he strolled past the gilt frames, but that did not keep his adoring parents from capturing his passing life for posterity.

He, on the other hand, did not have so much as a sketch of his likeness in the rambling house. His legacy was to be nothing more than a blemish upon the Graystone name. One that was to be forgotten as swiftly as possible.

Giving a shake of his head at his spiteful dislike of Simon (a man he had never so much as crossed paths with), Fredrick determinedly turned his mind to more important matters.

"How do things go at Oak Manor?"

"Much the same as ever, sir," Morgan replied, leading Fredrick up the magnificent oak staircase that had given the manor its name.

"The family is well?"

"Quite well."

"I suppose Father is busy overseeing the planting?"

"Yes, indeed."

"Is Lady Graystone in town for the season?"

"Yes, she had the townhouse opened last week."

"And my brother is with her?"

"Of course. Master Simon is always anxious to return to London."

Fredrick's humor returned at Morgan's discreet responses. He was the perfect butler, possessing the unshakable belief that "thou shall not gossip" was one of the Ten Commandments. Even among family members.

A saintly virtue when Fredrick was small and he had broken a window in the conservatory, or tossed several of Simon's expensive toys into the nearby lake. He had never feared that Morgan would reveal his guilt.

But now his reticence was less than a blessing. The older man's position in the household would mean he was privy to all sorts of sordid secrets. One of which might have forced Lord Graystone to pay Dunnington twenty thousand pounds to keep hidden.

Together they entered the formal drawing room. It was a splendid room with classical gods painted on the ceiling and arabesque tapestries covering the walls. Gilt edge plasterwork completed the image of tranquil elegance.

Whatever his complex feelings for Lord Graystone, Fredrick could not deny the man possessed excellent taste.

"If you will wait here, I will have Mrs. Shaw bring you a tray."

"Thank you, Morgan."

Morgan paused at the door, his stern expression softening. "You have been missed."

Fredrick smiled fondly. "As have you."

With a shallow bow the butler slipped from the room. Waiting until he was certain he was alone, Fredrick moved briskly across the room and quietly opened the door that led to his father's private study. A quick peek revealed the room was empty and he stepped inside to begin his search.

Not that he actually knew what he was searching for. Hell, he did not even know if he would recognize the deep, dark secret if he stumbled across it. But for the moment he had no brilliant notion of how to conduct his investigation. Nothing beyond asking his father bluntly why he had offered Dunnington twenty thousand pounds.

His lips twisted as he tugged open the drawers of his father's heavy walnut desk.

He had never shared a decent conversation with his father in his entire life. If he were to confront the wary man directly he would bolt before the words could finish leaving Fredrick's lips.

Discovering nothing more interesting than the usual papers and correspondence dealing with a large estate, Fredrick turned his attention to the book-lined walls. Unlike the rest of the house, this room was faintly shabby and well worn. Rather like a favorite pair of slippers that are kept for their comfort rather than their beauty.

It was a room that belonged exclusively to Lord Graystone. Even as a very young child, Fredrick had known better than to ever interrupt his father when he entered this room.

Now he felt a ridiculous sense of curiosity as he studied the collection of classical works and extensive farming texts that made up the bulk of the books.

With a shake of his head, Fredrick thrust aside his strange broodings. What did it matter that he had never known what authors his father loved? If he preferred to curl up with the classics of Plato or Coke's latest farming techniques? What he knew of his father could fit into a thimble, and he had managed to survive quite well in the world.

Dunnington, along with Ian and Raoul, had been all the family he had ever needed.

Fredrick made a swift search on the shelves, seeking for hidden safes, and even hidden doorways. He felt a fool tapping on wood, and tugging on books, but when he heard the unmistakable sound of approaching footsteps he was fairly confident that there was nothing to be discovered in the study.

With swift movements he was back in the drawing

room, staring aimlessly out the long bank of windows when the cook swept through the door with a large tray in her hands.

"Fredrick, my dear boy." Smiling broadly, the middle-aged woman with a dark braid curled at the nape of her neck and a plump, pleasant face set the tray on a low table. "Oh, but it is good to have you here."

"Thank you, Mrs. Shaw." Without hesitation Fredrick moved to pull the woman into a tight hug. Mrs. Shaw had been the one to comfort him when he cried as a mere tot, and baked him special treats to ease his loneliness. Stepping back, he took a deep sniff of the delicious smells filling the room. "Good God, do I smell plum pudding?"

Fussing with her apron, Mrs. Shaw managed to hide the tears of pleasure that filled her eyes.

"I have not forgotten your sweet tooth. There is also a tasty pheasant pie and green pea soup."

Fredrick promptly took his place on the sofa and filled a bowl with his favorite soup.

"A magnificent feast."

Planting her hands on her ample hips, the cook appeared ready to hover over Fredrick until he had eaten every morsel on the tray.

"Young gentlemen need plenty of plain, hearty food. Not that fancy stuff they serve in London. 'Tis no wonder that you are as thin as a reed."

He gave a small laugh at her obvious disdain for London chefs. "I assure you that I have yet to enjoy a meal equal to yours, no matter where I might travel."

A flush touched the round cheeks. "Such a flatterer."

"It is no more than the simple truth." Fredrick sampled the soup, his mind searching for the best means of interrogating the woman. Unlike Morgan, Mrs. Shaw was always prepared to enjoy a nice chat. "Tell me, Mrs. Shaw, how long have you been at Oak Manor?"

The woman blinked in surprise, but thankfully did not appear suspicious of his probing.

"Good heavens, let me think." She frowned as she pondered the question. "I was just turned twenty when I came as a scullery maid, so it must be near on twenty-seven years."

Twenty-seven years ago. The same time his father inherited the estate.

"I suppose you must have been born and raised in the nearby village?"

"No, indeed. The entire staff was hired in Winchester."

Fredrick narrowed his gaze. He had never realized that his father had hired an entirely new staff on his arrival to Oak Manor. It may be meaningless. In fact, it probably was. But it was the first odd detail he could jot into his notebook.

"Surely not the entire staff?" he protested. "There must be a few old retainers rattling about?"

"Nary a one." Mrs. Shaw gave a lift of her hands. "When your father took over the estate he pensioned off what few staff still remained and brought in a whole new lot. I always thought that Lady Graystone was behind it all. She was eager to take her place as mistress of the manor and she didn't want to be having anyone about who might compare her to the last mistress. After all, she was no more than a merchant's daughter, and it was rumored that your grandmother was a great dragon of a lady who was the terror of the entire district, even after she had been confined to her bed."

"I would not doubt that for a moment. Just walking past her portrait made me break out in hives," Fredrick retorted, recalling the painting of a silver-haired matron with a haughty expression and cold blue eyes. "Still, it is odd that even if Lady Graystone should desire a new staff she would not have hired a few from the local village. I believe that is the usual practice of large estates."

Mrs. Shaw shrugged, her expression revealing her less-than-complimentary opinion of Lady Graystone.

"Perhaps she thought to impress her neighbors by hiring city folk. She is always trying to prove she is as good as the rest of the nobs."

"Perhaps." Fredrick polished off his soup and reached for the plum pudding, his expression deliberately indifferent. "Are there any of the old servants still in the village?"

"I don't rightly know." The woman regarded him with a frown. "Is there something you are wanting?"

"I suppose that I am just curious. During my past visits I was too young to think about anyone but myself. Now I realize that I know precious little of those of you who helped to raise me, or even my own family."

"Is that why you have come back? To find your past?"

Fredrick resisted a wry smile. As far as he was concerned his past could stay bloody well buried. He was far more interested in his beloved father's past.

"Not at all," he said smoothly. "I have business in Winchester and it seemed churlish to be so close and not stop by to at least see how you and Morgan go on."

The plump face lightened. "Then you'll be staying?"

"Not at Oak Manor," he corrected gently. "But I intend to be in the area for several days. I hope to return as long as . . ." His words trailed away as he heard the sound of approaching footsteps, his stomach knotting with the familiar sense of dread and frustrated yearning.

Mrs. Shaw abruptly reached out to pat his shoulder. "He'll be happy to have you home, my dear," she whispered softly. "He may not ever admit it, but he's missed you."

Chapter Four

Portia was arranging a vase of flowers in the front salon when Molly abruptly burst through the door, her hand pressed to her heart.

"Oh, come quick, mum," she breathed.

Puzzled, but not unduly alarmed, Portia set aside the flowers and wiped her hands on the apron that covered her sensible gown.

"What is it? Is the coal wagon stuck again?"

"Nay, it is Quinn and that London gent," Molly said, tugging Portia through the door and toward a window that overlooked the yard. "It looks as if he were hurt."

"Good Lord, Quinn is hurt?" Portia demanded as she rushed to the window.

"Not him, the other one. Looks like he busted his head."

Portia's expression hardened as she caught sight of Quinn with his arm about the waist of her latest guest, assisting him toward the inn. It did not take a great deal of intelligence to realize Mr. Smith was deep in his cups and that he had somehow managed to take a blow to the head.

"Typical," she breathed in annoyance.

At her side, the ever romantic Molly heaved a deep sigh. "Gawd, but he is a handsome one. Just like an angel fallen from heaven."

Of course he looked like an angel, Portia thought sourly. How could a devil possibly seduce the innocent unless he had tumbled honey curls and features that could make a woman's knees feel weak?

Even in the fading light and foxed to the gills his beauty made her breath catch and her heart lurch in response.

"Heaven?" Her voice was sharp. "More like an imp from hell. Go to the kitchens and have clean towels and hot water sent to the blue chambers."

With a knowing glance, Molly bobbed a swift curtsy. "Aye, mum."

Giving a shake of her head, Portia moved to pull the door open and stood aside as Quinn managed to half carry the slender gentleman over the threshold.

"Take him upstairs, Quinn, before he bleeds all over the floorboards."

With an effort Mr. Smith lifted his head to regard her with pain-dazed eyes.

"Such sympathy, Mrs. Walker. You quite overwhelm me."

Turning away she led the way to the nearby stairs. "You do not need my sympathy, Mr. Smith. What you need is a thicker skull and the wits to stay off your horse when you are bosky."

"Now, Portia, the poor bloke was not bosky," Quinn interrupted, his breathing heavy as he struggled to help his companion up the steep steps. "It was that damnable cur of yers that was the trouble. Raced right beneath Mr.

Smith's mount with his yipping and yapping. It's a wonder the horse didn't break a leg and Mr. Smith his neck."

Sharp, biting guilt made Portia stumble on the stairs and she was forced to grab the banister or fall flat on her face. Drat it all. She had known when she had discovered the pup half starved in the ditch that he was bound to be a bother, but she had never encountered a stray she could resist.

Why else would her staff be made up of a collection of souls that had all been in the gutter at one time or another?

Reaching the landing, she turned back to regard her injured guest with an expression of regret.

"I . . . see. Forgive me, Mr. Smith. I had no notion that Puck had escaped from the garden."

A crooked, boyish smile touched his lips. A smile that oddly made her tingle to the tips of her toes.

"And it was much more fun to think that I had brought my own downfall upon my head, eh, poppet?"

God, he was just so . . . achingly beautiful.

Bewildered by her potent reaction to the man, Portia turned briskly on her heel and reached into her pocket.

"Come along, Quinn, I will get the door."

She opened the door with her master key and stepped aside to allow Quinn to drag Mr. Smith over the threshold.

"Ah, lovely Portia with her key to my room, and what of my heart?" the man crooned in a slurred voice. "Do you possess that key as well?"

Portia frowned as Quinn settled his burden on the wide bed. "Perhaps I should send for Jameson. He is becoming delirious."

Quinn gave a short laugh. "There's nothing the

saw-bones can do for a bump on the head. All he needs is a bit of rest."

Quinn was no doubt right, Portia acknowledged as she hurried to the side of the bed and perched on the mattress. The local doctor would not be thankful to be dragged from his dinner for a mere bump. And in truth, Portia trusted her own skills at nursing far more than the pompous Jameson. The man might be a master at boasting of his skills, but he was remarkably reluctant to actually put those skills to use.

"Take off his boots," she commanded Quinn, her gaze shifting toward the door. "Oh, Molly, bring that tray here."

Waiting until the maid had placed the hot water and towels on the small table next to the bed, Portia returned her attention to the man stretched on the bed.

He had closed his eyes, his brows furrowed in pain and his lovely curls tousled. Another wave of remorse raced through her, overcoming her instinctive distrust. The nasty gash on his forehead along with the rising lump was all her fault. The least she could do was attempt to soothe him to the best of her ability.

Once Quinn had dealt with his boots and pulled a blanket over his legs, Portia reached to tug at the tightly tied cravat. He could not possibly be comfortable with the thing wrenched about his neck.

Without realizing how close she had leaned toward his angelic countenance as she concentrated on her task, Portia was caught off guard when she felt the gentle warmth of his breath brush her cheek.

"If you intend to undress me, Mrs. Walker, I would prefer that we not have an audience," Mr. Smith whispered.

Her gaze jerked upward to discover him regarding

her beneath the thick tangle of his black lashes. In the muted light his grey eyes shimmered with a hint of pure silver. For a heartbeat she was mesmerized by the exotic gaze, forgetting even to breathe.

It was only when Quinn roughly cleared his throat that Portia realized that she had been staring at the man like the verist pea-goose. With an effort she abruptly regained her scattered wits.

"Just lay still, Mr. Smith," she commanded sternly. "I fear your head has been rattled quite enough for one evening."

"I need to return to the stables and see to his horse," Quinn abruptly announced, heading for the door.

"Make sure you check for injuries," Mr. Smith muttered.

"Oh aye, yer horse is in good hands." Quinn shot Portia a queer gaze as she dampened one of the cloths and began to gently dab at his wound. "As are ye."

Fredrick winced as she relentlessly continued her dabbing, determined to make sure there was not a speck of dust left in the wound.

"Beautiful hands, most certainly, but bloody painful. Must you keep prodding at my poor, aching head?"

She turned her head to send the hovering maid a wry smile. "Molly, would you find Spenser and ask him to unlock the cellars so you can retrieve a bottle of brandy? It seems as if Mr. Smith is one of those men who cannot bear a bit of pain."

"Aye, mum."

"A bit of pain?" the man protested as Molly scurried from the room. "My head has been cracked open."

"It is nothing more than a small gash." She forced herself to meet the silver gaze, ignoring that stupid tingle that continued to plague her. "Your brains are in no danger of leaking out."

"No thanks to that bloody cur."

She stiffened at his words. "I am sorry, Mr. Smith. I will ensure that Puck is kept properly locked away from now on."

"No." He reached up to lightly grasp her wrist, his thumb absently rubbing against the uneven pace of her pulse. "Do not imprison the dog on my account. At least Puck is honest in his dislike of my presence. I prefer that to spending an afternoon with a father who is forced to pretend that he does not consider me some loathsome creature that has crawled from beneath a rock."

Her eyes widened in surprise. "Your family lives in the neighborhood?"

"No, never my family." His eyes slid closed, his voice thick and unsteady with pain. "A bastard has no family."

Portia studied the elegant, decidedly aristocratic features with a sense of confusion. With his expensive clothing and fashionable carriage, she had just assumed he was of the upper orders.

She had *wanted* to assume that, a small voice whispered. If he were her enemy, then she had the means to keep him at a distance. God knew, she had years of experience at holding arrogant lechers at arm's length.

Now . . . now she did not know what to think.

"Oh."

He managed to lift his heavy lids and regard her wary expression. "Does that shock you?"

"I just thought . . ."

"What?" His lips twisted. "That I was just another cork-brained, frivolous dandy from London?"

"You have the appearance of a man of society."

"Not every man needs to inherit his place in the world. There are those of us who actually earn success."

"And a few women," she said tartly.

"Ah yes, you are a remarkable woman, Portia."

She battled the most ridiculous urge to blush at his soft words, suddenly aware that they were alone in the bedchamber.

"Hardly remarkable."

The silver in his eyes slowly darkened to smoke, his fingers easing their grip on her wrist to stroke up the length of her arm.

"Do not argue with a wounded man, poppet." His hand curled about the back of her neck. "You are remarkable, and so exquisitely beautiful."

"Mr. Smith . . ." Her words broke off in a gasp as he began tugging her head downward.

"Fredrick," he corrected.

"Halt this at once." She planted her hands on his chest, reluctant to struggle against his hold. "I do not wish to hurt you."

"You have been hurting me from the moment I caught sight of you," he breathed, his words still slurred enough to reveal he was not entirely in his right mind. "I have ached for this."

"Mr. Smith . . ."

"Fredrick."

The grey eyes flared with heat a heartbeat before he gave a firm tug on her nape and Portia discovered their lips clashing together.

Her first reaction was one of shock. After the death of Thomas it was not often she allowed herself to be touched, not by anyone. And most certainly not by a London gentleman.

But as his hand tugged her even closer, and his head angled to deepen the kiss, she realized that her shock was not one of disgust. Or even outrage at his daring.

Instead, all those strange tingles and flares of awareness she had felt since the man had arrived at her inn tangled together in the pit of her stomach. With a shocking force they all coalesced into a ball of searing excitement.

Her fingers curled into the fabric of his jacket as tiny shock waves raced through her body. His grip eased, his fingers lightly playing with the sensitive skin of her nape.

His lips also eased, teasing over her mouth with feather-light caresses and urging her lips to part for the thrust of his tongue.

Deep, soul-stirring delight raced through Portia's body like a sinful drug. She had never known a kiss could be so poignant, so affecting. As if she were being molded and changed by his light touch.

Against her will, Portia felt her muscles melting as she leaned more heavily against his chest, her breasts tight and aching beneath her heavy wool gown.

He gave a low growl as he nipped at her lips, outlining her trembling mouth with the tip of his tongue. His fingers flexed restlessly against her nape, his lips shifting to trail down the length of her jaw before nuzzling a path down the curve of her throat.

Portia unwittingly tilted back her head to give him greater access. With seductive cunning he discovered the pulse hammering in the base of her throat, wetting it lightly with his tongue before blowing his breath gently over the sensitive skin.

Heaven help her. She shivered beneath his touch. Had there ever been such exquisite pleasure?

She wanted to feel his clever fingers stroking down her body. She wanted to crawl on top of him and feel the heat of his body melt the bitter cold that had encased her for so long.

It was the sheer power of her need that at last jolted her out of the strange fog of bliss.

With a small moan of protest she lifted her head, her throbbing lips still parted as she regarded the man who had just revealed the true meaning of passion.

A shudder wracked Fredrick as he forced back the desire that pulsed through his body.

He had not actually intended to kiss Portia. Not when she was determined to brand him as a worthless lecher. But, whether it was the blow to his head, or the sheer potency of having her near, he had been unable to resist temptation.

And despite his aching arousal (and the knowledge it was not going to be eased any time soon) he was not a bit sorry he had tasted her sweetness.

Hell's bells but she was even more delectable than he had dreamed possible. He had done nothing more than kiss her, but his entire body was on fire. Suddenly he understood how Ian and Raoul could so easily toss aside all sense in the need to bed a particular woman.

He would never have thought himself susceptible to the demands of his body. At least not until he had tasted of Portia Walker.

Now he thought he might do anything, go to any length, just for the opportunity to have her in his arms again.

Breathing deeply, Fredrick allowed his fingers to travel up the curve of her neck to cup her cheek.

"Beneath all your starch and wool you smell of midnight roses, poppet," he husked. "A shockingly decadent scent."

She touched a nervous tongue to her lips, as if she could still feel the heat of him upon her lips. Her eyes briefly darkened with the passion she could not disguise, then, without warning she was stumbling off the bed and pressing a hand to her heart.

"No . . . I do not want this."

She was going to bolt, he realized with a flare of panic. And once she had disappeared she would devote her considerable will to convincing herself that he had just taken shameless advantage of her.

He had to do something. And quickly.

"Portia, forgive me." He raised his slender hands in a gesture of peace. "I did not mean to frighten you."

She blinked, as if an apology was the last thing she had expected. Good. If he could keep her off guard then perhaps she would not be so eager to judge him by her past.

"You did not frighten me. I just . . ."

"Do not wish to remember that you are a woman as well as an innkeeper?" he demanded.

She folded her arms around her waist, her expression hardening. "I just have no intention of being seduced by a stranger who will soon be gone."

"Fair enough."

Once again she was caught off guard. "What?"

Fredrick carefully shifted on the pillow, biting back a curse as a jagged pain lanced through his head.

"Portia, I kissed you because I have longed to do so from the moment I entered this inn. And I will not deny that I want you. Desperately." He entangled her wary gaze with his. "But I am perfectly capable of enjoying the companionship of a woman without demanding something that she is not yet comfortable offering."

She regarded him in wary silence until the sound of the maid returning made her give a sudden start.

"Here's the brandy, mum." Blissfully unaware of the tension clogging the room, the maid moved to set the bottle of brandy onto the table beside the bed. Once her task was complete she lingered long enough to cast a bold glance down Fredrick's reclined form, her dark eyes flashing with an unmistakable invitation.

"Thank you, Molly," Portia said dryly. "You may return downstairs and help with dinner."

"Aye."

With a small dip the servant left the room and Portia moved to pour a measure of the brandy into a glass.

"I doubt this is good for you, but gentlemen always seem to believe it will cure any ill."

Fredrick accepted the glass with a challenging smile. "Perhaps if nothing else, I can prove to you that not all gentlemen are the same."

A dark brow arched. "You would not be the first to try and to fail."

"My business has taught me that failure is merely one step on the path of success."

With a roll of her eyes she moved toward the door. "I will have Quinn bring you dinner when he returns from the stables."

As was her habit, Portia awoke early the next morning and washed herself with the cold water from the pitcher. Then, pulling her hair back in a smooth knot, she pulled on a fresh chemise. Instead of rushing through the rest of her morning routine, however, she discovered herself pausing before the oval mirror propped in the corner of the cramped chamber.

A rueful smile touched her lips as she studied the delicate lace inserts and pretty flowers that she had painstakingly stitched onto the fine lawn fabric.

Even her closest acquaintances would be shocked to discover that beneath her sensible gowns she wore such delicate, utterly feminine undergarments. To the world she had become a staid widow who devoted her life to her business. It was only in secret that she allowed herself to remember that she was still a relatively young woman who had once harbored the same hopes and dreams as any other.

Dreams she had thought buried until last night.

Stepping closer to the mirror, Portia considered her pale features and the delicate curves of her body. With vivid detail she remembered the feel of Fredrick's lips as they had traveled over her skin. The taste and scent of him had awakened sensations that still hummed through her body.

The knowledge was maddening, and yet, undeniably exciting. As if she had suddenly been jolted awake after years of sleep.

With a shake of her head, Portia forced herself to finish preparing for the day. For the moment she could not understand why Fredrick could so easily slip beneath her walls of defense. Or why her body reacted to him with such force. But one thing was certain, she could not hide in her rooms until he left.

Not only did her pride forbid such nonsense, but she had far too many tasks awaiting her attention.

Beginning with preparing a tray of breakfast for the

aggravating man, she acknowledged as she made her way down to the kitchen. It was, after all, entirely her fault that he had been injured. It was her duty to do everything possible to care for him until he was completely healed.

Ignoring the speculative glances from her staff, Portia loaded a tray with a variety of tempting dishes before she briskly headed back up the stairs. Not so briskly that her heart should be pounding against her chest, or her breath unsteady, of course, but it was a convenient excuse.

She halted at Fredrick's door, giving a brief tap on the smooth wood and awaiting his call for her to come in before pushing it open.

Entering the room, she crossed to set the tray on the table beside the bed. Only then did she allow herself to turn and regard the gentleman stretched on the bed.

Oh . . . this was a mistake, she realized too late. A horrid, terrible mistake.

Feeling as if she had just been kicked in the stomach, Portia forgot to breathe as her wide gaze traveled over the delicious angel lying beneath the rumpled covers.

A decadent angel, she corrected as her eyes skimmed over the rumpled honey curls and sleep-flushed features. Against her will her gaze lowered to the sight of his wide, smooth chest that was exposed in all its glory.

Mercy, she inwardly breathed, a violent explosion of awareness racing through her body. Who could have suspected that beneath those fine clothes were such sleek, powerful muscles? Or that his skin would be as smooth as polished velvet?

Her fingers twitched, they actually *twitched,* as she battled the overwhelming desire to reach out and explore the tantalizing flesh.

Thankfully unaware of her schoolgirl titillation at the sight of his half-naked body, Fredrick flashed that charming grin as he pulled the tray onto his lap and studied the thick slices of ham, eggs, kippers, and lightly toasted bread.

"Now this is a delightful surprise." He gave a low groan as he tasted of the ham, his grey eyes misty between the thick lace of his lashes. "Perhaps I shall take a tumble from my horse every evening."

Drawing in a deep, steadying breath, Portia managed to paste a cool smile onto her lips.

"I doubt that even your thick skull could withstand such punishment."

As always, he was undaunted by her aloof manner, his eyes shimmering in amusement as he continued to consume the large amount of food.

"Perhaps not." He polished off the eggs cooked in butter and chives, his eyes briefly closing in pleasure. "Where in God's name did you find your cook?"

Portia's heart skipped a beat as she studied the beautiful features that were softened by a faint shadow of whiskers. She remembered how those features had tightened with desire as he had kissed her. How those eyes had turned to smoke.

Portia wrapped her arms around her waist, willing her heart to resume beating. "Actually, I found her at a local gambling house in Winchester."

His eyes flew open with startled surprise. "Are you jesting?"

"Not at all." She gave a lift of her shoulders. "The . . .

establishment was as famous for its buffet as its selection
of house wenches. Perhaps more so."

"I can well believe it, but how did she come to work
at a respectable inn?"

"After the death of my husband I realized that I
must do something to attract the passing customers so
I traveled to Winchester and convinced Mrs. Cornell
that I could offer her more than her current employer."

"You went to a gaming hell? Personally?"

She met his curious gaze squarely. Over the past few
years she had learned to endure the shock and disapproval of gentlemen who thought business a purely
male domain. Women were too unstable, too weak,
too soft-hearted, too stupid . . .

She had heard every reason why she should sell her
inn and retreat quietly to a small cottage. Which, of
course, only made her more determined to succeed.

"If you truly are a businessman then you must know
that a faint heart can never survive," she challenged
in tart tones.

The expected expression of censure never appeared. Instead, Fredrick continued to regard her
with that mild curiosity.

"And it does not trouble you that she worked at
such a place?"

"No more so than the fact that two of my maids
were once prostitutes at that same gaming hell. Or
that Quinn was imprisoned for poaching. Or that
Spenser was once a smuggler."

Without warning Fredrick tipped back his head to
chuckle with unexpected amusement.

"You know, poppet, you are something of a fraud."

"What do you mean?"

"Beneath that hard-hearted businesswoman lies the soul of a saint."

A warm blush stained her cheeks at the low sincerity in his voice. She was quite prepared to defend herself against disdain, but it seemed she had no ready resistance to flattery.

"Not at all," she said, hoping she did not appear as flustered as she felt. "My servants possess a genuine appreciation for their posts. They work far harder than most staff."

"I do not believe that was your reason for hiring them, but I do agree that it is preferable to work with those who are eager to prove themselves."

She stilled as she realized that this was one gentleman who might actually understand the effort it had taken her and her staff to overcome the narrow, condemning view of others. Although he was clearly a well-educated gentleman, the mere fact that he was a bastard would have shut any number of doors in his face.

"As you were?"

"Yes." His smile twisted. "Had I been born an aristocrat I doubt I should ever have made the effort to make my own fortune. I suppose I should be grateful to my father for not bothering to give me his name."

"Oh, that reminds me." Silently chastising her scattered wits, Portia reached into her pocket to withdraw the small envelope. "This came for you earlier this morning."

Setting aside the tray, Fredrick reached for the envelope and slid his finger beneath the seal.

"It is from my father," he muttered, a frown tugging at his brows. "Bloody hell."

"Is something wrong?"

"Just an invitation to luncheon."

"You do not seem especially pleased."

Fredrick crumpled the paper in his hand before tossing it aside. "Considering that he could barely exchange ten words with me when I called upon him yesterday, it is rather odd he would desire me to share a meal with him."

"I presume that the two of you are not close?"

He ran a restless hand over his unshaven jaw. "As far as my father is concerned, I am nothing more than a mistake his conscience will not allow him to simply forget."

Against her will, Portia felt her heart softening at his bald confession. Blast the man. Why could he not just be another worthless rake? It was bad enough that her body reacted to him as if she were standing in the center of a lightning storm. But now he was in perilous danger of making her actually *like* him.

"I am sorry." She gave a short shake of her head. "Everyone should have family who loves them."

He regarded her with a searching gaze. "You sound as if you know something of the matter."

She hesitated only a moment before confessing the truth. Her past was hardly a secret in the neighborhood.

"My mother died giving birth to me and my father was a hardened gamester who lost his entire fortune at the tables before fleeing to India to escape his creditors."

"How old were you when he left?"

"Eighteen."

Fredrick sucked in a sharp breath, his eyes narrowed. "And they call me a bastard."

She smiled wryly. "Yes, well, when you are born a

nobleman you can be the worst sort of villain without ever raising an eyebrow."

"You will get no argument from me," he said softly.

No, she probably would not. Fredrick Smith had no doubt experienced any number of slights and snubs from gentlemen of the *ton.* Not that it seemed to have hampered him on his climb to success.

She had to admire him for that.

"Will you accept your father's offer to dine?"

His expression unexpectedly hardened. "Unfortunately, I have little choice in the matter. I have to accept."

"Are you sure you should be leaving your bed?" With a small frown she moved forward, her hand instinctively reaching out to lightly touch the gash on his forehead before she realized the sheer intimacy of her behavior. "The wound has closed over, but you still have a lump."

With a swift motion he had captured her wrist in a light grip, his eyes darkening with the awareness that crackled to life between them.

"Is it bad enough to tempt you to kiss it better?"

Portia sternly told herself to move away. His touch was light enough that she could easily break his hold. But as her gaze clashed with his own she realized that his fingers might as well have been steel shackles.

Mercy. His touch was as light as a feather, but it was sending tongues of flame licking up her arm and over her shivering skin.

"Certainly not," she breathed, her voice oddly husky.

His thumb brushed the pulse at her wrist. "Even if I tell you that it still aches like the very devil?"

"Perhaps I should call for the doctor."

"I would prefer a kiss."

The flames spread to curl in the secret depths of her stomach. Oh, yes. A kiss. A simple, delicious kiss.

It was what she had desired from the moment she walked into the room and saw him lying on the bed like some fallen angel.

No. It was what she desired from the moment she had awoken with the taste of him still lingering on her lips.

"Mr. . . ."

"Fredrick," he interrupted. "I have never seen such perfect skin. It is like ivory satin." He shifted her arm, bringing it lower so that he could sniff deeply of her inner wrist. "Satin scented with roses."

Her knees felt weak as she gulped in the elusive air. "I should go."

He gave a light tug on her wrist, steadily pulling her closer to his sinfully tempting lips.

"I will not try to halt you."

Tiny thrills of excitement feathered down her spine. A kiss, the voice of the devil whispered in the back of her mind. What was one kiss to recall during the long, endless nights?

Before the voice of reason could rise and destroy the moment, Portia leaned downward and touched her mouth to his own.

He gave a choked sound, as if he had been caught off guard by her daring. Then, before she could pull back, his hands had shifted to capture her face, his lips softening as they swept over hers with slow, drugging kisses.

Sweet, blissful heat flowed through her body as she instinctively parted her lips and allowed his tongue to explore ever deeper. Oh . . . God. Nothing in all her six and twenty years had ever felt like this.

Her hands fluttered before landing on the naked flesh of his chest. Another blaze of heat rocked through her, and barely aware of what she did, her fingers trailed a searching path over the warm skin, exploring the rigid muscles that flexed beneath her touch.

"Yes, poppet," he groaned, his mouth searching and finding the sensitive pulse at the base of her throat. "Touch me. Please, touch me."

She gave a low groan at the sound of his ragged voice. She wanted to touch him. Everywhere. From the thick, honey curls to the tip of his toes. She wanted to rub against him like a cat, heating her skin against his own.

As if sensing her shocking response, Fredrick allowed his slender, utterly clever fingers to slide down the curve of her neck and over the high neckline of her gown. Portia's breath evaporated, her knees nearly buckling as those fingers at last cupped the aching fullness of her breasts.

Blessed heavens.

That was what she wanted. Needed. For one insane moment she arched her back to thrust herself toward his touch, her nipples hard beneath her corset.

Oh . . . to have her stupid wool and whalebone magically disappear. To feel those wondrous hands on her bare skin.

It did not take a great imagination to know that the sensations that Fredrick Smith could inspire would be a world away from her previous experience.

He was no callow youth, intent only on his own pleasure. Nor was he elderly enough to consider her more a daughter than lover.

No, he would be patient and tender and he would teach her all the delicious secrets that other women whispered of.

The sound of voices in the corridor at last jerked Portia out of her sensual haze. Dear God, she had left the door wide open. Anyone could have walked by and seen her acting as if this were some bawdy house rather than a respectable inn.

With a small gasp she stumbled away from the lingering touch, her hand pressed to her pounding heart.

Fredrick sat up on the bed, his hand stretched out. "Portia . . ."

"No," she whispered, refusing to allow her gaze to lower to the vast amount of flesh exposed as his blanket tumbled to his waist. "I do not know why I did that. I cannot . . ." She gave a shake of her head and rushed toward the door. "Not again. Never again."

Chapter Five

Not again. Never again.

Portia's tortured words haunted Fredrick as he forced himself to bathe and dress for the upcoming meeting with his father.

Dash it all. He hadn't meant to startle her. In truth, he hadn't expected her to give into his coaxing for a kiss.

But once she had . . .

His body shuddered at the memory of her hands moving over his chest with those soft, tentative strokes. In that moment he would have given his fortune to have tugged her onto the bed beside him and eased his smoldering frustration in the heat of her body.

Instead she had once again bolted, leaving him alone and aching, with no genuine hope of relief in sight.

Bloody hell. The woman was enough to drive the most sane man to Bedlam. One moment she was the cold, aloof general who commanded all those around her with crisp precision, and the next she was melting in his arms as if she were a sweet, vulnerable woman who was in dire need of a man's touch.

No doubt if he had a lick of sense he would flee with all possible speed. For all Portia's obvious skill as an innkeeper, he sensed that beneath her careful control she was still struggling to understand the meaning of being a woman.

How could she not be, with a father who abandoned her when she was a mere babe, and a husband who had clearly left her wounded?

And yet, a small voice whispered, she was also warm, and passionate, and so tender-hearted that it made him smile to think of the misfits she had gathered beneath her wings.

A rare, exquisite woman who would put up a struggle worthy of Napoleon for any man stupid enough to try and get close to her.

Gathering his horse from the stables, Fredrick headed for his father's estate. Oh yes, she was an aggravating minx. And he was an idiot not to pack his bags and head for less dangerous grounds.

Idiot or not, however, he knew that he would not be packing any bags. At least not yet.

Mrs. Portia Walker might be the very definition of trouble, but she fascinated him like no other woman he had ever encountered. He would not be leaving until he managed to understand precisely what it was about her that entranced him.

Traveling up the tree-lined drive to the estate, Fredrick grudgingly put all thoughts of Portia aside and instead turned his attention to the upcoming meal with his father.

A far less fascinating subject, he acknowledged wryly. After the short, decidedly terse encounter only the day before he had never expected to hear from

Lord Graystone again. Certainly he had not expected to receive a gracious invitation to dine at his home.

He could only suppose the old bugger had experienced a belated sense of guilt at greeting his son with all the pleasure of a tooth-drawer. Or, more likely, he wanted to make sure that Fredrick had no intention of lingering near Oak Manor for any extended length of time.

In either case it at least offered the opportunity to pursue his original goal in coming to Wessex.

Leaving his mount in the hands of a groom, Fredrick entered the manor house and allowed a subdued Morgan to lead him to the back parlor where he found his father standing beside a long row of windows surveying the garden below.

For a moment, Fredrick hovered uncertainly on the threshold. As always he felt that tense, slightly sick feeling in the pit of his stomach when in the presence of his father. It was not that Lord Graystone was a frightening man. Like Fredrick he possessed a slender build and mild temperament.

But even as a young child Fredrick had been able to sense the terse discomfort that plagued Lord Graystone whenever he was in the company of his son.

As if it were only by grim determination that he could even bear a few moments in Fredrick's presence.

With a shake of his head, Fredrick resisted the urge to turn on his heel and rush from the estate. He was no longer a child to be hurt by his father's dislike. He was a man who had come on a mission.

One that he wanted done with so that he could return to London and his waiting business.

Perhaps sensing he was no longer alone, Lord Graystone slowly turned, his pale blue eyes briefly darkening with some indefinable emotion before he managed to paste a stiff smile to his lips.

"Fredrick, thank you for joining me."

Refusing to appear a coward, Fredrick forced himself to cross the Persian carpet to stand in the center of the room.

"I must admit I was surprised to receive your invitation," he said, his tone carefully bland. "Yesterday I sensed that you were not best pleased with my presence."

The older man flinched, almost as if Fredrick had managed to strike a nerve. "It was not that. Never that. I was simply . . . caught off guard."

Fredrick's lips twisted. "Yes, of course. I should have sent a letter warning you that I would be in the neighborhood and awaited a proper invitation. But my business came up unexpectedly and it seemed—"

"Fredrick, you will always have an invitation to this house," his father interrupted in a harsh voice. "If I have ever made you think otherwise then I am sorry."

It was Fredrick's turn to be caught off guard and he blinked in astonishment. It was the first time his father had ever indicated that he was anything more than an intruder that must be endured.

"Thank you, Father."

An awkward silence descended as Lord Graystone seemed to battle within himself as to how to treat the stranger that was his son. With an obvious effort, he moved toward a satinwood sideboard and busied himself with pouring out two small measures from the crystal decanter.

"Will you join me in a sherry?"

"Yes, thank you."

Handing Fredrick the small glass, Lord Graystone

stepped back, his gaze running over Fredrick's well-tailored grey jacket and black breeches.

"It is obvious that London agrees with you," he murmured.

Fredrick gave a faint shrug, thrusting aside his simmering resentment that unlike his half-brother, his own success had been hard won.

If he were to discover anything of value he would have to somehow lure his father into a sense of comfort.

"I have managed to survive," he said lightly.

"More than survive I should say." A smile touched the older man's lips. "I had always thought that engineers did no more than build bridges, but you seem to have a wide variety of interests."

Fredrick hid his stab of surprise. He would have bet his last quid that his father did not know he had created his own business, let alone that he was an engineer.

"I have built my share of bridges as well as a number of roads, but it is true that my interests are widespread. Perhaps too widespread," he admitted wryly. "I once had a very peaceful business with a handful of staff and now I seem to have acquired several warehouses and dozens of employees. They require an inordinate amount of attention."

"These employees are inventors, are they not?" his father demanded, once again surprising him.

"For the most part they are only hopeful dreamers who someday might see their various ideas become a reality."

"And you support them until that reality arrives?"

Fredrick nodded, not adding that he also assisted the inventors with his own skill when necessary. Dreamers, he had discovered, rarely possessed simple common sense. They might conjure the most fabulous inventions, but failed to realize that their design was far too complex to be replicated, or so ridiculously obscure there was no market for them.

"I consider them an investment, much like my investments in various patents."

His father studied him intently, almost as if he were genuinely interested in Fredrick's work.

"So you invest in dreams."

Fredrick gave a startled laugh, discovering that he liked the notion. Most considered him a practical man. A man who lived by his lists and schedules and calculated logic. Few were ever allowed to know that deep in his heart a poet lurked.

"I suppose that is one way of putting it." He allowed his gaze to study the features that were so painfully similar to his own. "May I inquire how you have come to know so much of my business?"

"Even so far from town the stories of your business genius manage to circulate," his father said evasively. "It was written in the *Post* that you possess the Midas touch."

Fredrick gave a short laugh, picturing the endless days of toil he had put in for his famous Midas touch.

"I could only wish it were that simple."

"True." The smile faded from the lean, elegant features. "There are too few who understand that success is the result of hard work, not just luck. And sacrifice." His voice lowered, a tinge of sadness threaded through his words. "There is always sacrifice."

Sacrifice? An odd choice of words.

What had he been forced to sacrifice?

"You seem to understand hard work well enough." Fredrick waved a hand around the recently refurbished room. "The estate appears quite profitable."

"It was not always so." Lord Graystone drained his sherry and set aside his glass. "Before I inherited the title my father had managed to run the estate into dun territory and my brother promised to follow in his footsteps. They both believed that they could continue to take from the estate without ever bothering to reinvest in the land or the people."

"Having traveled a good deal throughout England I must say that it is not at all an uncommon practice among landowners," Fredrick could not resist pointing out.

Being a bastard was at times awkward, but it was nothing compared to the lives of too many tenants.

"You are right," his father readily agreed. "I attempted to be the voice of reason upon occasion, but as the younger son my opinions were not requested, nor were they at all welcomed. My brother accused me of attempting to undermine his authority with the tenants and forbade me even to speak with them."

It was the first true insight his father had ever given into his life and Fredrick discovered himself grudgingly intrigued.

"That must have been a difficult position."

"It was damn well impossible." Lord Graystone smiled wryly. "In truth I was relieved when I was forced to leave . . ."

The words were broken off sharply as Lord Graystone abruptly turned to pace toward the windows. It was obvious that he had revealed far more than he had intended and Fredrick was careful to keep his manner casual.

"That I can well imagine," he said, setting aside his own glass. "It would be frustrating for anyone to be forced to stand aside and watch his home being ruined." He paused, knowing better than to blatantly demand why his father was forced to leave Oak Manor. He was a fool, not a stupid fool. "Did you go to London?"

"Winchester," his father retorted in clipped tones.

"Of course. That is where Lady Graystone comes from, is it not?"

"Yes." Turning, Lord Graystone regarded his son with the guarded, closed expression that Fredrick had become all too accustomed to. The brief few moments of intimacy were at an end. "I believe luncheon should be ready. Shall we?"

"Of course."

In awkward silence they moved through the hushed corridors to the dining room. Despite the long, polished table that could easily seat twenty guests, there was a cozy warmth to the darkly paneled room with its vast fireplace and towering windows that provided a fine view of the rose garden.

The silence remained as they were seated and the footmen arrived with trays of turtle soup, stewed trout, and Fredrick's favorite lobster curry.

It was not until his father had waved the servants from the room that the older man made a visible effort to lower the stiff guard he had built around himself.

"Are you comfortable at your inn?" he demanded as he poured them both a glass of wine.

Fredrick hid his startled expression. What the devil was his father up to? He never made personal inquiries of his bastard son. Not even bothering to ask after his health.

Savoring the lobster curry, Fredrick gave an inward

shrug. Whatever odd compulsion had come over Lord Graystone, it suited Fredrick's purpose.

The man had already revealed that he had been forced to leave Oak Manor when he was young. And that after his inheritance he had made some painful sacrifice. Vague clues that might lead to precisely nothing, but still it was more than he had before he arrived.

Besides, his father's past sins were not the only puzzle currently plaguing him.

Perhaps Lord Graystone could assist with unraveling the mystery of Mrs. Portia Walker.

"I am quite comfortable," he said with a faint smile. "I do not believe I have ever rented rooms that are quite so ruthlessly clean or enjoyed meals so exquisitely prepared. Mrs. Walker possesses a true talent in running a first-rate establishment."

"Walker?" His father frowned as if the name were somehow familiar. "Of course. Melford's daughter."

"You know her?"

"I know *of* her," his father corrected. "Her father was a friend to my brother. As I recall they shared many interests, including their addiction to expensive courtesans and the gaming tables."

Which meant that Portia's father was definitely an aristocrat. The Graystones did not rub elbows with the unwashed masses.

"It is rather odd that a woman of her obvious social standing would become a proprietress of an isolated inn."

His father shrugged. "I seem to recall there was some scandal attached to the woman."

Fredrick reached for his wine. "I did happen to

learn that her father disappeared to India when his debts became too great."

Lord Graystone frowned, as if scouring his mind for memories of the long ago gossip.

"Yes, it had something to do with that . . . ah, now I recall. The daughter was engaged to some minor nobleman or another, not a local man, and he turned out to be a true bounder."

Fredrick stiffened. "What do you mean?"

"The cad left her standing at the altar. It was only a few days later that her father fled from his creditors." Lord Graystone gave a wave of his hand. "I suppose he had hoped his new son-in-law would settle his accounts and when that did not come to pass he was forced to flee."

Fredrick downed his wine in one swallow, a dark anger flaring through his heart. What sort of man would abandon his young daughter just days after her heart and her future had been destroyed?

And who the blazes was the minor nobleman who would leave his bride at the altar? A woman so beautiful, so extraordinarily talented, that she would make any man proud to call her his own.

No wonder Portia regarded men as treacherous beasts who were doomed to disappoint her.

"This Melford sounds like a genuine rotter," he muttered, hoping that the man had managed to offend one of the natives once he reached India. Being roasted over an open pit was appropriate punishment for the louse.

His father grimaced. "From what I recall of Melford he was always a weak and self-centered dolt. It is hardly surprising that he would think only of himself when it came time to pay the piper."

"So Mrs. Walker was forced to wed to survive," Fredrick said softly.

"I suppose she was."

Fredrick forced himself to polish off the last of his lobster curry. Mrs. Shaw had gone to a great deal of effort to prepare his favorite dishes. He did not take such acts of kindness for granted. They were far too rare in his world.

"What do you know of Mr. Walker?" he at last demanded.

His father regarded him with a narrowed gaze. "Nothing more than that he was considerably older than his bride." He paused, as if choosing his words with care. "Is there a particular reason for your interest in Mrs. Walker?"

Fredrick smiled as he reached to refill his wine glass. "I am always interested in the unusual and the unique." The image of vivid blue eyes set in a perfect oval of a face burned through his mind, his body hardening with anticipation. "And Mrs. Walker is most certainly unique."

Chapter Six

Fredrick left Oak Manor in a mood he could only describe as bemused.

Good God, he had spent nearly two hours in his father's company. And they had actually spoken to one another. In full sentences rather than stilted grunts and mutters.

Fredrick did not know whether it was a miracle, or if the sky was about to fall, but as he traveled back toward the Queen's Arms he discovered that the smothering resentment he always endured after being in the presence of his father was not nearly as overwhelming as usual.

The question was why?

Why had his father invited him to luncheon and then actually treated him as a welcomed guest? Why had he known so much of his bastard son's business?

Could it be that he actually regretted their estrangement over the past ten years? Could he have followed his career from afar, regretting that he never bothered to so much as pat his own son on the back?

Fredrick gave a sharp shake of his head. Who could

say what might be going through the mind of Lord Graystone? Or why he had decided to behave in such an odd manner?

Come tomorrow he more than likely would return to the cold, remote man of Fredrick's past.

And besides, he had not come to Oak Manor with the futile hope of forging a relationship with the man who had fathered him. He was here to discover the reason Lord Graystone had ever been willing to hand over twenty thousand pounds to Dunnington.

Turning his thoughts back to his father's confession that he had been forced to leave his home, Fredrick pondered the best means of discovering the reason for the family feud.

The current servants would clearly have no knowledge. Not if they had all been hired after his father had inherited the title. But surely there must be someone who knew the family history still rattling about.

The question was how to discover their whereabouts, and then question them without causing undue curiosity.

A delicate task that would require some thought. He would not risk floundering around and calling undue attention to himself.

Pulling his notebook from his jacket, he managed to jot down his various options without ending up in a ditch or becoming lost. At last reaching the inn, Fredrick tucked away his notebook and entered the yard.

He frowned at the thick mud that remained despite the pale sunlight. Mrs. Portia Walker might have many skills, but comprehending proper drainage was not one of them.

Heading directly to the stables, Fredrick dismounted

and went in search of Quinn. He found the old servant in the tack room enjoying a peaceful smoke.

Not bothering with preliminaries, Fredrick explained precisely what he desired of the man and the various tools that would be needed to accomplish the task.

Quinn listened in silence, with only the lift of his brows revealing that he found Fredrick's request out of the ordinary.

At last he turned his head to spit. "Drainage ditches, eh?"

Fredrick smiled, leaning against the workbench with his arms folded over his chest. He breathed in deeply of the rich scent of hay and leather and polish. Earthy scents that reminded him that he was far from his London townhouse.

A knowledge that for the moment did not trouble him a whit.

"Unless you prefer mucking about in the mud?" he demanded.

The servant gave a wry grin. "Nay, I can't say as I do. Still, it seems a mite odd that Mrs. Walker hasn't spoken of this notion."

"Not odd at all considering that I have yet to speak with her about it. I thought it would be a pleasant surprise."

"Oh aye, a surprise." Rubbing his chin, Quinn narrowed his gaze in a quizzical manner. "Why?"

"I beg your pardon?"

"Why would a fashionable gent who be just passing through want to be plotting surprises for an innkeeper?"

"If I were truly a fashionable gent I would tell you to mind your own business, you damned old goat," Fredrick said lightly, his expression carefully bland. "But as it is, I am merely a man of business who cannot halt my compulsion to tinker and fix anything in my path. Including a muddy yard in an obscure inn." A rueful smile touched his lips. "My friends will assure you that I have yet to be invited to their homes without finding something that needs to be altered."

Quinn gave a snort at the perfectly logical explanation. "And this has nothing to do with getting Mrs. Walker in yer bed?"

Fredrick swallowed a soft groan at the thought of Portia in his bed. Hell, he would dig a ditch to London if it would mean having her delicate body warm and welcoming beneath him. His rampaging lust, however, was not solely the reason for his desire to teach her that men could offer more than betrayal.

It was all becoming far more complicated.

Complicated enough that he had no desire to actually sort through the strange impulse that compelled him to prove his worth to the aggravating woman.

Aware that Quinn was studying him with that all-too-knowing gaze, Fredrick conjured a small smile.

"I am a man who is perfectly capable of recognizing a beautiful woman when she crosses my path, but I do not force the unwilling."

"But ye are willing to seduce her with drainage ditches?" Quinn persisted, clearly feeling it his duty to protect the woman who had taken him in when no one else would.

Fredrick did not doubt that the entire staff felt the same protective urges. Which meant that he would have to take care not to give any of them a reason to consider him the enemy.

"For the moment I would be pleased if she could learn that not all gentlemen are created for the sole purpose of making her life miserable."

The older man pondered for a long moment, debating between bringing Fredrick's plot to a swift end and allowing him to continue.

"Clever, but I fear yer destined for a nasty set-down," he at last warned. "Mrs. Walker don't take kindly to those who interfere. Especially not London gents."

"She is a woman of sense." Frederick gave a lift of his shoulder. "Once she realizes that my changes are best for the inn, she will be happy that I offered my expertise."

Quinn gave a short laugh. "Aye, she might, but then she might just geld ye. Should be interesting to see which it is."

Fredrick would have found the words a good deal more amusing if there weren't more than a bit of truth in them. Portia Walker was certainly capable of doing a bit of gelding if the urge should hit her.

"Interesting, indeed," he said dryly. "So you will assist me?"

"Yer playing with fire."

"It will not be the first time."

There was another pause before Quinn gave a wide grin. "Very well, I'll gather the lads. But do not blame me when you find yerself being hauled like a carcass over the coals."

By late afternoon, Portia found herself near exhaustion. Her own fault, of course. After overseeing the daily laundry, she had sorted through the linens in search of those that needed darning, spent an hour of haggling with Mr. Patrick, the local butcher, inventoried the cellars, and tackled her account ledgers with grim resolution.

That did not even include the departing and arriving guests who demanded her attention.

Portia rubbed her lower back as she made her way through the back corridor to the kitchen. She had accomplished a great deal over the past few hours, she acknowledged wryly, except the one thing she had hoped to accomplish.

Damn Mr. Fredrick Smith.

She did not want to be plagued by thoughts of those heartbreakingly beautiful features. Or the feel of his clever fingers sliding over her skin. Or the taste of his finely carved lips.

She did not want those whispers in the back of her mind that urged her to forget her sworn promise never to trust another man.

And she most certainly did not want those scandalous daydreams of scented spring nights lying in a pair of warm, strong arms.

Portia muttered beneath her breath as she entered the bustling kitchen. Soon enough Mr. Smith would be on his way and she could put him firmly from her mind. Until then . . . well, until then she would grit her teeth and hope no one noticed her ridiculous distraction.

Crossing the freshly mopped flagstone floor, Portia halted beside her cook.

"Mrs. Cornell, have you seen Tolly?"

Busy shelling peas, the older woman gave a nod of her head toward the back door.

"Aye, he's outside helping that London gent."

Portia frowned. London gent? That could only mean Fredrick. But what the devil could he want with young Tolly?

"Thank you," she murmured, moving swiftly out of the inn and into the back garden.

Absently frowning as she realized that Tolly was nowhere in sight, she paused long enough to pet the ecstatic Puck, who danced about her feet before heading toward the stable yard.

She rounded the corner of the inn, coming to a sudden halt at the sight of her entire male staff busily digging along the edges of the yard.

Picking up her skirts to keep the wool from being stained, she hurried to where Quinn was filling one of the ditches with a mixture of gravel and sand.

"Quinn?"

The older man straightened, an odd glint of humor in his eyes. "Aye?"

"Whatever are you doing?"

"Ye had best ask yer guest." He nodded his head toward the stables where Fredrick was using a hoe to mark lines in the mud. "He was the one who decided yer yard was in need of drainage."

Portia's heart gave a startled jerk as she studied the slender, honey-haired man. He had stripped down to no more than tight breeches and a fine lawn shirt. Not nearly enough to hide the smooth muscles that rippled with a predatory grace, or the glimpse of pale golden skin that was exposed by the open buttons.

Holy heavens. Her mouth went dry even as her palms began to sweat in the most peculiar manner.

It was no wonder that custom dictated that a man remain properly attired in the presence of a lady. At least a man who could make a poor woman gape and gawk at his sheer male beauty.

It was indecent.

Nearly as indecent as the heat curling through the pit of her stomach.

With a shake of her head, Portia forced her attention back to the man at her side.

"I do not care if he decided my inn needed wings so it might fly, he has no right to interfere. And you had no business giving into his ridiculous commands," she added tartly.

Quinn pulled a handkerchief from his pocket and wiped his damp brow. "He promised ye would be pleased."

"Pleased?" She gave a click of her tongue. "The man dares to treat my property as if it were his own, and he believes I will be pleased?"

"Well, ye must admit that the yard does get a boggy mess when it rains, and the man seems to know a thing or two about these ditches. Why toss away a fine gift jest because ye have no liking for the ribbon?"

Portia rolled her eyes. "Mr. Smith has caused quite enough chaos at the Queen's Arms. I will not tolerate any more."

Spinning on her heel, Portia marched across the muddy ground to the stables. Fredrick Smith might be the most beautiful man she had ever encountered, but he was also the most annoying.

A dangerous combination to her normally even temperament.

Halting directly before the aggravating man, Portia planted her hands on her hips and conjured her most commanding expression.

"Mr. Smith."

Without even bothering to glance up, Fredrick continued to pull his hoe through the mud.

"I thought we had agreed to Fredrick," he murmured softly.

A shaft of anger shot through Portia even as she shivered at the sight of his half-naked form. Gads, it was even more disturbing up close.

Despite the cool air, the linen shirt was damp enough to cling with loving precision to the width of his chest and the scent of warm male skin reached out to tease at her nose.

Her entire body tingled with a sharp, delicious tension that threatened to distract her from the reason she had approached him in the first place.

It was hard to be furious when her thoughts were consumed with the picture of ripping that shirt from his body and running her hands over that hard chest.

Snapping her teeth together, she grimly thrust aside the treacherous sensations.

"Mr. Smith, please put my hoe down and attend me."

"My name is Fredrick."

She glared at the top of his honey curls as he continued with his self-imposed task.

"Fredrick," she forced herself to grit.

Slowly straightening, Fredrick allowed the hoe to drop and pulled a handkerchief from his pocket to wipe at his hands.

"Yes, Portia?"

"Would you mind telling me just what the devil you think you are about?"

Tucking away the handkerchief, Fredrick at last allowed his gaze to meet her cold glare.

"I would not mind at all," he said with a faint smile. "I am offering you the benefit of my expertise. I assure you that many pay a fortune for my skills."

"And if I had desire of your skills then I would

willingly pay you such a fortune," she informed him
in icy tones. "As it is I would prefer that you reserve
your expertise for those who request it."

"Why?"

"Because I do not appreciate your interference."

A chiseled brow arched as he studied her with an
unnerving intensity. "And how am I interfering?"

"You know very well that you have taken my servants away from their duties and have them wasting
their time digging in the mud instead of tending to
my guests."

He shrugged, the simple movement causing the
muscles of his chest to ripple in a fascinating manner.

"Actually what they are doing is providing proper
drainage so your yard will not become a treacherous
swamp whenever it rains," he said, as if it were all perfectly logical. "I assure you that your guests will be
delighted to avoid ruining their footwear. And you
will have far more carriages willing to halt if they need
not fear becoming stuck in the mire."

He was right, of course. She had been meaning to
have the yard properly repaired for the past year. That
knowledge, however, did nothing to ease her smoldering frustration.

She did not want any man interfering in her life. Especially not this man. It was aggravating enough that
he set her senses aflame just by being near. Did he
have to thrust his way into her business as well?

"That is not the point."

"Then what is the point?" he pressed.

"This is my property."

"And?"

Her fingers clenched into tight fists. He was being
deliberately obtuse. And worse, she did not know if

she wanted to throttle him or rip off that shirt and kiss her way down his gorgeous chest.

Portia sucked in a deep breath, deliberately jutting out her chin. "And you have no right to make decisions here."

"Even if they are good decisions?" he demanded.

"They are *mine* to make," she gritted.

Without warning he had reached out to grasp her hand and tugged her into the nearby stables. Portia stumbled behind, too startled to put up a proper fight.

Or at least that was what she told herself. Otherwise it would mean a secret part of her actually wanted to be alone with the man in the shadowed stables.

Pulling until they were out of sight of the servants, Fredrick at last halted and regarded her with a narrowed gaze.

"I admire your independence, poppet, but surely a gentleman can offer you a gift without threatening it?"

She gave a jerk on her hand, attempting to free herself from his grasp. When it was obvious he would not loosen his grip without a futile struggle, Portia was forced to content herself with an aloof expression.

"You consider this a gift?"

That charming grin curved his lips. "You did not seem the sort of woman who desired the traditional posies or pretty trinkets."

Her heart slammed against her chest as she felt his thumb lightly caress the skin of her inner wrist. Her eyes widened as they clashed with the shimmering gray gaze.

Oh . . . mercy.

Concentrate, Portia. Just . . . concentrate.

"Why would you offer me any gifts?"

"To please you, of course."

A sharp fear arrowed down her spine. "No, Fredrick, do not . . ."

Her words stuttered to a halt as he stepped closer, his hands lightly running up her arms to grasp her shoulders. His touch was soft, but it sent a shock of heat to the tips of her toes.

"I am asking nothing of you, Portia," he said, his tone low and as smooth as honey. "And I do have an ulterior motive."

"What is that?" The words came out strangely hoarse.

"I have already ruined one pair of boots." The silver eyes danced with amusement. "If I ruin my last pair I shall be forced to go about in my stockings."

She lowered her gaze, unable to think clearly when he was so near. "Please do not jest."

"Portia—"

"This is not just a business to me," she interrupted, far too conscious of his proximity. It would be so easy to reach out and touch that beautiful face. To run her fingers through his tangled curls. Gads, it was actually painful to resist. "This inn is my . . . security. So long as it is in my charge I know that I need never fear for my future."

"I understand, poppet," he murmured. "I truly do."

With a sharp movement she had pulled from his distracting touch. "You could not possibly understand."

The elegant features hardened as he caught and held her wary gaze. "Portia, I was born a bastard. There is no one in the world who better understands what it is to be completely alone in the world. My mother died when I was born, and until the age of eight, I was forced to live with an elderly widow in Winchester who took great delight in beating me with her cane. I had no friends, no one who cared if I cried myself to sleep at night." His lips twisted in a humorless smile. "Not even my beloved father who did not even acknowledge me as his bastard until I was sent to school in London."

She bit her bottom lip, touched in spite of herself by his stark words. "I am sorry."

"I did not reveal my sordid past for your pity," his features softened. "I only want you to know that I understand your need to feel that you are in control of your life. When one is forced to endure uncertainty and constant upheaval, it is inevitable to crave a need for security."

He did understand. Perhaps more than she wanted.

This man had felt the terror of being helpless against the whimsy of fate. Of knowing that he had no one but himself to depend on if he was to survive.

Which in some ways only made it worse, she acknowledged. If he would just primp and prance and flutter about like any decent dandy she could freeze him with one slaying glare.

But a kindred spirit?

That she did not know how to battle.

Portia wrapped her arms about her waist as she regarded him with a wary frown.

"If you understand, then why are you so determined to meddle where you do not belong?"

The grey eyes became misty as he allowed pleasant memories to overtake him.

"Because I was fortunate enough to be given into the care of a very wise man who taught me that being strong and independent did not mean a person cannot appreciate the kindness offered by others. In fact, it is in sharing our lives with others that brings a richness to our days."

"I share my life with many people," she protested. "The people who work for me are more than mere servants, they are my family."

"And dependent on you for their livelihood."

Portia stiffened, oddly stung by his words. "What is that supposed to mean?"

Slowly he stepped toward her, his gaze deliberately lowering to her mouth.

"They are no threat to you, poppet," he whispered.

"And you are?"

A wicked fire abruptly sparked to life in the silver eyes. "Perhaps."

She resisted the urge to lick her lips. That breathless tension was swirling between them. A near tangible heat that brushed over her skin and made her breath unsteady. The slightest movement and she would be in his arms.

Where she wanted to be.

"I need to return to the inn," she husked.

He gave a soft chuckle, as if amused by her less-than-subtle need to flee. Then he slowly bent his head toward her.

Portia instinctively prepared herself to battle his kiss, but she was unprepared when he tilted his head and pressed his face in the curve of her neck. He drew in a deep breath, inhaling her scent.

"Exquisite," he murmured. "Midnight roses."

A shudder wracked Portia's body. "Fredrick."

Before she could even begin to struggle (always assuming that she had the strength or the will to struggle), he was pulling away to regard her with a searching gaze.

"Shall I continue with my drainage ditches?"

For a moment Portia fought to regain command of her scattered wits. She did not want to think of drainage ditches. Or the danger of letting down her guard in the presence of a heart-rendingly handsome gentleman. She wanted him to yank her into his arms and quench the ache that was becoming near unbearable.

At last she gave a shake of her head and smoothed her trembling hands down the folds of her apron.

If she were at all sensible she could command this man to leave her inn at once. He was worse than any mere rake.

He was bossy and interfering and capable of turning her mind to mush with a single glance.

Unfortunately, at the moment she was not feeling sensible. She was feeling as giddy and fluttery as the worse sort of henwit.

Clearly a swift retreat was in order.

"If you wish to play in the mud, then by all means enjoy yourself," she muttered, turning toward the door and hopefully the sanity beyond. "I have learned to indulge my guests, no matter how strange or annoying they might be."

"If you truly wish to indulge me, poppet, I have a better means of . . ."

Rushing out the door, Portia picked up her skirts and dashed across the muddy yard.

The devil take Fredrick Smith.

Portia tried any number of tricks to put thoughts of angelic features and wicked grey eyes from her mind.

She assisted Mrs. Cornell in the kitchen, she took Puck for a long walk through the woods, she took a hot bath, and she even laid down for a short nap.

Nothing, however, was effective in keeping her mind from dwelling on Fredrick Smith.

Time after time she discovered herself drawn to a window simply to catch sight of him. There was such a confident assurance in his movements, such a natural ability to command those about him. It was not arrogance, but more the absolute knowledge that he knew precisely what needed to be done and how to accomplish the task.

A part of her knew that she should have been furious at his outrageous interference. She had battled her entire life to at last acquire her sense of independence. He had no right to thrust himself into her business.

But it was not fury that was plaguing her as she slowly left the inn and headed for the stables. Instead it was a confusing mixture of fear and bewilderment, and a treacherous excitement that refused to be squashed.

Entering the stables, Portia moved past the stalls toward the back rooms that Quinn claimed as his own.

"Quinn?" she called softly.

A narrow door opened and the elderly servant appeared to regard her with a hint of surprise.

"Aye?"

Portia smiled as she moved to stand before him. She had known Quinn her entire life. He had been a groom for her father before Lord Melford had been forced to sell off his stables and turned his faithful servant away without so much as a reference. Not surprisingly, Quinn had been forced to survive by whatever means necessary and more than once he was punished for daring to poach for his food.

When her father disappeared, Quinn returned to the estate and silently took command of keeping the roof from falling in upon her head and planting a small garden to provide a bit of food for the table.

She would never forget his patient kindness toward the lonely, scared child she had once been.

Certainly he was more a father to her than Lord Melford had ever been.

"I wanted to assure myself that you did not overtax yourself today."

He gave a lift of his shaggy brows. "Nay, I can still handle a shovel if need be."

"Yes, I know, but you are bound to be sore in the morning." She held up her hand to reveal the small ceramic pot she had brought with her. "I have brought you some of Mrs. Cornell's ointment."

Quinn reached for the pot with a smile. They had all learned to depend upon Mrs. Cornell's salve for their various aches and pains.

"That was right thoughtful of you."

She smiled as she studied the weathered face. "You are important to me, Quinn. I think of you as part of my family."

His expression abruptly softened as he gave her shoulder a gentle pat. "Aye, me dear, you have managed to cobble together a fine clan, even if we are a mixed lot."

Portia gave a laugh, thinking of the diverse staff she had managed to collect.

"Definitely a mixed lot." She gave a small shrug. "Still, there is something to be said for actually choosing your family members rather than simply inheriting them."

"Aye, that be true enough. No one would choose your rotter of a father."

"No." Portia shuddered, firmly blocking the

unpleasant memories of the weak, shallow fool who had fathered her.

A small silence fell as Quinn regarded her with a narrowed gaze. "Is there something troubling you, Portia?"

Her gaze dropped as she absently plucked at a thread that had frayed from the hem of her sleeve.

"Why did you agree to assist Mr. Smith today?"

"Because the yard was in need of work and he had the skills to make it the finest in the county." Reaching into his pocket, Quinn pulled out a folded sheet of vellum. "Ye see, he has written a recipe for a mixture to spread over the ground to keep it dry. Soon enough travelers will know that they need never fear being stuck in the mud when they halt at the Queen's Arms."

He had a point, of course. She had been in the business long enough to know that those who frequently traveled the roads were well aware of which yards could be depended upon not to mire them during a rain.

And she did not doubt that Fredrick had ensured that her yard would be the best tended in the entire county. She might not know a great deal about Mr. Smith, but she did sense that he would demand nothing less than absolute perfection in anything that he attempted.

She gave a faint shake of her head. "That is all very well, but you know how I feel about others interfering with my inn. Especially strangers," she said.

Quinn shrugged. "Yer a fine woman, Portia, but ye can be a mite too stubborn. We needed the work done and Smith gave us the direction we was needing. I saw no purpose in cutting off me nose to spite me face."

Was that what she was doing? Had she become so isolated that she could no longer determine the difference between a simple act of kindness and meddling in her affairs?

Gads, she did not know what to think.

"Where is Mr. Smith now?"

"He said something of a hot bath and a tray in his room." Quinn grimaced. "I fear he is still suffering from the blow he took to his noodle. Not that he would admit as much. In some ways he is as stubborn as ye."

Her brows lowered. She had nearly forgotten that he was still recovering from a dangerous blow to his head. Drat, the infernal man. He could have made himself seriously ill spending hours shoveling and hauling that mud about.

"I will see to Mr. Smith," she promised before pointing a finger toward Quinn's beak of a nose. "You are to have an early night and do not forget to put the ointment on before you go to bed. It will do no good if it is left in the pot."

Chapter Seven

Fredrick felt considerably better after his bath, but there remained a dull ache in his temple.

What a blasted fool, he chided himself as he pulled on a brocade robe and ran a comb through his damp curls. He possessed his fair share of intelligence. Some might claim that he possessed more than his fair share. So why had he blithely pressed himself to continue even when his head began to throb and his muscles shake with weakness?

Because he was so bloody eager to impress a woman who did not possess the least interest in being impressed.

Quinn had been quite forthcoming during their afternoon together. He had not only revealed that while Fredrick was attempting to display his skills in her yard the aggravating woman was napping in her room, but that the only reason she had so often appeared in his chambers was because she did not want her maids left alone with him.

She felt it her duty to attend to Fredrick to protect the hapless maids from his ungovernable lust.

Fool, indeed.

Moving toward the window, Fredrick watched as the sun set behind the line of trees just beyond the inn.

His only consolation was that Ian and Raoul were far away in London. The last thing he needed was to have his friends witness his rather pathetic attempts to capture the interest of a reluctant lady. He doubted that either of them had ever encountered a female who did not leap into their bed with eager anticipation. Hellfire, the two probably had to lock their doors to keep them out.

Certainly they had no need to flaunt themselves like a shameless popinjay.

A soft knock on the door thankfully interrupted his uncharacteristic broodings and, turning from the window, he called for the servant to enter.

Expecting Quinn with his evening dinner tray, Fredrick felt his chest tighten and his blood heat at the sight of Portia Walker sweeping over the threshold.

She was tiny enough to fit into his pocket, and yet, she managed to fill the room with her feminine power and the sweet scent of midnight roses.

Momentarily captivated by her unexpected arrival, Fredrick watched in silence as she glided across the room. Dash it all, she was a beautiful wench. Even in the ugly grey gown that was fit for nothing better than the rubbish heap, she managed to appear exotically beautiful with her raven dark hair and porcelain skin.

That now familiar fire stirred in his groin as she neared the bed. Oh yes. That was where she belonged. All he need do was take a few steps forward and he could scoop her off her feet and . . .

The heated fantasy was destroyed as Fredrick

belatedly noted the heavy tray she was setting on
a low table.

By gads, he disliked the notion of her waiting on
him as if she were a mere servant. And more, he disliked the notion that she attended upon him because
she feared he was some sort of animal that was just
waiting for the opportunity to rape some poor maid
who happened across his path.

At the time Quinn had confessed the truth, Fredrick
had been rather startled to think he could be mistaken
for a lecher. God knew, it did not often happen.

But now, with his head aching and his body tormented with frustrated need, he discovered his
usually placid temper distinctly on edge.

"Portia, what are you doing?"

She straightened to regard him with a faint surprise
at his sharp tone.

"You did request a tray in your room, did you not?"

"Yes, but I presumed that you had staff to deal with
such requests."

She faced him squarely, her arms folded. The
army general quite prepared to quash a renegade
subordinate.

"They have duties to attend to."

"And you fear I might force myself upon any poor
maid who might stray into my lair?"

Her aloof expression faltered at his blunt accusation.
"What?"

"Quinn told me that you had warned the maids to
avoid my presence."

A sudden color stained her cheeks. "Quinn should
learn to keep his mouth shut."

"Is it true?"

"I . . . I will admit that I often protect my maids from those gentlemen I fear might be a danger to them."

He gave a short laugh as he turned back to gaze blindly out the window. "Charming."

There was a rustle of wool before Fredrick was enveloped in the warm scent of roses. Not that he needed the tantalizing scent to inform him that Portia had halted close behind him. The flames licking through his body were warning enough.

"But that does not include you, Fredrick," she said softly. "Never you. I do not believe you would harm any woman."

His hands clenched with the effort not to turn around and jerk her into his arms.

"Then why are you here?"

"I am here because Quinn is concerned that you have not entirely recovered from your fall."

He gave a short laugh. He supposed pity was marginally better than viewing him as a potential rapist.

"Do not fear, poppet, I have no intention of cocking up my toes anytime soon."

"Good, I am far too busy to bother with your funeral," she said briskly. "Now come and eat your meal while it is still warm. I hope that you like roasted venison and potatoes in rosemary?"

Fredrick heaved a sigh as he slowly turned to meet her searching gaze. His frustration remained, but the need to keep her here in his rooms, to keep her where he could at least gaze at the perfect Madonna face and hear her sweet voice, was overwhelming.

Pathetic.

But what was a man caught in the throes of such an irresistible fascination to do?

"You know, you should be careful, poppet, I might

just steal your cook when I return to London," he said in deliberately light tones.

Her own expression eased and a hint of curiosity sparkled in those magnificent blue eyes.

"You do not have a cook in your home?"

"I have a housekeeper who is capable of producing a meal, but I am so rarely at home the effort of hiring a full staff seems a waste."

Clearly unaware that her proximity was causing his body to stir and harden beneath his robe, Portia tilted her head to one side.

"You work so many hours?"

"A great number." Fredrick struggled to keep his mind on something other than soft curve of her breasts. "And I also travel."

"Do you like it?"

"Traveling?"

"Yes."

Fredrick searched the delicate features that appeared genuinely interested before giving a slow nod of his head.

"I enjoy exploring places that I have never been and meeting people that intrigue me. I have increased my business substantially and more importantly discovered friends that I would never have met if I had remained in London." He felt an odd sense of melancholy as he thought of his empty townhouse. For all his pride in having achieved such a status of success, he had become increasingly aware of a haunting loneliness when he walked into the house. "Still, as I grow older I have discovered a growing desire to create a home of my own and put down roots."

She gave a startled blink, as if caught off guard by his words. "You intend to wed?"

"Most certainly." He wondered why she seemed so surprised. Did not most men marry and produce families? "Ever since I was a young boy I have dreamed of possessing a family I could claim as my own."

"If it is so important to you then I am surprised that you are not already wed."

A faint smile touched his lips. "Not surprising at all."

"And why is that?" The blue eyes hardened. "Because you have enjoyed your life as a bachelor too much?"

Fredrick narrowed his gaze, sensing that she was thinking back to the man who had abandoned her at the altar. Of course, was there ever a moment that she was not comparing him to some man or another that had disappointed her?

"Because I have not yet met *her*," he said simply.

"Her?"

"The woman who is meant for me."

He once again managed to surprise her. The blue eyes widened as she studied him with a bemused expression.

"You believe there is one true woman for you?"

Fredrick shrugged, only vaguely shocked that he would reveal such an intimate secret to this woman. Why would he start behaving as a rational man at this point?

"What can I say? Beneath all my logic beats the heart of a romantic."

She gave an unsteady laugh. "Astonishing."

"And what of you, Portia?" he demanded. "Are you a romantic?"

Her lashes lowered to effectively shield her emotions. "I believe that people wed for all sorts of reasons and that it is only for the fortunate few that love is actually involved."

Although Fredrick was forbidden from reading her inner thoughts, Portia could not entirely hide the edge of haunting pain in her voice.

Taking care not to startle her, he stroked his hands lightly up her arms to rest upon her shoulders.

"Did you love your husband?"

Portia sucked in a sharp breath at his touch, but thankfully she did not pull away.

"I cared for him, but as I am sure you have already discovered, he was a number of years older than me."

"Was he good to you?"

Her gaze abruptly lifted. "Thomas was very good to me. Without him . . . I do not know what I would have done."

Fredrick frowned at her obvious sincerity. "And yet, you have not married again."

Something that might have been panic at the mere thought of marriage flashed through the blue eyes. Peculiar.

"I have not been asked."

"Oh come, poppet." Fredrick smiled wryly. "I do not doubt with very little effort you could have any number of gentlemen anxious to kneel at your feet."

"Very pretty, but I am no longer a young maiden with stars in my eyes. I have no interest in flirtations."

"Now, that I do not believe for a moment."

"Why?" She tilted her chin. "Cannot a woman be more interested in her business than chasing after some man or another?"

Fredrick allowed his fingers to drift down her back in a gentle caress.

"There are none of us that enjoy being alone, even

when it is by choice. We all have the need to feel the warmth of another, to share our most intimate selves."

Just for a moment her eyes darkened with the same heat that pulsed through his body. Then, with a choked sound she took an abrupt step backward to break his hold.

"It is a simple matter for a man to share his intimate self. He pays no consequences for his pleasure. A woman is not so fortunate."

Fredrick frowned. "Consequences?"

She made an impatient sound. "If a woman weds then she is under the complete authority of her husband. If she takes a lover she risks her reputation and the very real possibility of getting with child."

Well, he could hardly argue with that.

It was true that women risked much when placing themselves in the hands of a man.

His mother had paid with her very life.

But the thought of this woman remaining frigid and unloved throughout the endless years was unbearable.

He wanted her to discover that there were men who could be trusted. Men who could offer her more than disillusionment.

Stepping forward, he grasped her hands before she could elude him. "Portia, there are means for a woman to enjoy pleasure without risking her reputation or becoming with child."

Her gaze lowered to his hands that held her captive. "A man will promise anything when he seeks to seduce a woman."

Slowly he lifted her hands to his mouth, stroking his lips over her slender fingers.

"Not all men are alike, poppet, just as not all women

are alike." He turned her hands over to nuzzle the center of her palm. "I would never lure a woman into my bed and then abandon her to her fate. I would treat no woman as my mother was treated."

She shivered beneath his touch, her breath unsteady. "Fredrick . . ."

"Do you want me, Portia?" he demanded, capturing her wary gaze with his own.

She stilled, as if she were struggling to erect those barriers that kept others at a distance. Sensing her battle, Fredrick stroked his thumb over the sensitive skin of her inner wrist, willing her to admit the truth.

At last she heaved a frustrated sigh.

"I do not *want* to want you," she muttered.

Fredrick could not halt his soft chuckle. "It is rarely a matter of choice."

"Of course it is a matter of choice," she protested, her voice husky. "There might be an . . . attraction between us, but we have a choice of whether or not we act upon it."

He held her gaze as he touched his tongue to the center of her palm. "Shall I tell you what I choose?"

A shudder wracked her body. "I do not need to be able to read your mind to know what you would choose," she breathed.

"It is a fortunate thing that you cannot read my mind." He sucked the tip of her finger between his lips as a raw heat flowed through his veins. He wanted to taste every inch of her satin skin. To feel the smooth velvet rubbing against him as he thrust into her. "If you actually knew the deliciously wicked thoughts that have plagued me since I first caught sight of you, poppet, you would have me chained to the wall."

Her breath caught, her eyes darkening with a need she could not disguise. "I have not yet ruled out that possibility," she muttered.

"You can chain me anywhere, so long as you promise to stay here with me," he murmured, lightly nipping her finger before he tightened his grip and pulled her inexorably forward. "In fact, the notion of being at your mercy is a most intoxicating image."

Portia did not struggle as he tugged her against his hard body, not even when his arms carefully encircled her body. Instead she regarded him with wide eyes that held a confusion of fear and vulnerable longing.

"Fredrick, I do not think this is a wise notion," she whispered.

He trailed his fingers up the curve of her back, his head lowering to brush his lips over her temple. "If you want me to stop, Portia, all you need to do is tell me," he promised. "My only desire is to please you."

She clutched at the lapels of his robe, her lashes fluttering down to hide her expressive eyes.

"Why? Why do you want to please me?"

Fredrick drank in the sight of her ethereal beauty in the flickering candlelight. His heart squeezed as his gaze drifted over the porcelain perfection of her features. The narrow line of her nose, the dark sweep of her raven brows, the lush curve of her rose-kissed lips. She was by far the most lovely creature he had ever held in his arms, but it was not her beauty that captivated him.

It was the strength in the line of her jaw, and the hint of mulish determination in her firm chin that kept him beguiled. There were pretty women in every village he passed through, but it was rare to discover such a combination of intelligence and staunch courage.

This woman had overcome every obstacle that life had thrown into her path and still was capable of gathering others in need beneath her wing.

And yet, for all her strength and sheer willpower, she possessed hidden wounds that kept her from allowing anyone truly near.

"Because I know what it is to be alone," he said, his lips kissing a path to the curve of her ear. "I know what it is to be wary of allowing another close because you fear they will hurt or disappoint you."

She instinctively arched into his body, her unsteady breath brushing the bare skin of his neck.

"What do you want from me?" she demanded.

Fredrick's muscles clenched as a wave of desire flooded through him. What did he want from her?

Everything, a voice whispered in the back of his mind.

Every beautiful, stubborn, mysterious inch of her.

But he would begin with her delectable body.

"This," he muttered, he dipped his head to nuzzle the long line of her neck, his fingers dealing nimbly with the buttons that ran down the back of her gown. As the heavy wool loosened, he gave a gentle tug on the material to reveal the curve of her shoulder. "And this." His mouth savored the smooth skin of her shoulder as he continued to pull the gown steadily downward.

She gave a soft moan, her fingers locked in a death-grip upon his robe.

"Fredrick."

Fredrick bit back a foul oath as he forced himself to lift his head from the addictive sweetness of her skin.

"Do you want me to halt?"

Her eyes reluctantly lifted to meet his smoldering gaze. "I . . ."

"Portia?" he prompted. As much as he longed to overwhelm her with the passion that he could sense trembling through her, Fredrick had given his promise. He would not have her accusing him of treachery.

She sucked in a deep breath before giving a slow shake of her head. "No, do not halt."

Holding her gaze with his, Fredrick gave another tug on the gown, smoothing it over her hips to pool at her ankles. Then, with more haste than skill he was unknotting the laces that held her corset in place.

"You are exquisite. As beautiful as the finest jewel," he murmured, stripping away the corset to leave her standing in her thin shift. Lowering his head he allowed his gaze to drift over her slender body. "Bloody hell," he choked out as he caught sight of the delicate chemise that was paneled with fine lace and delicately embroidered with flowers. It seemed designed for the sole purpose of inflaming a man's fantasy.

And he was definitely inflamed, he acknowledged as his groin hardened and his erection thrust against the heavy folds of his robe.

Sensing his shock, Portia pulled her head back to regard him with eyes shadowed by desire.

"Fredrick?"

"You are a woman who never fails to surprise, poppet," he husked, his fingers reverently trailing a path along the deep plunge of her neckline. "Who could have suspected that beneath all that wool and starch was such a delicate garment?"

She shivered as his touch brushed the curve of her breasts. "It is merely a chemise."

"No," he breathed, lowering his head to replace his

fingers with his lips, goaded beyond bearing by the sight of her tightly budded nipples peaking through the thin lace. "It is temptation."

"Oh." Her eyes fluttered shut as her hands crept upward to tangle in his hair.

Cupping her breasts, Fredrick found the tip of her nipple and sucked it between his lips, using his teeth and tongue to tease her.

"Your scent has been driving me mad," he murmured as he shifted to discover the taste of her neglected nipple. "I shall never again be near roses without thinking of you."

"This is . . ."

His hands moved down her slender waist, the heat of her body searing through the thin fabric.

"This is what?" he demanded, relentlessly continuing to pleasure her swollen breasts.

"Dangerous," she whispered.

It was dangerous, Fredrick realized as his body throbbed with the need to lower her to the ground and thrust into the heated silk of her body. This pounding, consuming passion was the sort of thing that made men toss aside pride and loyalty and honor.

It was the sort of thing a man would trade his very life to possess.

His arms tightened about her body and with one smooth movement he had her off her feet and was heading toward the bed. Her eyes widened, but she gave no protest as he gently set her on the edge of the mattress and sank onto his knees between her spread legs.

"What are you doing?" she demanded as he captured the hem of her shift and tugged it up her legs to expose the pretty ribbons that held up her stockings.

"Do not fear, Portia," he murmured, untying the ribbon to remove a white stocking. "I only want to please you."

"Dear God," she hissed, as he lowered his head to trail a string of kisses down the inner softness of her exposed thigh.

Lost in his haze of desire, Fredrick managed to relieve her of the small slippers and the remaining stocking before spreading her legs wide enough to expose the tiny patch of raven curls that hid her most intimate secrets.

He gave a hungry groan as he tasted of the tender skin of her shivering thigh. He wanted to consume her. To make love to her for hours as he discovered every sweet inch of her body. But for tonight it was enough to offer her a glimpse of what paradise could be.

Forcing himself not to rush her, Fredrick took his time as he nipped and licked at her skin, rewarded by her low, shaky moan as he headed discreetly toward his goal.

"Fredrick, what are you doing to me?" she rasped as her fingers threaded through his hair.

He smiled in satisfaction as he realized that no man had ever made the effort to please her in such a manner. It was little wonder that she had so easily turned her back on the pleasures of the flesh.

Placing his hands on her legs to keep her from closing against him in shock, Fredrick at last shifted to stroke his tongue through the satin heat of her cleft.

Portia gave a small shriek at the intimate kiss, her hands tugging painfully on his hair.

"Oh, mercy."

"You shall have no mercy on this night, poppet," he

swore, his tongue searching until he found the small nub of her pleasure.

"Fredrick."

Her grip eased as her fingers ran a restless path through his hair, her breath coming in small pants as he laved her with tender care.

Fredrick moaned as the taste and scent of her filled his senses. His erection was so hard he thought it might explode at any moment, but with a grim determination he forced his thoughts away from his own needs.

Tonight was for Portia.

Opening himself to her every gasp and soft sigh, Fredrick tormented her with soft licks that brought her to the edge of the precipice without allowing her to tumble over. Over and over he plundered her sweet heat, feeling her legs trembling beneath his fingers.

"Fredrick . . ." she at last pleaded on a small sob, "please."

"Whatever you desire, poppet," he breathed, taking the tender flesh between his lips as he suckled her to an explosive release.

Crying out in shocked pleasure, Portia fell back on the bed, her entire body shivering as she struggled to breathe. Fredrick rose to his feet and just for a moment allowed himself the pleasure of gazing down at her delicate body sprawled on the bed.

Attired in the thin chemise, with her raven curls spread across the blanket and her features flushed with passion, she had never appeared more beautiful.

His erection throbbed as it brushed against the fabric of his robe. He had never been so painfully aroused. Dash it all, playing the role of tutor rather than lover was a brutal business. If he did not have relief soon he might end up in Bedlam.

Then Portia's lashes fluttered slowly upward, the dazed glow of wonderment managing to ease the wrenching frustration that held him in its grip.

With a small smile, Fredrick climbed onto the bed and pulled her into his arms, burying his face into the rose-scented tresses.

There would be other nights, he promised himself. Nights when she would trust him enough to give of herself freely.

Until then he would gladly accept whatever she felt ready to offer.

Chapter Eight

Portia was floating on a cloud of bliss. Mercy. She had never dreamed of such exquisite sensations. Certainly not by merely having a gentleman put his mouth between her legs.

It had been decadent and delectable and wickedly, madly delicious.

And most wondrous of all there was no fear that her life was about to be plunged into some ghastly nightmare to punish her for her sins.

Instead there was nothing but a serene satisfaction and incredible warmth as she snuggled into Fredrick's strong arms. At the moment she was quite certain she would be content to lay beside him for the rest of eternity.

Long moments passed until Fredrick gently trailed his fingers over her cheek.

"Portia."

"Mmmm?"

"Will you look at me?"

His finger slipped beneath her chin to angle her face upward.

Vibrantly aware of the robe that had fallen open to reveal a vast amount of his pale, golden skin, she astonishingly felt a flicker of excitement race through her sated body. She did not know what it was about this man that set her senses ablaze, but it obviously hadn't been ended by their brief encounter.

At last she allowed her eyes to meet his gaze, her heart squeezing at the genuine concern that smoldered in the silver depths.

"Are you well?" he demanded softly.

An unsteady smile touched her lips. "I am not entirely certain. I have never experienced anything like that."

His concern eased as his finger strayed to outline her lips. "You are pleased?"

A sudden flush stained her cheeks as she recalled her cries of pleasure.

"You must know that I am. I did not know that . . . that a woman could find pleasure in such a manner."

His chuckle whispered over her cheek as he slid his palm down her back and pressed her against the hard length of his arousal.

"There are many pleasures yet to be discovered, poppet. All you need do is trust me."

A shiver raced through her. Not of fear. That, she was prepared for. But instead it was a stunning desire to arch her body against his hardness. To brush aside the heavy robe and run her tongue down that smooth chest while he pressed her onto her back and thrust deep inside her.

She swallowed a small gasp as the shocking images tumbled through her mind, making her heart pound and her body clench with need.

"No," she breathed softly, pushing from his lingering hold and scrambling from the bed.

In a blink of an eye he was standing beside her, watching as she struggled to tug the gown over her head with a puzzled frown.

"Portia, what is it?"

Dipping her head she hid her expression behind her hair as she hastily tugged on her stockings and slippers.

"I must go before I am missed."

She heard him heave an aggravated sigh as she clumsily tied the ribbons around the top of her stockings.

"So after all we have shared you intend to scurry back behind your barriers?" he rasped.

Portia gave a shake of her head as she struggled to reach the buttons that lined the back of her gown.

"I do not know what I intend," she muttered, unable to think clearly with him so near. Gads, she had sensed from the beginning that Fredrick was different, but she had no notion just how different. After all, the last time she had offered herself to a man she had experienced nothing more than relief that it was all over.

How could she suspect that she could actually find such paradise? That she could possess a near overwhelming desire to crawl back into that bed and forget the world in a haze of lust?

Still fumbling with the aggravating buttons, Portia felt her hands being brushed aside as Fredrick stepped behind her.

"Here, let me," he muttered, swiftly dealing with the buttons. When the last slid into place, his hands skimmed across her shoulders in a tender caress.

Portia softly moaned as she felt his lips brush the side of her neck. "Portia."

Her eyes began to flutter downward as enticing prickles of anticipation spread through her body. It would be so easy to lean back into his body. To snuggle her head in the small hollow beneath his shoulder and allow him to seduce her all over again.

Far too easy, a voice whispered in the back of her mind.

She took a hasty step away, grudgingly turning to meet his smoldering gaze.

"Please, Fredrick, I really must go."

He gave a lift of his hands, his expression tight with frustration. "I have told you that I will never do anything against your will, Portia. You are not my captive."

Portia swallowed a near hysterical laugh as she moved toward the door, her body still tingling from the magic of his touch.

"You do not need to do anything against my will to make me your captive, Fredrick," she whispered as she pulled open the door. "And that is why I am leaving."

The tiny village that lay nestled in the valley near Oak Manor was just as Fredrick remembered.

The small stone church that the Graystone family had attended for the past three centuries still slumbered with an ancient peace beneath the pale sunlight. The tidy Green still boasted a crumbling wishing well. And High Street was still lined with a handful of shops that catered to the locals.

Beyond the shops were a dozen or so whitewashed cottages with thatched roofs and small gardens that had been the home to villagers for countless eons.

It was a pretty enough village, Fredrick acknowledged as he passed the curious onlookers who gawked from various windows, but so steeped in tradition that it felt as if he were traveling back in time.

No doubt the citizens enjoyed the sense of being separated from the rapidly changing world, but Fredrick was a man who very much appreciated the future.

Even as a child he had felt stifled when he managed to slip from his father's estate to wander the cobblestone streets. It was as if he could smell the stale mustiness in the air.

Of course, in all fairness, it was not entirely the sense of cloistered monotony that had caused his discomfort.

As a lad he had been drawn to the village by the sounds of children playing on the Green. For hours he would watch them dart across the grass, always harboring the hope that just once he would be invited to join in their games.

In hindsight it was perhaps understandable that the neighboring children had avoided him. To the villagers he possessed the blood of Graystones and was considered far above their touch, while the local nobles would never allow their precious offspring to be contaminated by a bastard.

At the time, he had known only that he was being shunned and the pain had cut deeper than any dagger.

He had, however, discovered one friendly face among the throng of strangers.

Pulling his mount to a halt, Fredrick motioned toward a lad lounging near the corner. The urchin hurried forward with an eager grin, readily catching the reins that Fredrick tossed toward him.

Fredrick dismounted and placed a coin in the boy's grubby hand as he headed into the nearby pub. A wry smile touched his lips at the hint of deference in the boy's manner. It was amazing what the proper clothes and unmistakable polish of wealth could do.

It was the first time he had arrived at the village as a man of substance rather than a bastard.

Entering the narrow pub, Fredrick was forced to halt as his eyes adjusted to the murky shadows. Slowly he was able to discern the open-beamed ceiling of the tap room along with the small tables that were scattered over the worn planks. With a cautious step he made his way through the gloom, smelling the scent of ale and stale tobacco.

Oddly familiar scents, he realized, as he halted at the heavy walnut bar that ran along the back of the room. As familiar as the barrel-chested man enfolded in a white apron who was sliding glasses into the notched rack above the bar.

Oh, there was no doubt that there was more grey than brown in the thick mane of hair, and that there were considerably more lines on the pug face, but he would recognize Macky anywhere.

This was the man who always had a jovial word and place at the end of the bar for a lonely child. He had even whittled Fredrick an entire regiment of soldiers to play with when he visited the pub.

Fredrick had never forgotten him for his kindness.

Taking a seat on one of the high stools, Fredrick waited for the man to finish his task. It was far too early for most patrons to have worked up a thirst, which had been Fredrick's intention.

Macky might have extended a friendly hand to Fredrick as a child, but his loyalty was to the Graystone family, and especially to the current Lord Graystone. The man would not readily spread old gossip.

It would take a bit of coaxing if he were to discover anything of worth. Something that would be impossible if Macky was busy waiting on a dozen customers.

Besides, a voice whispered in the back of his mind, if he had remained at the inn he would have been unable to resist his obsessive need to seek out Portia.

Despite every scrap of logic that warned it would be a mistake to put pressure on the aggravating woman while she struggled to accept the powerful attraction that smoldered between them, there was a ridiculous part of him that fiercely needed to be close to her. Even if it was just to catch a glimpse of her face.

Bloody hell.

With an effort he thrust aside the thought of Mrs. Portia Walker. It was bad enough that he had spent the entire night hard as a rock with the scent of her clinging to his blankets. And that his dreams had been filled with memories of her soft moans as she had reached her first climax. Today he was determined to concentrate upon his search for his father's past.

At last sensing he was no longer alone, Macky turned about and regarded him with a curious frown. It was not often his pub was patronized by strangers, and certainly not by strangers who could afford a coat cut by Weston.

Wiping his beefy hands on a towel, he moved to stand directly opposite Fredrick.

"What'll you have?"

Fredrick smiled at the suspicious tone. "A pint of your best, Macky."

The man blinked in confusion. "Do I know you?"

"Fredrick Smith."

Macky made a choked sound as he regarded Fredrick's fine clothes and the ruby stickpin that sparkled in the folds of his crisply tied cravat.

"Little Freddie?" He gave a shake of his head before a wide grin split his face. "Bloody hell, it is good to see you, lad."

Fredrick chuckled. "Not so much a lad anymore."

"No, I suppose not." With expert ease Macky had a tankard of ale sitting before Fredrick. "Are you visiting the Manor?"

Fredrick took a drink of the dark ale, considering his best approach. "Actually, I am in the neighborhood on business, but I could not pass through without calling on my father, and of course, my old friends."

"About time, lad. It has been too long since you were last here."

Fredrick felt a small pang in the region of his heart. He had worked so hard to put his childhood behind him. Even those who had reached out to make his days a bit more bearable.

"I suppose it has been," he said, a hint of apology in his tone. "I fear I have been rather occupied."

Always reluctant to have his tender heart exposed, Macky gave a gruff laugh. "Oh aye, you've been busy making a fortune for yourself in the city. I always knew you would make something of yourself."

Fredrick shrugged. "I am not certain I have actually made something of myself, but I will admit that I have been lucky in my investments."

Macky gave a click of his tongue. "There is no luck in business. Only hard work."

"Perhaps."

There was a short silence before Macky cleared his throat. "The Baron is right proud of you, you know."

"Proud?" Fredrick's smile faded. How could a father be proud of a son he viewed with shame? "I think you must have me confused with Simon, old friend. Bastards do not make their fathers proud."

"Now there you are far off the mark, Freddie. Lord Graystone has long known that you have become a respectable businessman while Simon is nothing more than a wastrel." His lips thinned as he gave a shake of his head. "Damnation, you should see that boy prancing about the village in his fancy clothes and sniffing after everything in skirts. A pity."

Until yesterday Fredrick would have laughed at the mere notion his father could even recall his name, let alone kept track of his success. Now . . . who the hell knew what was going on behind that guarded composure?

He grimly refused to dwell on the notion. He had long ago halted his attempts to please his father.

"Well, Simon is young and the Graystones are rather notorious for their indiscretions," he said lightly.

Macky looked surprised by the accusation. "Perhaps your grandfather and uncle were gamblers and whoremongers, but your father has always been more like his ancestors. They built an estate here that any man could be proud of. And what's more, they never forget those in their care."

"My father has certainly proven his ability to manage the estate, but his younger years were clearly devoted to reckless pleasure." Fredrick smiled wryly. "I am proof of that."

"Now, no more of that sort of talk, Freddie. Your father was no scoundrel." There was another silence as Macky debated in his own mind. At last he heaved a sigh. "He loved your mother."

Fredrick froze in shock. Never in all his years had anyone spoken of his mother. Not his demon-spawned foster mother, not his father, and certainly not those who were dependent upon the Graystone family.

"Did you know my mother?"

Macky grimaced. "I suppose it does no harm to speak of her after all these years."

"Macky?" he pressed, his heartbeat unsteady.

"Aye, I knew her." He held up a hand as if sensing the shocked questions that hammered through Fredrick. "Not well, mind you. But she occasionally came to the village and was always polite to those she met."

Another gust of astonishment rushed through his body. He had always assumed that his mother had been some servant that his father had encountered in Winchester or even London. After all, if she had family in the neighborhood then surely at least one of them would have stepped forward to claim him?

"My mother lived here?"

Macky gave a lift of his hands. "She came to the Manor house as a companion to your grandmother after Lady Graystone was forced to her bed."

"A companion?" Fredrick frowned, his hands clenching on the brass railing that ran the length of the bar. "That means she had to be from a respectable family. My grandmother would have accepted nothing less."

"The daughter of a Scottish doctor, although I don't recall her name. She had the sort of nursing skills that Lady Graystone needed to ease her discomfort."

"Good God." Fredrick's shock was beginning to shift to smoldering anger. "My father seduced a gently bred female beneath his own roof?"

"Not seduced," Macky hastily protested, a hint of concern tightening his heavy features. The man would drown himself in his own ale rather than to think ill of his powerful patron. "They fell in love."

Fredrick gave a sound of disgust. "A gentleman in love does not abandon the woman he has impregnated."

"Now you just mind you those unworthy thoughts, Freddie," Macky warned, his faced flushed. "Your father did not abandon her. Although your grandmother was right set on turning the poor lass away without so much as a shilling, it was your father who stood by her side. He said if she were to be tossed from the house, then he would go as well. They left for Winchester just a few days later."

Fredrick felt as if he had taken a blow to his stomach.

His father's words echoed through his mind.

In truth, I was relieved when I was forced to leave. . . .

Christ, the reason he had left Oak Manor had not been for the mysterious scandal Fredrick had hoped to learn about. It had been because of him.

Even worse, he was forced to accept that his father was not the cold-hearted beast that he had always presumed him to be. Lord Graystone had not turned his back on his mother. Instead he had allowed himself to be thrown from his own home to be at her side.

Dash it all. . . .

With an effort, Fredrick pushed the revelations to the back of his mind. He would consider what he had discovered later. When he could sort through them in a logical manner.

It seemed to be becoming a habit of his since arriving in Wessex, he acknowledged wryly.

Draining the last of his ale, Fredrick managed to

clear his wits. At least enough to notice the belligerent glint in Macky's eyes.

He had allowed himself to be distracted by the mention of his mother and had effectively ensured that Macky was in no humor to confess any of Lord Graystone's past scandals.

Ah, well, it had been only a distant hope to begin with. The neighbors were far too dependent upon the goodwill of Lord Graystone to readily confess any hidden sin he might have committed.

"Thank you for telling me the truth, Macky," he said, placing a coin on the counter before rising to his feet. "You are the first to do so."

The older man's expression eased at the soft words. "Perhaps it was not my place, but I cannot have you thinking ill of your father. He is a good man."

A good man? That was debatable, Fredrick silently mused. After all, Lord Graystone had fostered a bastard on a well-bred lady and harbored some secret he was willing to pay a fortune to keep buried.

Still, he was proving that he was not quite the monster of Fredrick's childish imagination.

"You are no doubt right, old friend." On the point of retreat, Fredrick paused, suddenly struck by a new thought. "Oh, I wanted to ask you if you have ever heard of a gentleman by the name of Dunnington?"

Macky furrowed his brow. "Dunnington?"

"I believe he once worked as a tutor in the neighborhood."

The man gave a shrug. "I can't say as I have. Of course, I don't rub elbows much with tutors."

Fredrick smiled. "No, I suppose not."

"What's your interest in this Dunnington?"

"Business."

"A pity." Macky leaned his elbows on the counter of the bar. "You are old enough that you should be seeking out tutors for your own sons."

Fredrick should have laughed at the gentle reprimand.

Although he was hardly in his dotage, it appeared that once a gentleman gathered a large enough fortune, society believed it was his duty to share it with a wife and horde of children.

It was not amusement, however, that made his stomach clench with a sudden longing.

Instead it was the uninvited image of a raven-haired angel round with his child.

Just for a moment his heart refused to beat. Why the devil would such a thought even enter his mind? It certainly had not with any other female.

Could it be that she was the one?

The woman he had been awaiting his entire life?

The answer seemed to tease at the edge of his mind, but noticing that Macky was regarding him with a quizzical glance, Fredrick forced a nonchalant smile to his lips.

"Perhaps you are right, Macky," he murmured as he headed toward the door. "'Tis certainly a matter I intend to explore while I am in the neighborhood."

Chapter Nine

When Portia left her restless bed, she fervently promised herself that she would do her best to avoid Mr. Fredrick Smith.

It was not anger, or frustration, or even guilt that had brought on her decision. No, those emotions were far too familiar to trouble her. She had worn them like a threadbare gown since she was a child.

Instead it was the strange sense of anticipation that raced through her blood as she pulled on her clothes and smoothed her hair into a tidy braid. Almost as if for the first time in years she was eager to face the day.

And that was frightening, because she could not even pretend that her peculiar, almost giddy mood was not directly connected to Mr. Fredrick Smith.

She was precariously close to becoming obsessed with the wicked, fallen angel, she was forced to accept. And she knew that she had to make some decisions before she once again found herself caught in his potent spell.

There could be no doubt that Fredrick hoped to enjoy a brief affair during his visit to the inn. Or that he possessed the skills necessary to make such an affair a truly wondrous experience. Beyond wondrous, she acknowledged as she shivered from the memories of the previous night.

He was the first man to stir the sensuality in her nature that she had forgotten she even possessed.

A sensuality that she had buried years before.

But while it was an exhilarating experience, she was wise enough to hesitate before simply plunging headlong into desire. It was all very well for Fredrick to blithely claim they could conduct a private affair with no consequences, but she was far from convinced.

The complications of even a brief encounter were not easily overcome. And until she came to a decision of whether or not she intended to give into Fredrick's seduction, it was unfair to continually place herself in his path.

He was no callow youth to be teased by her heated kisses one moment and then rebuffed by her panicked refusal the next.

No, he was a gentleman who had offered her nothing but respect, and he deserved her respect in return.

A mature and intelligent decision that proved to be quite easy to keep.

At least as long as Fredrick remained conveniently absent from the inn. It was an entirely different matter when he returned and promptly retreated to the back garden with a bottle of brandy.

For two hours she staunchly attempted to ignore the slender male who sat in such splendid solitude. He was obviously content to work his way through the bottle of brandy without interference.

But as the darkness began to descend and the

breeze became chilled, she could no longer ignore the growing concern that gripped her.

Something had clearly occurred to trouble him.

And while her logic was steadfast, her heart was not nearly callous enough to leave him alone and cast to the wind in her garden.

Heaving a sigh at her own foolish weakness, Portia gathered her cloak before slipping out the kitchen door and entering the small garden.

With a sharp series of barks Puck rushed to greet her arrival. Oddly, however, the gentleman seated on the marble bench did not so much as turn his head. Instead he remained sprawled with negligent ease, his legs thrust out and the brandy bottle held precariously in his hand.

Offering the prancing spaniel a swift pat on the head, she shooed him away and moved to take a seat on the bench.

"Fredrick?" she murmured softly.

Still he continued to gaze at the distant sky, his elegant profile softly outlined by the light spilling from the inn.

Good God, but he was exquisite.

Such delicate features that still managed to be utterly male. Features that must have been crafted by the most skilled angels.

It was only with the greatest effort that she kept her fingers hidden beneath the fold of her cloak so they did not reach up to brush a stray honey curl from his forehead.

"Good evening, Portia," he husked, speaking with that careful effort that revealed he had consumed a good deal of the brandy.

"Dinner is being served in the public rooms."

A small smile tugged at his lips. "No more private trays to my chambers?"

Her heart jerked sharply before she managed to give a small shrug. "I believe you have demonstrated you have recovered sufficient strength to make your way down the stairs."

Slowly he turned his head to regard her with those far too perceptive grey eyes, although they were not quite so focused as usual.

"Perhaps, but my food never tastes quite so delicious as it does when it is being delivered by your sweet hands."

His voice was lightly teasing, but Portia did not miss the grim set of his features.

"What is troubling you?"

"How do you know that anything is troubling me?"

"For such a successful businessman you do not hide your emotions particularly well." She glanced around the empty garden. "Besides, you have been brooding out here with that bottle of brandy for the past two hours."

He offered a boyish grin. "You noticed."

"I was waiting for you to leave so that I could feed Puck."

With a sharp laugh he lifted the bottle to his lips. "Of course."

"Fredrick, did something happen today?"

"It is a . . . personal matter. Nothing that would be of interest to anyone."

"Perhaps I should be allowed to decide whether or not it would be of interest."

His smile faded as he held her gaze. "Why do you care, poppet?"

"Does it matter?" she demanded, her mind shying from the blunt question.

He studied her in silence for a long moment and Portia was prepared for a rebuff when he at last heaved a deep sigh.

"I had an intriguing conversation today with an old friend," he said softly. "A conversation that included my mother."

Before she could halt herself, Portia had settled her fingers on his rigid forearm. As if she could ease the darkness shrouded about him with a mere touch.

"Is it painful to speak of her?"

"Not so much painful as astonishing, since I never speak of her," he confessed, his lips twisting. "In truth, there was nothing to speak of. I have never known anything of my mother other than the fact that she died at my birth."

"Your father never spoke to you about her?"

He gave a derisive laugh. "My father never spoke to me about anything, at least nothing beyond the state of the weather and the progress of his harvest. He certainly never encouraged any intimate confidences."

Portia's heart clenched at the thought of a young, vulnerable Fredrick being denied even the barest comfort at the loss of his mother. She at least had her mother's belongings to give her a sense of the woman who had given her birth.

"And so you have never known anything of her?"

"Nothing."

She unconsciously gave his arm a comforting squeeze. "What did you discover today?"

His gaze lowered to where her fingers lay on his arm. "That she was a true lady. She was the daughter of a doctor and she came to Oak Manor to be a companion to my grandmother."

Portia sensed his confusion at the discovery, but more than that, she sensed his pain. A pain, she realized, that she ached to take away.

"You must resemble her," she said softly.

Fredrick lifted his gaze with a startled blink. "Why do you say that?"

"You have implied that your father is a . . . distant gentleman, while you are obviously a warm and caring person."

His hand shifted to cover her fingers that lingered on his arm, a wicked smile teasing at his lips.

"Very warm, at least when I am in your presence."

Suddenly the night did not seem nearly so chilled. In fact, her entire body was tingling with a heat that nearly stole her breath.

"Did you discover anything else?" she forced herself to demand, her voice not quite steady.

"Yes." Without warning, Fredrick was off the bench and pacing toward the low brick fence. "I discovered that my father did not abandon her as I always supposed he had. Indeed, he left Oak Manor to take my mother to Winchester when my grandmother discovered she was with child."

Even in the thickening shadows, Portia could make out the stiff set of his shoulders and the tension of his rigid back as he drained the last of the brandy and tossed aside the bottle. Rising from the bench, she moved to stand at his side before common sense could halt the urge to soothe his grief.

"Then he must have loved her," she said softly.

"So it would seem."

She frowned at his clipped words. "Why does that trouble you?"

There was a long silence. At last he gave a slow shake of his head. "I have always assumed that my father disliked me because he resented my mother becoming pregnant and forcing a bastard on him. Now . . . now it appears he held at least some affection for my mother. So why did he never care for me?"

Pain sliced through Portia's heart and she knew with absolute certainty that if Lord Graystone ever dared enter her inn that she would take a horsewhip to him.

Damn his worthless hide.

With an effort she ignored the smoldering desire to punish Fredrick's unworthy father and instead concentrated on the man standing stiffly at her side.

"You said that your mother died during your birth?"

"Yes."

"Perhaps you were too distressing a reminder of what he had lost," she suggested. "After all, he turned his back on his family to be with the woman he loved, only to lose her in a tragic manner. It is only natural that your presence would conjure memories he would prefer to put behind him."

He turned his head to regard her with a shimmering gaze. "Clearly you have never encountered Lord Graystone."

"It is possible, you know."

His lips twisted. "If you say."

Once again Portia felt compelled to reach out and touch his arm. "Whatever his reason for keeping you at a distance, it cannot be any worse than knowing that your father disliked you simply because you were not born the proper sex."

As Portia had hoped, Fredrick was distracted by her low words, his strained expression easing as he turned to regard her with a searching gaze.

"Your father desired a son?"

"Of course." For once the memory of her feckless father did not bring with it the familiar jarring anger. Instead she was aware of nothing beyond the nearness of Fredrick's lean body and the warm male scent that spiced the air. "A daughter could not join him in his hunting or gambling or whoring. And even worse, I possessed the audacity to lecture him on tossing away his fortune."

He reached out to cup her cheek. "He was a weak, cowardly idiot."

"Yes, he was," she promptly agreed.

"We are a fine pair, are we not, poppet?" he sighed.

She shrugged. "It would seem to me that we have done well enough without the assistance of our families. In fact, I would say that we are far more successful for having been forced to make our way in the world. How many noblemen do you know that have become nothing more than worthless fribbles?"

A chiseled brow arched. "You think I should be grateful to have been abandoned by my father?"

"I think you should be grateful that you were born with the fortitude to overcome your past and the intelligence to create business that provides for you and for your employees. You could be living in the gutters and begging for a coin."

"You are right, of course." The silver eyes slowly darkened to smoke as he deliberately lowered his gaze to her lips. Portia's heart stuttered, but she made no move to pull away as his arms encircled her waist and he tugged her close. "And in truth, at this moment I have no wish to think of the past. I would much rather concentrate on the present."

A hint of panic fluttered through her mind. Not at his touch. But at the savage pang of longing that clutched at her lower stomach.

She wanted to lean into that hard body. To slide her fingers into the silk of his honey hair. To tug his lips down to cover hers in a deep, hungry kiss.

"Your dinner . . ." she breathed.

"Portia, just let me hold you for a moment," he commanded as he lowered his head to touch his lips to the sensitive skin of her temple. "I need to feel you in my arms."

"Someone might see us."

"I do not intend to ravish you in the garden." His fingers flexed against her lower back. "Not that I would mind, but I am not quite lost to all reason." He breathed deeply of her curls. "God, it feels so right to hold you."

It did feel right. Perfect, in fact.

Portia allowed her eyes to slide shut as she savored the feeling of being wrapped in Fredrick's arms. Oh, mercy. It was more than the aching desire that she had come to expect.

Standing in the chilled garden she felt warm and safe and . . . and cherished.

Sensations she had never thought to experience with any man.

Sensations that were far more perilous than mere desire.

With a dangerous ease she allowed herself to soak in the heat of him, arching as his palm inched up her spine to cup her nape in a possessive grip. Even when he stroked soft kisses down the curve of her cheek, she made no effort to pull away.

"Portia," he murmured just before his lips captured her mouth in a startling fierce kiss.

She made a low sound in her throat. He tasted of brandy and male desire, his masterful touch sending jolts of excitement through her body. Her fingers clutched at his coat as his hand cupped her bottom to haul her firmly against the straining muscles of his groin.

Muttering beneath his breath, Fredrick thrust his tongue into her mouth, plundering her with a restless hunger that caught her off guard. Tonight he was not the tender, careful lover she had come to expect. Instead he was urgent and demanding, as if his control had been shattered.

Perhaps Portia should have been shocked by his brazen need. She had, after all, put considerable effort into becoming a rigidly respectable lady. The sort of lady who could run her own business without lifting a brow among the highest sticklers.

But far from shocked she was instead shuddering beneath a blast of passion that nearly sent her to her knees. This was what the poets wrote of and what prompted sane women to toss aside everything they held dear.

His mouth shifted to plant hot, damp kisses down the curve of her neck. Portia readily tilted back her head, her heart thundering and her breath coming in small gasps as Fredrick tucked her more firmly between his spread legs and rocked the length of his arousal against her.

A moan was wrenched from her throat as a frustrated need speared through her lower body. She wanted to be far away from the garden. Far away from the inn with its prying eyes.

Someplace where she could be utterly alone with this beautiful man.

It was the sound of a carriage entering the yard that managed to recall Fredrick to the fact they were standing within easy sight of the inn. With a low groan, he reluctantly lifted his head to regard her with dazed eyes.

"Bloody hell," he at last breathed, his voice unsteady as he lowered his arms and stepped from her. "I never thought to say this, but I fear I am not at all trustworthy to be alone with you on this night."

Still caught in the throes of passion she swayed toward him. "Fredrick?"

"No, poppet." He wrapped his arms around his chest, as if he were waging a war within himself. "The brandy has stolen more than my wits, and I am not certain I possess the power to halt myself from taking more than you wish to offer. You should return to the inn."

Portia bit back the urge to protest that in this moment there was nothing that he could take that she would not willingly offer.

If she did give herself to him it would not be when he was aching from the pain of his bitter youth and befuddled with strong spirits.

The man was just foolish enough to awaken in the morning and presume it had been nothing more than sympathy that had led to her capitulation. That she would not allow.

Stepping back she wrapped the cloak more tightly about her shivering body.

"Will you be well?" she demanded, disliking the

thought of leaving him alone with his haunting memories.

As if he could not halt himself, Fredrick reached out to lightly touch her hair, his expression impossible to read in the shadows.

"Do not fret, poppet, I intend nothing more than to wallow for a while longer in my self-pity before seeking my bed," he said wryly. "In the morning I shall have returned to my interfering, arrogant, annoying self."

A smile twitched at her lips. "Along with a painfully thick head."

"No doubt." With obvious care, Fredrick leaned down to brush his lips over her forehead. "Run along, poppet, before my good intentions disappear entirely."

It took far more effort than it should have for Portia to turn about and make her way through the dark garden. She desperately wanted to remain and offer him the comfort that he needed. Thankfully, she possessed enough wits to realize that if she lingered comfort was not all she would be offering.

Entering the bustling kitchen, Portia ignored the raised brows and hidden smiles from her staff.

She knew that she looked flushed and mussed and thoroughly kissed.

Even worse, she knew that she looked as if she had *enjoyed* being thoroughly kissed.

With an inward shrug she slipped off her cloak and headed toward the front of the inn. Despite her distraction with Mr. Fredrick Smith, there were guests arriving.

Business was business, she reminded herself sternly.

* * *

Portia's prediction of a thick-head proved all too accurate when Fredrick awoke the next morning.

A thick-head that was not improved by the crack to his skull that had not yet fully healed.

Cursing his stupidity, Fredrick resisted the urge to linger in his bed and made his way down to the public rooms for an early cup of tea.

Dash it all, he never drank to excess. At least not since his younger years when Ian and Raoul would occasionally lure him into Dunnington's attics to share a bottle of blue ruin.

Of course, his day had been the sort to drive any gentleman to drink, he acknowledged wryly.

And perhaps he had needed a few hours to adjust to the revelations that Macky had revealed. His only true regret was that he had held a warm and willing Portia in his arms and had been forced to send her away.

With a sigh, Fredrick reached beneath his jacket and pulled out his small notebook.

He had wasted yet another day without being one step closer to completing his task in Wessex.

Today he was determined to accomplish something, anything.

The question was where to begin.

There were perhaps a few in the neighborhood that might have some knowledge of his father's past. But would any of them be willing to reveal any sordid secrets?

And more importantly, could he be certain that his father's secret sin had occurred while he lived here?

After all, Dunnington had managed to uncover the truth. And there was no indication that the tutor had ever been near Oak Manor. God knew that if he had ever resided in the neighborhood Macky would have full and complete knowledge of him. The taproom gossip flowed with the same liberal excess as the ale, and even the most obscure resident would have been fully debated and dissected by the locals.

Perhaps it was time that he turned his attention to Winchester, he told himself, scribbling notes on the paper. He might not have much information to discover where his father had lived while he was in the city, but he was well enough acquainted with Dunnington to know precisely where to begin.

If his beloved tutor had one weakness it was for books. The tutor could not possibly have lived anywhere without having haunted every bookstore and circulating library in the area.

Pleased to have at least decided on a direction to continue his search, Fredrick abruptly stilled as a tingle of pleasure spread over his skin.

There was only one thing, or rather one person, who could make his entire body shiver with awareness by simply entering the room.

Lifting his head he watched as Portia moved in his direction, a glass of some mysterious substance in her hand.

He hid a smile at the God-awful beige gown that hung loosely on her slender form. He could only suppose that her tender heart had led her to hire a blind dressmaker.

Nothing that ugly could have been deliberately created.

Of course, the hideous gown could not disguise the luminous beauty that shimmered in the early morning sunlight. His heart slammed against his chest as the world melted away to leave only the sight of pale, delicate features and cobalt eyes.

He might not yet be utterly certain that this was the woman of his dreams, but he could not deny that he had never before been so wholly captivated.

Rising to his feet, Fredrick gave a shallow bow as she halted at his table.

"Good morning, Portia," he murmured, his voice soft enough it would not travel to the handful of guests scattered about the various tables.

"Good morning." Her expression was carefully composed as if aware of watching eyes, but there was a warmth in her gaze that eased his lingering fear he might have frightened her with his stark hunger in the garden. "I am surprised to discover you up and about at such an early hour."

Fredrick grimaced, knowing his lingering pain was etched on his wan countenance. "I did consider nursing a sore head in the hopes you might take pity upon me and bring a tray to my room."

"Actually, I have indeed chosen to take pity upon you."

"Ah." He allowed his gaze to slide to her soft lips. "Shall I return to my rooms?"

The faintest hint of color touched her cheeks as she thrust the glass she was holding into his hand.

"Only if you wish to enjoy Mrs. Cornell's cure in privacy."

"Cure?" Fredrick tentatively sniffed at the strange brown brew. "Good God, it smells vile."

"No matter what the smell, I assure you that it will ease your aches," she said.

"If I am forced to drink this swill then the least you can do is have a seat and keep me company," he cunningly negotiated. He would drink a dose of arsenic to have a few moments with this woman. "I might very well need someone to bury my remains."

She gave a sniff at his teasing, but with a brisk motion she took her seat opposite the table.

"I will have you know that Mrs. Cornell's potions and ointments are renowned throughout the county."

Fredrick took his own seat as he studied the disgusting mixture. "Really? Perhaps I should speak with her about bottling them," he murmured before forcing himself to take a swallow of the potion. A shudder wracked his body, his stomach revolting at the disgusting concoction. Christ. It was worse than drinking sludge. "Then again, perhaps not," he groaned. "No matter how effective they might be, I do not believe that many will be eager to lay down good coin to drink something that tastes as if it came from the gutter."

"I shall expect a full apology once you begin feeling better," she informed him, indifferent to his battle to keep from casting up his accounts. Callous wench.

Ah, well. It was no less than he deserved after becoming bosky in her garden.

"Actually, you shall have my apology long before I begin to feel better," he said softly.

Her brows lifted in confusion. "And why is that?"

"I was not at my finest last eve—"

"No, Fredrick, do not apologize," she interrupted with that edge of command in her voice. "There is no need."

Fredrick resisted the urge to snap a salute. "At least allow me to assure you that I am not a gentleman who makes a habit of being deep in his cups."

"I did not believe that you were." With an obvious attempt to change the subject, Portia pointed a finger toward the notebook still clutched in his hand. "What are you working upon?"

With practiced ease, Fredrick flipped through the pages to tug out a sheet that was covered with a series of sketches. Placing the sheet on the table he covertly slipped his notebook back into the pocket sewn into the lining of his jacket.

He was not yet prepared to share his reasons for being in Wessex. Not until he knew something more of his father's secret.

"Actually, I have a few notions that I believe you might be interested in," he said.

Studying the paper, Portia sent him a narrowed gaze. "What on earth is this?"

"A series of block and tackle pulleys." A smile touched Fredrick's lips. "They would be a vast improvement over those you currently use."

She rolled her beautiful eyes even as a reluctant laugh tumbled from her lips.

"You truly are impossible."

Fredrick shrugged. "I do try."

A silence descended as Portia studied him with a searching gaze. "Why are you here, Fredrick?"

Caught off-guard by the abrupt question, Fredrick slowly lowered his gaze to study the worn wood of the table. He would not deliberately lie to Portia. Not when he sensed she had been deceived and manipulated by men her entire life.

"I have business in the area," he murmured evasively.

"What sort of business?"

"I am . . ." He slowly lifted his gaze to encounter her frown. "Seeking information."

"You are being remarkably mysterious."

"My business demands secrecy." That at least was

the absolute truth. He had learned early in his career that there were any number of unscrupulous cads among both inventors and investors. "You would be shocked by those who are willing to pay a small fortune to discover what I am currently working upon."

She gave a choked sound, as if she were attempting to swallow an impetuous laugh.

"You believe that there are people who spy upon you?"

"Do not laugh, it is not at all unusual." He leaned back in his chair and folded his arms over his chest. "I devoted the past month to seeking out which of my staff had been bribed to steal information on our design for a nail-making machine for a competitor."

Her smile faded, as if she sensed the distress it had caused him to discover that a man he had trusted for the past three years was no more than a traitor.

"How horrible."

Fredrick shrugged. He had already come to terms with Richardson's betrayal. The young man was not the first to have sold his soul for a few pounds, and he would not be the last.

"The price of investing in dreams, I suppose," he admitted wryly.

"Dreams?" she murmured. "Is that how you think of your business?"

"It was my father who suggested it first, but it does seem to describe my career well enough," he admitted.

Rising to her feet, Portia regarded him with a mysterious smile.

"Actually I think it describes *you* well enough, Fredrick."

Before he could demand an explanation for her

odd words, Portia had turned and was threading her way through the tables.

Fredrick leaned back in his chair as he watched her retreat.

What had been in that Madonna smile?

A possibility? A promise? Dare he hope an . . . invitation?

Fredrick rose to his feet, suddenly realizing the throbbing in his sorely abused head disappeared.

It could, of course, be proof that Mrs. Cornell's ghastly potion did indeed possess healing ingredients. It was believed by many that the nastier the taste of a medicine the better it worked. And he could not imagine anything that tasted any worse than the brown sludge.

In his heart, however, he knew that it had been the smile of a Siren that had cured his ills.

Chapter Ten

The city of Winchester was a pretty town that was dominated by a Norman cathedral that contained a long Gothic nave. Astonishingly, the entire structure was built upon rafts that floated upon the peat marsh.

Dunnington had taught Fredrick that the city had begun as a Celtic hill fort before the invasion of the Romans and had once been the capital of Wessex beneath King Alfred the Great.

A city rich in history and tradition, although Fredrick would never travel through the narrow streets without recalling his years of misery spent beneath the roof of Mrs. Griffin, a pious woman who firmly believed that the son should suffer for the sins of his father.

Passing through Kingsgate, Fredrick grimly kept the unpleasant memories at bay. It was already well past noon and he had no time to waste upon a past that was not worth recalling.

Leaving his mount in the care of the local stables, Fredrick headed for the center of the city with its medieval shops that draped over the narrow street.

He would begin his search in the center of the city and work his way outward.

A fine, practical notion that unfortunately took far longer than he had originally calculated. No doubt because he allowed himself to be distracted by purchasing the necessary materials to replace the ancient pulleys at the Queen's Arms.

Dusk was already descending when Fredrick entered the narrow bookstore near Winchester College. Pushing open the heavy door he winced at the jarring sound of the bell that echoed through the musty silence.

His eyes widened as he regarded the jumble of worn leather-bound books that were inexorably consuming the towering shelves, the small tables, and even the warped floor. There was barely room left to step through the door and make his way to the small counter.

At his approach, a small, silver-haired man with a pair of thick spectacles perched on the end of his nose lifted his head from a book spread on the counter to regard him with a hint of impatience.

"Yes, what do you want?"

"I have a few questions that I hope you can assist me with."

"What sort of questions?"

Fredrick conjured his most charming smile. "To begin with I wish to know how long you have owned this establishment."

"Near on thirty years. Why the devil do you want to know?"

Fredrick hid a small smile at the gruff suspicion. It was little wonder the establishment looked as if it were about to tumble into a pile of rubble. The owner might be a genius when it came to books, but he possessed the charm of a hedgehog.

"I am in search of a gentleman that I believe was a patron of your shop years ago."

The shaggy brows lowered in a forbidding manner. "What gentleman?"

"His name is Dunnington. Mr. Homer Dunnington."

"Dunnington?"

"A slender gentleman with brown hair and eyes," Fredrick prodded. "He made his living as a tutor."

"Bah. I've known a hundred tutors. Can't remember them all."

"Beyond Dunnington's love for history he possessed a weakness for lurid Gothic novels. I believe he lived in the area some twenty-five to thirty years ago."

"Gothic novels, you say?" As Fredrick had hoped Dunnington's clandestine addiction to melodramatic romances managed to strike a memory. The bookseller pulled off his glasses and absently polished them with a grubby handkerchief. "It does seem that I once knew such a man. A sensible chap, although quite thick-skulled when it came to the superiority of the English." The man gave a disapproving shake of his head. "Can you believe he actually argued that Chinese society was our equal? As if those heathens could do more than make vases and paint lacquer. A contrary sort."

Fredrick could not resist a short laugh. Dunnington had shocked more than a few with his belief that pagan societies could possess sophisticated and highly intellectual cultures.

"Yes, that would be Dunnington." With an effort he dampened his thrill of excitement. It appeared that he could at last connect Dunnington to Winchester, but it was still no more than a theory that he had encountered Lord Graystone during his time here. "Do you happen to recall if he lived in the neighborhood?"

Astonishingly the brows managed to lower even further, the bristly hairs nearly hiding his pale eyes.

"Why do you want to know?"

Thankfully Fredrick had rehearsed his story on the ride to Winchester. With a charming smile he moved to absently study a nearby stack of books.

"He recently passed and he has left a small inheritance to his nearest heir."

"An inheritance, eh?"

"Yes. Unfortunately he left few clues to any relatives he might possess."

"There, you see, he was just as I told you, contrary," the bookseller retorted, as if pleased to have his opinion of Dunnington's obstinate nature confirmed.

Fredrick gave a small shake of his head. The jealousy between scholars never failed to astonish him. Anyone who considered intellectuals as timid and meek creatures had never encountered rivals in a full-scale battle.

Far more frightening than any duel.

"Did he live in the vicinity?" he demanded.

The man gave a click of his tongue. "Lud, it must have been near on three decades ago, how should I know?"

Fredrick glanced pointedly at the large ledger book that was visible at the end of the counter.

"Do you write down the name and direction of your customers?"

"Only those who I extend credit to."

"Would you still have records from Dunnington's time?"

The bookseller perched his glasses on his nose

before glancing absently about the overcrowded room. "I suppose they might be in the attic."

Fredrick did not doubt for a moment they were either in the attic or stuffed among the other books. The man did not appear to have tossed away anything, including the rubbish, in the past thirty years.

"Would it be possible for me to have a look at them?" As the man opened his mouth to deny the request, Fredrick smoothly reached beneath his jacket to reveal a leather purse. "Of course I would not expect to make such a request without compensating you for any inconvenience."

The bookseller glanced toward the dusty windows where it was barely possible to discern the growing shadows.

"'Tis late. My housekeeper will have dinner awaiting me."

Pulling a handful of pound notes from the purse, Fredrick tossed them onto the counter.

"Why do you not go enjoy your dinner while I take care of the search? It should take me no more than a few hours and you can return and lock up."

"Well, I . . ." The man wavered, caught between his suspicion that Fredrick was plotting some nefarious scheme and the unexpected windfall that was spilled across his counter. At last greed overcame good sense and he plucked the notes from the counter and stuffed them in his pocket. Then, with a hurried step he was rounding the counter and heading toward the door, no doubt worried that Fredrick might have a change of mind. "I suppose it would do no harm. The ladder to the attic is in the back of the store. I will return in two hours."

Fredrick grimaced as the bookseller shut the door

and a cloud of dust swirled through the air. Dash it all, he could not begin to imagine the filth that awaited him in the attics.

Still, if there was a remote chance that he could find information on Dunnington, then he could not allow a bit (or more likely, a choking deluge) of dust to stand in his path.

Pulling out his handkerchief, he held it over his mouth as he headed toward the back of the shop.

The truth could be a messy business.

By half past ten that evening, Portia had come to an end of any legitimate tasks to keep her from climbing the stairs to her chambers. The guests were settled, the public rooms were nearly empty, and Molly was on duty to see to any guests who might make an appearance.

Unless some disaster occurred there was no reason at all to linger in the front salon.

So why was she here, peering out the window and pacing the floor as if she were expecting some momentous occurrence?

Because she was awaiting a honey-haired gentleman with the face of an angel to return to the inn, a disgruntled voice whispered in the back of her mind. And there was absolutely no possibility that she would seek her bed until she had managed to catch a glimpse of him.

Mercy, but she was in a mess.

Giving a shake of her head, Portia moved from the window as she heard the sound of approaching footsteps. The last thing she desired was to be caught wandering about like a lost soul.

She was vigorously arranging a vase of dried flowers

when Quinn entered the room and regarded her with a faint smile.

"Good evening, Portia."

Portia regarded her groom with a lift of her brows. As a rule the elderly man preferred the solitude of his rooms in the stables after dinner. It was the one place that he could smoke his pipe without Mrs. Cornell chiding him at the nasty smell.

"Quinn, is anything the matter?"

His smile widened as he folded his arms across his chest. "I thought I recognized that pretty little nose."

Portia gave a puzzled blink. "I beg your pardon?"

"I was walking across the yard and I noticed a nose being pressed to the window."

Portia lowered her head toward the flowers as a heat stained her cheeks.

"I may have glanced out the window," she muttered.

"Glanced?" Quinn gave a low chuckle. "More like a hound on the scent of a fox."

"Is there something you need, Quinn?"

"I was about to ask ye the same question, luv." Crossing the patterned carpet, Quinn halted directly beside Portia. "Ye have been pacing around here like Tolly the night before the carnival comes to town."

"That is ridiculous." Lifting her head, Portia intended to slay her companion with a glare only to heave a sigh at his knowing expression. "Oh, gads. I do not know what is the matter with me," she admitted, wrapping her arms about her waist. "I feel as if I am a top that has been wound too tightly."

"I vaguely recall such sensations." Quinn smiled in a wistful manner. "Ach, I miss those days."

"I cannot imagine why," Portia groused. "I just want peace."

Quinn gave a click of his tongue. "I suppose peace is well enough, but it is not what makes a person happy."

"Of course it does."

"Nay, luv." Reaching out a gnarled hand, Quinn lightly patted her shoulder. "Peace is merely an excuse to hide yerself from the world. Happiness is wading through all the messy, exciting uncertainty that is life."

Portia shuddered. Good God, she had spent most of her life battling her way through the muck life offered her.

"I have endured all the messy uncertainty that I desire, thank you, Quinn," she said.

"Mayhaps." Stepping back, Quinn regarded her for a long moment. "Do ye know what I like best about this inn?" he abruptly demanded.

"What?"

"I like to stand at the stairs in the morning as the children scramble down the steps, so eager to discover what wonderful adventures that the day holds for them that they can't bear to remain abed." A smile touched his lips. "We should all discover something in our lives that makes us rush down the stairs in the morning."

Portia's breath lodged in her throat. Good heavens, that was precisely how she had felt the past few mornings. That delicious thrill of excitement that she had not felt since she had been an eager, young child.

She regarded her friend with a suspicious frown. "You are not a mind-reader, are you, Quinn?"

Quinn's smile widened as the sound of the front door opening followed by a swift set of footsteps echoed through the near-silent inn.

"Enough of a mind-reader to know when me presence

is no longer needed." With a wink the elder man headed for the door. "Sweet dreams, luv."

Portia took an impetuous step forward, a sensible part of her urging her to follow Quinn from the room and retire to her chambers. Surely it was bad enough her old friend had caught her waiting for Fredrick's return like a . . . what had he said . . . a hound on the scent of a fox?

The last thing she desired was to have anyone else speculating on her presence in the salon.

Her brief bout of sanity, however, was swiftly overtaken by that lingering need to know that Fredrick was once again beneath her roof and that he was well.

She was standing in the center of the salon when the footsteps slowed and Fredrick paused in the doorway to regard her with a heart-melting smile.

"Good evening, poppet."

Her mouth went dry as faint candlelight brushed over the elegant features that never failed to steal her breath. And his eyes . . . they glowed like the purest silver.

Reminding her heart to beat, Portia allowed her gaze to lower to the dark jacket and breeches that clung to his lean body. They were beautifully tailored, as were all his clothes, but tonight they were coated with a thick layer of grey dust.

Her eyes widened as she took a step forward. "Good heavens, did you take another spill?"

Fredrick grimaced ruefully as he shoved a hand through his tangled honey curls. "I can occasionally manage to remain seated, poppet. I am not an utter greenhorn."

"I never thought you were," she murmured, hiding her amusement at the realization that she had managed to prick his pride. "It is just that you are covered in dirt."

"Ah." He gave an absent shrug as he prowled steadily forward. "Most of the dust came from an attic I was searching."

Portia struggled to pay attention to his words as her body tensed with an exquisite awareness.

"Why ever were you searching through an attic?"

"Actually there are the most fascinating objects to be discovered among the rubbish."

The only fascinating object that Portia found herself interested in was the firmly chiseled mouth that held her nearly hypnotized.

Oh, the magic in those lips.

A rash of heat tingled over her skin.

"I presume that must mean that your business is going well?" she managed to husk.

"I am not yet certain," he murmured in distracted tones, his attention focused on the fingers he trailed down the curve of her cheek. Portia's heart lodged in her throat. He was going to kiss her. Thank God. She swayed forward as his head slowly began to lower, only to abruptly halt as Molly bustled past the doorway, covertly shooting a swift glance into the room. With a smile that was tight with a healthy dose of frustration, Fredrick stepped back. "I suppose I should go to my chambers and deal with this mess before I am reprimanded by my very stern innkeeper for spreading dirt about her establishment."

Portia ran her shaky hands down her skirt. Drat it all. What the devil was Molly doing wandering the inn at this time of night? She should be waiting near the foyer for any guests to arrive.

"Have you . . ." She was forced to halt and clear her throat. "Have you had dinner?"

"I purchased something that was masquerading as a meat pie, but I was wise enough to toss it to the dogs after one bite."

"Perhaps Mrs. Cornell . . ."

"Thank you, poppet, but I do not intend to disturb your cook at this hour," he said firmly. There was another sound from the doorway as Tolly and Spenser tromped past, both of them eyeing Fredrick with a hint of warning. Fredrick held up his slender hands in a gesture of defeat. "Indeed, it would appear my late arrival has already created enough of a disturbance. I shall take myself off to my bed before the entire staff joins in the parade." He offered her a faint bow before heading toward the door. "Good night, Portia."

Portia clenched her hands as Fredrick disappeared down the hall.

She should be pleased, she told herself sternly. She had managed to speak with Fredrick and was assured that beyond a bit of dust he had returned safely.

There was nothing left to do but seek her bed for the night.

Standing alone in the room, however, she realized that she was not pleased. She was not pleased at all.

So, what did she do now?

Chapter Eleven

Fredrick managed to wash away most of the dust he had accumulated from the bookstore attic, unfortunately, the cold water did nothing to ease the aching frustration that plagued his body.

Pulling on his robe and running a comb through his damp curls, Fredrick struggled to concentrate on his unexpectedly successful evening.

It had taken near three hours, and a search through endless ledgers, but he had at last stumbled across the name of Dunnington.

He now had an address of where Dunnington had resided during his stay in Winchester. Tomorrow he would return and discover if there was anyone in his previous neighborhood that remembered the old tutor, or better yet, remembered Fredrick's father.

He was one step closer to achieving his goal, but at the moment he did not feel at all satisfied.

Indeed, he was feeling distinctly *unsatisfied*.

With a growl at the heavy throb in his groin, Fredrick was reaching for the nearby bottle of brandy when there was a soft scrape on his door.

Frowning at the unexpected noise, Fredrick crossed the room and pulled open the door. His surprise deepened as his gaze landed upon the slender, raven-haired beauty that stood in the hallway, a tray held in her hands.

"Portia?"

"Shhh . . ." Sweeping past his frozen form, Portia sent a chiding glance over her shoulder. "Close the door before we are seen."

Fredrick's lips twitched as he obeyed her clipped command and turned to watch the lovely sway of her hips as she moved to set the tray on a low table.

"What are you doing here, poppet?" he demanded.

She fussed with the plates upon the tray for a long moment, her trembling hands revealing she was not nearly as composed as she desired him to believe.

"I knew that you must be hungry so I brought you a tray." At last she forced herself to straighten and meet his searching gaze. "The ham is cold, but it should be filling and the bread is fresh."

"I am sure that it is delicious. Mrs. Cornell is a consummate artist in the kitchen."

She managed a nervous smile. "Oh, and I managed to uncover a few apricot tarts from Spenser's hidden supply."

Holding her gaze, Fredrick moved forward, not halting until he was standing directly before her with his hands on her shoulders.

"Portia."

She licked her lips, sending a jolt of warmth through his already overheated body. Bloody hell, if she were only here to offer food then he was in deep trouble.

"What?" she demanded warily.

"Why are you here?"

"I told you. I thought you might be hungry and—"

"And so you deliver trays to all of your hungry guests?" he interrupted as he relentlessly tugged her closer and closer.

"A few."

He chuckled softly as his arms lashed about her waist. "Poppet, is it so difficult to admit that you wanted to be with me?"

"Yes," she grudgingly conceded.

"Why?"

With a sigh, she lifted her hands to smooth them over the satin lapels of his robe. "I do not know."

"Tell me." Fredrick lowered his head, stroking his lips over the soft skin of her temple. "Tell me why you are here, Portia."

"I wanted . . ." Her words broke off in a jagged sigh as his lips stroked down to investigate the hollow behind her ear. "I wanted to see you. Be with you."

He breathed deeply of her midnight rose scent as his hands skimmed downward to grasp her hips. With one tug he had her firmly pressed to the hard muscles of his groin. A bittersweet pleasure considering the thick folds of her gown.

"You are here with me, poppet," he murmured softly. "Now tell me what you want from me."

She stiffened at his demand, her breath rasping in the air as she struggled against her instinctive fear of such intimacy.

At last she sucked in a deep breath and then, without warning, she tugged open the lapels of his robe to expose his bare chest. Fredrick gave a choked sound of pleasure as her lips blazed a path across his skin.

"I want you," she whispered, her hands slipping beneath his robe to clutch at his shoulders.

Fredrick shuddered at the feel of her soft, tormenting mouth. Still, he possessed enough sense to make sure that Portia understood what she was offering.

"You are certain, Portia? You will not wake in the morning filled with regrets?"

She tilted back her head to meet his narrowed gaze. "Fredrick, I do not know what the morning will bring, I only know that in this moment I do not want to be alone. I want to have your arms around me. I want to be with you."

"You want to be with me fully?"

Her lips curved in a smile of pure temptation. "Fully."

Fredrick released a shaky breath, his tightly coiled desire busting through his body in a small explosion.

Tomorrow he might once again be the enemy, but for tonight she was warm and willing.

For once in his life he would live for the moment.

"Then so be it."

Portia was aware of the moment that Fredrick allowed his rigid control to slip. It was in the compulsive flexing of his fingers as they dug into her hips, and the shimmering blaze of his silver eyes.

Heat charged and crackled in the air, but rather than the fierce, overwhelming passion she had braced herself for, Fredrick's lips were as gentle as the brush of a feather as they moved down the line of her jaw.

"My midnight rose," he whispered against her skin, the rasp of his whiskers sending a blaze of excitement down her spine. "I have ached for you."

She gave a low moan as she allowed her hands to stroke over the heated silk of his chest. On the last occasion she had been too caught in her own pleasure to enjoy the sensation of returning Fredrick's caresses. Now, she fully absorbed the feel of his skin lightly roughened with golden hair, the fascinating play of his muscles that hardened beneath her touch, the way his flat nipples pebbled as her tongue teased them.

Intent on her joyful discovery, Portia was barely aware of his own practiced movements, and it was not until she felt a cool breeze on her back that she realized he had managed to unbutton her gown and was efficiently unlacing her corset.

"Yes," she breathed as she felt the heavy gown slip away to leave her standing in her pretty shift. Somehow having the ugly brown fabric stripped away made her feel deliciously feminine.

"I want you, Portia Walker," he said thickly.

Lifting her eyes she met the searing silver gaze. "And I want you, Fredrick Smith."

Her words had barely managed to tumble from her lips when his head lowered and he stole her breath with a fierce kiss that held all the pent-up hunger he had kept sternly leashed.

Of their own will her lips parted to welcome the thrust of his tongue. Before Fredrick, she had thought such an intimate kiss offensive, but as her tongue instinctively moved to meet his caress, Portia was reeling from the pleasure that poured like warm honey through her blood.

It was this man, she bemusedly accepted. His touch, his taste, even his warm male scent that combined to make her senses tingle to life. No other could stir her to such a fever-pitch.

Arching against his hard body, Portia shivered as his hands skimmed up the curve of her waist, tenderly cupping the sensitive fullness of her breasts.

Her knees threatened to buckle as his thumbs played over her aching nipples. Oh, mercy. The intense pleasure arrowed straight to the pit of her stomach, searing each nerve along its path.

She struggled to choke back a groan when Fredrick eased his kiss to playfully nip at the corner of her mouth.

"No, poppet, do not hide what you are feeling," he murmured. "I want to hear your sweet sounds when I please you."

Portia's head fell backward as his marauding lips burned a path down the curve of her neck. She did not think that it was possible to hide what she was feeling. Not when her entire body was trembling beneath his exquisite touch.

"And how will I know when I please you?" she murmured.

He chuckled softly as he clasped her hand and led it down to where his erection was already visible between the edges of his robe.

"I have no means to disguise my reaction," he said, his breath catching as Portia readily allowed her fingers to explore the hard, straining proof of his desire. "Bloody hell."

"Do you like that?"

"God . . ." he husked, his eyes squeezing shut as she found the soft sack. "Yes, I like it. I like it very much."

Portia discovered she liked it as well. She liked the small, strangled noises that she could coax from his lips as she encircled him with her fingers. She liked his ragged struggle to breathe when she stroked over the rounded tip. She even liked the musky scent of his arousal that was filling the air.

It offered a sense of power she had never before experienced in the arms of a man.

For long moments Fredrick allowed her to fully discover the delights of stirring his passions, then with a deep groan, his arms tightened around her and with a smooth motion he had her swept off her feet.

Expecting to be carried to the bed, Portia was caught off-guard when Fredrick instead moved to the side table set against the far wall.

"Fredrick?"

"Trust me," he urged, settling her on the edge of the smooth wood.

Waiting until she met his gaze, he slowly tugged her shift upward, deliberately rubbing the silk over the tips of her breasts before pulling it over her head and dropping it onto the floor.

"By all that is holy, you are exquisite," he breathed, his gaze running a reverent path over the curves of her breasts and down the slender line of her stomach. Portia gasped as fingers followed in the wake of his smoldering gaze, moving downward until he reached the curls between her legs.

Good heavens, she was already feeling that delicious tension beginning to build. A tension he had taught her would be followed by sweet paradise. But it was too soon. As much as she had enjoyed having Fredrick pleasure her, she wanted to hold him close as he reached his own release.

She needed to know that she could offer him the same pleasure.

"Not yet," she muttered, her hands reaching to tug at the belt of his robe. "I want to see you. All of you."

"Whatever you desire, poppet," he husked, readily parting the thick robe and allowing it to slip from his body.

Portia sucked in a deep breath. Unlike most men that she knew, Fredrick was not a mass of bulk and hair. Instead he was as sleek and elegant as the marble statues of Greek gods.

Unable to resist, she reached to smooth her hands over his chest, lingering on the rapid beat of his heart.

"I did not know a man could be so beautiful," she whispered.

He laughed softly as he parted her legs to step between them. "Not nearly so beautiful as you."

A shiver wracked her body as his erection brushed against her heated core.

"Must you always have the last word," she teased in a breathless voice.

"Always," he assured her before he lowered his head and kissed her with hungry demand.

Her hands instinctively lifted to encircle his neck, her lashes lowering as his clever fingers stroked along her inner thigh with a relentless caress. A blaze of sensations flared from the light touch, her legs quivering as his searching fingers neared the heart of her need.

Any lingering fear or hesitation was forgotten beneath the force of her aching need. She had been alone for so long. She needed the feel of his warm touch, the sound of his voice as much as she needed the pleasure of his intimacy.

Perhaps more.

Growling low in his throat, Fredrick plunged his tongue between her lips at the same moment that his finger slipped into her moist heat.

Portia forgot to breathe as he stroked deeper and

deeper, his thumb strumming over a small peak that created tiny sparks of delight. Her fingers restlessly tangled in his hair as her legs widened in silent invitation.

Scattering kisses over her upturned face, Fredrick at last reached down to position his shaft. She prepared for his entry, but unexpectedly he instead rubbed the hard length against her cleft.

She pulled back to regard him with a puzzled glance. "Fredrick?"

The silver eyes glittered beneath his half-lowered lids. "I told you to trust me, poppet," he murmured.

His hands lowered to grip her hips, pressing his arousal firmly against her. For a moment Portia was lost in confusion as he thrust upward, refusing her silent pleas to enter her body.

It was not until his erection stroked over her sensitive nub that she realized his intention.

"Oh . . ." she rasped, her lashes fluttering downward as his relentless strokes made her body tighten and arch.

"Wrap your legs around me," he urged, his lips nibbling along her collarbone. Portia readily obeyed his command, a soft cry tumbling from her lips as he relentlessly stroked her toward the beaconing bliss. "Yes, poppet," he groaned, his mouth moving down to capture a straining nipple between his lips.

The feel of his tongue flicking over the sensitive tip was enough to send Portia tumbling over the edge of pleasure. Her head fell back as the tiny eruptions wracked through her body, her breath rasping loudly.

Fredrick shifted to bury his face in the curve of her neck, his hips continuing to pump until he gave a low shout and Portia felt his warm seed spread across her stomach.

Wrapped tightly in his arms, Portia snuggled against his chest and allowed a satisfied smile to curve her lips.

Once again Fredrick had managed to offer her a means of intimacy that did not threaten her future.

Clearly his talents of invention were not solely confined to his business.

Fredrick was oddly shaken as he felt Portia snuggle into his chest with a sigh of contentment.

It was not the climax they had just shared, although that had been rather wonderful. Spectacular, in fact. Or even the sheer relief of easing the frustration that had plagued him for days.

No, it was the complete sense of rightness in the moment, he decided as he scooped her into his arms and carried her toward the bed.

So terrifyingly, perfectly right.

Laying her slender form onto the mattress, Fredrick moved to swiftly wash himself, then dampening a cloth he returned to the bed and stretched out beside her. With gentle strokes he began to clean her smooth ivory skin.

As she remained still beneath his ministrations, Fredrick lifted his gaze. A tiny shock raced through him at the sight of her pale features in the candlelight, her expression soft and sated, her eyes darkened and her curls tumbled across the pillow like a veil of ebony satin.

There was very little of the commanding general about her now. Instead she was all tempting female.

His body responded with a randy eagerness and

swallowing a groan, Fredrick gently pulled her into his arms and eased her head onto his chest.

"You are being very quiet, poppet," he murmured, his fingers absently running a path through her satin curls.

"I am not quite certain what to say," she replied, her own fingers skating over his chest.

"Well, you could say that I am the most talented lover you have ever encountered." He kissed her forehead. "And that you are utterly, completely, wholly enthralled." He kissed the tip of her nose. "And that you will adore and worship—"

"Worship?" she interrupted, giving his arm a small pinch. "Not bloody likely."

He gave a chiding click of his tongue. "Such language, poppet. I am shocked."

"I do not know why you should be. As the owner of an inn I am accustomed to hearing the sort of language that would make a sailor blush."

Fredrick frowned at her light tone. Dammit, this woman should be draped in lace and jewels and surrounded by the most delicate of society. The men in her life had failed her miserably.

"Does it trouble you?"

"To hear foul language?"

"No, to be isolated at this inn when you should be gracing the drawing rooms of London."

He felt her body stiffen beneath his hands, her head deliberately lowered to hide her expression.

"I have never possessed the desire to grace any drawing room."

He slipped a finger beneath her chin and tugged her countenance up so he could examine her guarded expression.

"That cannot be entirely true, Portia. Every young girl dreams of her debut among society, surely you were no different?"

She was silent a long moment, as if debating whether to ignore his intimate prying.

"Perhaps when I was very young and very foolish," she at last admitted with a faint sigh.

"Why was it foolish?"

"Because my father was never going to spend the money to offer me a proper season." She gave a short, humorless laugh. "More often than not I was forced to sew my own gowns if I desired to attend the local assemblies."

Fredrick could not halt a low grunt of disgust. He already knew that Portia's father was a jackass. Now it appeared that he was a lobcock as well.

"Damnation, was the man entirely daft?"

She met his glittering gaze with a hint of surprise. "He was often weak-willed and self-absorbed, but I am not certain he was actually daft."

"He must have been daft or he would have devoted himself to making sure that you were placed on the Marriage Mart." Fredrick allowed his finger to skim over the warm silk of her cheek. "My God, with your beauty you would have landed a husband that would have willingly supported your father for years to come."

"My father believed that my prickly nature would frighten away most suitors," she explained. "Especially those suitors who were in a position to choose a more amenable debutante." Fredrick grimaced at the thought of Portia's tender years in the care of the heartless bastard. Hell, it was a wonder the poor woman had not been crushed and dispirited beyond repair. Her own expression was one of resignation.

"You cannot imagine his surprise when Edward actually proposed to me."

Fredrick's heart gave a small jerk as he realized that she had revealed far more than she had intended.

"Edward?" He kept his tone deliberately nonchalant, not yet willing to reveal he had already heard of her treacherous fiancé who had left her at the altar. "I thought your husband's name was Thomas?"

He could hear her sharp breath. "Yes. Yes, it was."

"Portia?" He shifted to lean on his elbow, studying her pale features. "Who was Edward?"

Her eyes darkened, a combination of anger and resentment and more disturbing, a lingering pain, smoldering in the cobalt depths.

"He was . . ." She struggled to keep her voice steady. "He was a mistake."

"You were engaged to him?"

"For a brief time."

"Why did you not wed?"

Her eyes narrowed, clearly unhappy at his probing. "Edward decided he preferred the life of a bachelor rather than becoming a husband. To the best of my knowledge he continues to enjoy his unfettered existence in London."

"Did you love him?"

Her lashes lowered to hide her reaction to his blunt question. "It was all a very long time ago."

"Did you love him, poppet?"

Without warning she lifted her hands to press them against his chest, her expression warning that she had reached the end of her patience.

"I will not discuss my past, Fredrick. It no longer matters."

Fredrick smiled wryly. "If it no longer mattered

then you would not allow the memory of your ex-fiancé to haunt you."

"Fredrick . . ." She gave another shove on his chest, arching backward as he firmly wrapped his arms around her to prevent her escape.

"Lay still, poppet, you can keep your secrets," he murmured, tracing his lips over her troubled brow. "At least for now."

"How very generous of you." Her eyes narrowed, although she halted her struggles. "I suppose I should return the favor and assure you that you shall be allowed to keep your secrets as well, Mr. Smith. At least for now."

Fredrick elevated a honey brow. "My secrets?"

A challenging smile touched her lips. "There is more to your journey to Wessex than just business, is there not?"

Portia watched the perfect, finely chiseled features for his reaction to her accusation. If Fredrick desired to poke and prod into matters that were none of his business, then why should she not return the favor?

Being the owner of an inn had taught her to keep a careful watch upon her guests. It was the only means of knowing which customers might be overly demanding upon her staff, which might create trouble with the other guests, and even which might attempt to slip out without paying their bill.

She had sensed from the beginning that there was more to Fredrick Smith's arrival at the Queen's Arms than mere business.

If she hoped to catch him off guard, however, she was doomed to disappointment. Instead of alarm, his expression was merely one of curiosity.

"Why do you believe there is more to my journey?" he demanded.

She met his gaze squarely. In some ways this man was as skilled as herself at keeping others at a distance when he desired. The only difference was that he was clever enough to use that heart-rending charm as a shield.

"There is a . . . distraction about you. Almost as if you are searching for something."

His lips twitched, his eyes darkening with that ready passion. "That is hardly a secret, poppet," he husked, his fingers creating chaos as they skimmed down her stomach. "I can promise you that I have never been quite so distracted in my entire life. Although I believe that my search is about over . . ."

"Fredrick," Portia squeaked as his fingers brushed through her lower curls to the opening between her legs. "I am trying to have a conversation with you."

He merely laughed as he tugged her legs wider, giving him even great access to her tender flesh.

"I am listening, poppet." He gave her earlobe a nip before outlining the shell with his tongue. "What do you wish to say to me?"

The hands that had been pushing him away now rubbed over the satin heat of his chest.

"Are you attempting to divert me?" she demanded, not nearly as annoyed by his devious tactics as she should be.

His lips nuzzled the corner of her mouth. "I should think it was rather obvious what I am attempting to do, but if you would like a detailed explanation I would be happy to clarify as I go along."

Her breath became lodged in her throat as his clever fingers stroked through her gathering dampness.

Oh . . . mercy. The aggravating man was clearly attempting to avoid her questions. It was a blatant manipulation of her passions.

At the moment, however, she found that she did not particularly care why he was arousing her to a fever-pitch. Only that he not halt the sensual assault.

"Actually, I do not believe there is any need for explanations," she murmured.

"Are you certain? I have a few deliciously wicked details that I could . . ."

"Fredrick, would you please just kiss me?" she demanded as her body shuddered in need.

Surprise, swiftly followed by stark desire, rippled over the golden countenance at her unexpected daring. Then, with a low groan he was kissing her with a fierce urgency.

"Is that what you want?" he whispered against her lips.

"Oh, yes." Portia shivered as his hands were skimming up the curve of her waist and cupping the fullness of her breasts. "That is precisely what I want."

She gave a small gasp that was swallowed by his devouring lips. His thumbs lightly encircled her nipples, teasing them into tight buds.

Sweet heavens. How had she never known that this wondrous bliss existed? How had she survived so long without the touch of this man?

Her eyes fluttered closed as he branded her face with restless kisses.

"I have never wanted a woman as I want you," he rasped as he pressed his hard arousal against her hip. "You are more than a distraction. You are rapidly becoming an obsession."

Her hands clutched at his arms as he gently nibbled

his way down the curve of her neck. He paused at the pulse that beat wildly at the hollow of her throat, his tongue reaching out to taste of her skin.

Portia moaned at the heady sensations that poured through her body. She wanted to close her eyes and drown in the pleasure that his touch created, but just as insistent was the need to return his heated caresses. She wanted to hear his soft moans echoing her own.

Trailing her hand down his chest, she lingered on the carved muscles of his stomach, a faint smile touching her lips as Fredrick sucked in a sharp breath.

Portia skimmed her hand ever lower, at last encountering the strong thrust of his erection. Encircling him with her fingers, Portia gently stroked over the silky skin that covered the hard length.

A low growl rumbled in Fredrick's throat as his hands swept down her heated skin and he grasped her hips. Then, without warning, he was turning her over so that she faced the mattress.

Startled by his strange behavior, she turned her head to regard him over her shoulder. "Fredrick?"

"Do not fret, poppet," he murmured as he shifted to press himself to her back. He gave her shoulder a small nip. "There is still an endless variety of pleasure to be discovered."

"But, you cannot . . . oh."

Her words came to a shocked halt as his fingers once again slid down the gentle swell of her stomach and then through her dark curls.

"Do I please you, my love?" He buried his face in the curve of her neck while his finger began to stroke with a slow insistence. "I need to hear the words from your sweet lips."

Her eyes slid shut as his finger dipped into her

damp heat. "Yes, you please me," she sighed, a delicious pressure beginning to build within her. "Oh . . . yes. Yes."

She felt his hard shaft pressing against the back of her thigh, his thrusts mirroring the stroke of his finger. Portia's fingers dug into the pillows as her breath came in short, shallow pants. A part of her desperately longed to feel the hard length of him buried deep between her legs. To be so intimately connected to him would surely be paradise.

But even as she opened her lips to beg him to enter her, she was giving a startled moan. That sharp pleasure was racing out of control and before she could slow the building pressure a sharp explosion of bliss quaked through her body, stealing her breath and clearing her mind of everything but the delight of Fredrick's touch.

Chapter Twelve

It was no surprise that Fredrick awoke with a sense of utter contentment. Spending the night making love to a beautiful woman tended to improve the mood of the most surly gentleman.

Of course, he would have been a good deal more content if he had awoken with his arms still clutching her warm body close, he acknowledged as he forced himself to climb from the bed that still held her sweet scent and attired himself in a dove grey jacket and black breeches.

Obviously he would have to find some means of whisking the lovely Mrs. Portia Walker away from the Queen's Arms, he abruptly decided.

Not only because he desired to spend a few days in her company without being forced to sneak about like a pair of naughty schoolchildren, but he was beginning to suspect Portia would never reveal her deepest self so long as she was constantly fretting over the local gossip of her servants and guests.

And he wanted to know all those secrets she kept

hidden. Her every hope and dream and fear. All the bad and all the good.

He wanted to know her heart and soul.

A delightful notion. Unfortunately, he was wise enough to realize that dragging Portia from her beloved inn, even for a few days, would be akin to dragging a badger from its lair. And there was still the small matter of his father's dark secret that needed to be uncovered.

A small smile touched his lips as he headed down the stairs and entered the public rooms. Whatever the difficulties in luring Portia into a clandestine journey, he would overcome them.

Overcoming difficulties, after all, was what he did best.

Taking a seat at a table near the door, Fredrick paid little heed to the three elegantly attired gentlemen who were gathered at the back of the room. A mere glance was enough to reveal that they were the usual pampered louts who possessed too much money and too much time. The sort who always had to be loud and flamboyant enough to attract the attention of everyone in the room.

Ridiculous twits.

Instead he trained his attention on the plump maid who scurried to his table with a welcome cup of tea.

"Good morning, Molly," he murmured, the smile that had been curving his lips when he awoke this morning still clinging to his lips.

The woman gave a low, knowing chuckle as she caught sight of his expression. Despite her youth she possessed the sort of experience to recognize a well-satisfied gentleman.

"Aye, a very good morning, sir. At least for some of us. Will you be having yer usual breakfast?"

Fredrick's stomach rumbled at the scent of baked ham that filled the air. "Yes, I believe I will. Is Mrs. Walker down yet?"

Expecting another one of those wicked chuckles, Fredrick found himself intrigued when instead the maid appeared almost flustered by his question.

"Oh aye. She was up at the crack of dawn." Molly managed a thin smile. "She is never one to lie abed. Always busy doing something."

"Is she in the kitchen?"

"I . . . I believe she is in the garden. Or perhaps it's the stables."

Fredrick resisted the fierce desire to grab the maid and shake her until she confessed the truth of Portia's whereabouts. It was not the hapless servant's fault that her employer was one of the most secretive, irksome, exasperating women ever to plague a man.

"If you happen to see her, will you tell her I would like to have a word with her?" His pleasant words came out between gritted teeth.

"Aye." With a hasty dip the maid was charging back toward the kitchen and Fredrick was left alone to ponder the one woman in the world who could alter his joyous mood to one of brooding annoyance in a matter of seconds.

Where the devil had she gone at such an hour? And why was her staff so furtive about her disappearance?

A dozen different reasons, each more implausible than the last fluttered through his mind as he consumed the large breakfast that Molly delivered to his table.

Lost in his thoughts, he failed to notice the gaggle

of dandies who strolled from the back of the room to halt at his table. It was not until the tallest of the frivolous idiots deliberately jostled Fredrick's elbow that he bothered to glance up.

"Well, well," the gentleman with a weak chin and thinning brown hair sneered. "If it isn't Graystone's bastard. I heard the nasty rumors that you were skulking through our neighborhood."

Fredrick leaned back in his seat and folded his arms over his chest. He was far too accustomed to the various snubs and insults he endured to react. If he allowed himself to be baited by every idiot who crossed his path he would never do anything but indulge in battles.

"Hardly skulking," he drawled. "Have we been introduced?"

"Introduced?" The man glared down the length of his too-thin nose. "Not bloody likely. I do not associate with by-blows. Not even my own."

"Charming. Is there some purpose for interrupting my breakfast?"

"I want you to leave here."

Fredrick smiled. "And I want to build a machine that will allow me to fly, but I doubt that either of us will get what we desire. At least not today."

The man appeared briefly caught off-guard by Fredrick's casual indifference to his rude attack. With a glance toward his two portly friends for support, he stiffened his cowardly spine.

"Your presence is an insult to Simon."

Ah. So that was the reason for this nasty little encounter, Fredrick acknowledged. Clearly the three buffoons were friends of his brother and having

heard of his presence in the neighborhood had come
to play the petty game of badger-the-bastard.

With an inward sigh, Fredrick rose to his feet. The
intruders would not be satisfied with a few passing
taunts. He wanted to be prepared in the event that
the encounter came to blows.

"An insult to Simon?" He gave a genuinely amused
laugh. "Now that is rare. From all I have heard, Simon
manages to be an insult just by walking into a room."

The dandy sucked in a sharp breath, his hand instinctively smoothing over his gaudy velvet coat with
oversized buttons that appeared absurd among the
common guests.

"How dare you?"

"Very easily." Fredrick shrugged. "My beloved
brother is nothing more than an insufferable cox-
comb who is laughed at by the entire neighborhood.
Would you like to know how they describe him and
his friends?"

A hint of color touched the thin countenance.
"Only a bastard would presume that a true gentleman
gives a fig for the opinion of turnip-headed farmers."

"No doubt he is satisfied with the opinion of his
fellow coxcombs. Hardly surprising considering the
lot of you possess the same appalling habit of attiring
yourself like molting peacocks."

The man's countenance darkened to the same
shade of cranberry as his velvet jacket. "Why, you
worthless bastard . . ."

His arm pulled back, as if he were contemplating
the perilous notion of taking a swing at Fredrick. At
the same moment there was a stern, decidedly feminine voice slicing through the air.

"Is there something I can do for you?"

As one the gentlemen turned to regard the woman who stood like a diminutive general surveying her disorderly troops.

"Well, well." The velvet-coated jackass smiled in a far too familiar manner as he took in the stunning beauty of Mrs. Portia Walker. "There is without a doubt any number of things you can do for me, my sweet. But for the moment I will settle for having this . . . piece of filth thrown into the nearest gutter."

The magnificent blue eyes snapped with disapproval as Portia folded her arms and glared at the gentleman.

"Mr. Smith happens to be a guest in this inn and if anyone is to leave it will be you and your friends."

The man gave a small jerk at the obvious rebuff. "Do you know who I am?"

"I do not, and in truth, I am not particularly interested."

Fredrick would have been amused by Portia's ready defense if he had not been acutely aware of the attention they were attracting. The last thing he desired was to have her business disturbed by an ugly brawl.

"We shall see about that," the man growled as he stepped toward Portia.

With a swift motion, Fredrick had placed himself in front of the seething gentleman, his expression cold with warning.

"Portia, there is no need to trouble yourself," he drawled. "I am certain that this can be resolved without creating a fuss." His gaze narrowed as he studied the three intruders. "Perhaps we should step outside to finish our conversation?"

Typically, Portia was not satisfied to leave matters in

his hands. She was a woman who very much preferred to be in command of every situation.

Grasping his sleeve she tugged at his jacket until he reluctantly turned to meet her glittering gaze.

"This is my inn, Mr. Smith. I will decide whether or not to trouble myself."

He leaned close to whisper in her ear. "I am accustomed to dealing with such arrogant pests, poppet. The more attention that the idiots draw to themselves, the more satisfied they will be. It is far better that I escort them from your establishment and sort this out in private."

"No, Fredrick," she hissed. "There are three of them. You will be hurt."

"Good God, has no one taught you not to question a man's fighting prowess?" he demanded with a low laugh. "You might as well question my very manhood."

She pulled back to stab him with an annoyed frown. "This is not the time for jests, Fredrick."

There was a rude sound from behind him as the dandy gave his shoulder a slight shove.

"I suppose I shouldn't be surprised that a bastard is hiding behind the skirts of his trollop . . ."

The word "trollop" was still hanging on his lips when Fredrick spun about and connected his fist with the man's weak chin.

There was a low grunt and then the peacock tumbled backward to land on the flagstone floor with a pleasing thud. Fredrick peered down at the fool, a violent flare of satisfaction racing through him.

He would endure any number of insults with a smile on his face if it would avoid unpleasantness in the middle of the public rooms. But he would be damned if he would endure one insult directed toward Portia.

With a rather childish spite, Fredrick prodded the unconscious lump with the tip of his boot, fully appreciating the sight of his handiwork. His moment of distraction, however, nearly proved to be disastrous as the injured man's friends managed to gather enough courage to rush him.

More concerned with making sure that Portia was kept safely out of the fray than the bumbling attack of the pathetic fribbles, Fredrick was preparing to shove the two backward when a dark, well-built gentleman stepped through the doorway and grasped the two charging men by the scruffs of their collars.

"Bloody hell," Ian Breckford drawled. "I never expected to find such good sport when I came in search of you, Freddie boy."

Perfectly stunned by the unexpected arrival of his friend, Fredrick could do no more than gape at him in shock.

"Ian? What the blazes are you doing here?"

Oblivious to his astonishment, Portia grasped his hand and lightly touched his knuckles that were scraped and bleeding.

"Fredrick, you have been hurt," she exclaimed.

"It is nothing," he muttered absently.

Ian lifted his brows, the eyes the exact shade of antique gold shimmering with a dangerous fire.

"You allowed these slow-tops to hurt you?"

Recognizing that expression, Fredrick stepped forward. "Ian . . . no," he commanded, but too late.

With one smooth motion Ian had managed to jerk his two captives toward one another, cracking their heads with a sickening thud. The sharp blow managed to knock both of them unconscious and with a pleased smile Ian dropped them onto the floor and calmly dusted his hands together.

There was a loud round of applause for Ian's theatrics, but Fredrick was far from pleased. Stepping forward, he grasped his friend by the arm and dragged him out of the room.

"Damn you, Ian."

"Fredrick, have you lost what few wits you once possessed?" Ian protested as Fredrick tugged him ruthlessly down the corridor.

"Very likely," Fredrick readily agreed.

"Bloody hell, do you know how many hours I spent at the gaming tables to pay for this jacket you are determined to ruin?"

"We both know that you now have an ample amount of money to pay for any number of jackets."

Ian made a rude noise. "That is not the point."

Reaching a private salon, Fredrick pulled Ian into the empty room and closed the door. He ignored the recently refurbished sofa and overstuffed chairs that Portia had taken such care to choose for the darkly paneled room. All that mattered was that they were away from the curious onlookers.

"We should not be interrupted here," he muttered.

Wrenching his arm from Fredrick's grasp, Ian smoothed his hand over the fabric of his champagne superfine jacket.

"Really, Fredrick, is this any way to treat an old friend who has not only traveled a considerable distance to be with you, but also just managed to vanquish your enemies with a single blow?"

"I did not ask that you vanquish my enemies, Ian."

"Ah, so that is the trouble." A sudden smile light-ened the dark features, revealing a straight row of star-tling white teeth. "You were hoping to impress that raven-haired beauty I glimpsed at your side by slay-ing a few dragons. Forgive me, I did not intend to steal your glory."

Fredrick swallowed a sigh. "I was hoping to deal with the ridiculous buffoons without creating a distur-bance that will be the talk of the neighborhood."

"What does it matter?" Reaching beneath his jacket, Ian pulled out a silver flask that was always filled with top-notch whiskey. "It seemed to me that the neigh-bors were pleased enough to watch the mincing pea-cocks knocked onto their backsides."

Fredrick winced at the memory of the smattering of applause as Ian had tidily dealt with pinks of the *ton*. It was all very amusing for the guests, but it was not their livelihood that was being threatened by the un-pleasant encounter.

"Those peacocks have powerful families who might very well cause trouble for Portia," he said with an edge in his voice.

The golden eyes narrowed as Ian took a deep sip of the whiskey. "Portia?"

"Mrs. Walker, the owner of this establishment."

A smile of pure male appreciation curved Ian's full lips. "Ah, the raven-haired beauty."

Fredrick abruptly turned to pace toward the fine bay window that overlooked the stables. Why bother attempting to convince Ian that an ugly brawl with the local dandies was a poor notion? The rogue's favorite sport was humiliating the upper crust.

"What the devil are you doing here, Ian?" he at last demanded.

With a nonchalance that did not entirely hide the hint of wariness on the dark, beautiful features, Ian took a deep drink of his whiskey.

"I came to visit an old friend. Surely that is not so strange?"

"How did you know I was staying at this inn?"

Ian shrugged. "Your father was gracious enough to give me directions."

Fredrick gave a strangled cough as he stepped toward his friend. "You spoke to my father?"

"Yes." The dark, smoldering gaze flared over Fredrick's near delicate form. "You know, you look a great deal like him. Much more so than that squishy, sallow-faced boy I saw in portraits *ad nauseam* throughout the house. Oh, and before I forget, Lord Graystone requested that I offer you an invitation to dine with him tonight, and I of course, am included in the generous invitation."

"Dammit, Ian, this is no time for your games," Fredrick rasped. For some reason the thought of Ian calmly chatting with his father was more than a trifle bothersome. Perhaps because he had always managed to keep his life in London so completely separated from his painful existence at Oak Manor. "Why are you in Wessex instead of Surrey where you belong?"

There was a thick silence before Ian gave a sharp laugh. "Actually, I did leave London with every intention of visiting Surrey."

"And?"

Ian drained the last of the whiskey and shoved the flask back into the inner pocket of his jacket.

"And somewhere along the road I managed to end

up in Wessex. I never did have much of a sense of direction."

A wave of sympathy flooded through Fredrick. Ian would skewer himself on a hot poker before he would admit that he had lost his nerve on the road home.

"Ian, there is no need to travel to Surrey, you know," Fredrick said gently. "Return to London and enjoy your fortune. It is what we would all do if we had any wits."

"I have the feeling that you are attempting to rid yourself of my presence, Freddie boy," Ian drawled as he moved to settle himself in one of the gold and ivory striped chairs. "Is it just a general dislike for my companionship or does it have something to do with that lovely little angel that was so concerned for your wounds?"

Fredrick ignored the hint to reveal his relationship with Portia. He never spoke of the women who caught his interest. And certainly not one who was beginning to mean a great deal more to him than a passing fancy.

"I am always pleased to have your company, Ian. You know that."

The cynical expression that Ian wore like a mask softened at the unmistakable sincerity in Fredrick's words.

"Thank you." He templed his fingers beneath his chin as he studied Fredrick with a curious gaze. "Tell me what you have managed to discover."

"Precious little thus far, I fear." Fredrick gave a frustrated shake of his head. "At the moment, the only thing I have to go upon is the fact that Dunnington and my father both resided in Winchester for a brief time."

"Winchester, hmmm." Ian considered a moment. "It is at least something."

Fredrick was struck by a sudden thought. Ian was already aware of his reason for being in the neighborhood, so there was no need to hide his search for Dunnington's boarding house. And in truth, he could use a measure of the man's indecent luck.

"Actually, I intend to visit Winchester later this afternoon if you would be interested in joining me?"

"Why not?" Ian stretched out his legs and crossed them at the ankle. "While I am there, I can see about renting a room for the next few nights."

Fredrick gave a lift of his brows. "Why not remain here?"

"For once you appear to have enough sense to enjoy the attentions of a beautiful woman." Ian flashed his wicked dimples. "I would not desire to steal away her heart."

"You fear that your charm is irresistible?"

"Of course," Ian agreed with a casual arrogance. "I am known as Casanova, after all."

Fredrick chuckled at his companion's blatant confidence. He was not at all concerned at being cut out by his more dashing friend. Although most women were captivated by the dark, restless passions that smoldered about Ian, Fredrick was confident in Portia's unwavering dislike for well-practiced rakes.

"Somehow I am quite certain that Portia would be indifferent to that practiced charm," he murmured with a faint smile. "Still, it might be best if you stay in Winchester. I do not desire any unnecessary questions as to the reasons for my stay in the neighborhood."

"What excuse have you given?"

"Business."

Ian rolled his eyes. "Predictable."

"Which means that it is believable," Fredrick pointed out in reasonable tones.

Ian smiled wryly, his long fingers tapping a steady tattoo on the padded arm of the chair.

"Your father was quite . . . delighted when I appeared at his door," he said without warning, the golden eyes watchful. "In fact, he refused to allow me to leave until I had tasted of his particularly fine brandy and he had managed to ply me with a dozen questions."

Fredrick stiffened. "What sort of questions?"

"About your life in London. If you are happy." His smile widened with a taunting amusement. "If you have a particular female you have shown an interest in. If you have need of anything. He did not appear nearly as indifferent to you as I expected him to be."

Fredrick grimaced. "I will admit that he has been behaving in a distinctly odd manner since my arrival. If I had to guess I would say that he is feeling guilty for forgetting my existence during the past ten years."

Ian caught and held his gaze. "Are you so certain that he forgot you?"

"How could he not?" Fredrick paced across the room, his emotions tightly coiled as he refused to consider the notion of his father giving a bloody damn. "Lord Graystone has not bothered to so much as scribble me a note in the past decade. Not even when he was staying in London. Hardly the behavior of a devoted father."

"Perhaps not, but—"

Fredrick held up a warning hand. "It does not matter, Ian. I am not here to win my father's affection. I am here to discover why he willingly paid Dunnington twenty thousand pounds for his silence, nothing more."

The golden eyes twinkled with a sudden fire. "And to seduce a certain innkeeper?"

Portia.

Sucking in a sharp breath, Fredrick headed directly toward the door. Dammit, he had allowed Ian to distract him. He needed to get rid of the unconscious noblemen before they awoke and created difficulties.

"Remain here," he commanded in stern tones. "I will return in a moment."

Chapter Thirteen

Portia kept her composure firmly intact as she commanded Quinn to seek out the unconscious gentlemen's servants. With a minimum of fuss the three noblemen were carried to their waiting carriage and the public rooms were returned to a semblance of normality.

Inwardly, however, she was battling a most astonishing fury toward the idiotic fools. How dare they enter her inn and insult and attack Fredrick? Could they possibly believe that they were superior to a gentleman who had managed to build a vast business with nothing but his own wits? That they possessed any redeeming value just because of their name?

What had they ever accomplished beyond drinking and gambling and whoring?

Gads, Fredrick was worth a dozen of the worthless fribbles.

Managing to smile and chat with the lingering guests, Portia was wise enough to move toward the door as she caught sight of Fredrick marching down the hallway.

"Where are the bodies?" he demanded, his eyes dark with a shimmering emotion.

Threading her arm through his, Portia calmly turned him away from the public rooms and toward the kitchens. Although Fredrick was blessedly above the stupidity of most males, he was clearly still in a temper. It seemed best to conduct their conversation in privacy.

"I had them dropped in the nearest well," she teased, futilely hoping to lighten his dark mood. "I do not believe the magistrate will search for them there."

He frowned, clearly not amused. "What?"

Portia heaved a faint sigh. "I had their servants collect them and sent them on their way. It is hardly the first occasion I have had to deal with loutish guests or a boxing match over breakfast."

A muscle worked in his jaw as he struggled to hide his seething anger. "No, I do not suppose it is. Still I regret being the cause of such an ugly encounter in your establishment."

"It was not your fault, Fredrick." Coming to a halt, she turned to confront him. "Men such as that will always find some means of causing difficulties. As you said, they must have attention constantly drawn to themselves."

"Yes, but these buffoons were friends of my . . . brother," he gritted. "And I suspect that they deliberately chose to come to the Queen's Arms because they had learned I was staying here."

A hint of unease trickled down her spine. His expression held a grim hardness that was not at all like him.

"So what if they did?"

"Portia, perhaps it would be best if I went to stay at another inn."

"No." She clenched her hands at her side. "Fredrick, that is absurd."

"Actually, it makes very good sense." His lips twisted in a humorless smile. "If Simon's friends desire to create difficulties for me I will not have you and your establishment caught in the mess. They could do your business a great deal of harm."

Did Fredrick mean to leave her inn and never return?

No. It was unthinkable.

Never to see his elegant, beautiful countenance again? Never to have him interfering in matters that were none of his business? Never to feel those clever, wicked fingers skimming over her skin?

Portia swallowed her biting fear. She would brood on her strange, panicked reaction later. Much later.

For the moment she was intent on making sure that he did not disappear in some spat of glorious nobility.

Men could be such idiots.

"I am not without my own power and connections, Fredrick, and I do not need you to protect me from petty autocrats." She regarded him with an expression of offended pride. "I have been taking care of my inn for a number of years without interference from you or anyone else."

He frowned in concern. "Portia—"

"The gentleman who arrived, he is a friend of yours?" She interrupted as she turned and began to move down the hall.

Fredrick absently fell into step at her side. "Actually, he is more a brother than a friend."

There was no mistaking the warmth in his voice at the

mention of the unexpected gentleman. "Will he wish a room for the night or is he just passing through?"

"He will be staying in Winchester. Portia . . ."

"I must speak with Mrs. Cornell about dinner this evening," she muttered, intent on escape before he could say another word. Her companion, however, had an entirely different notion. Before she could take more than a step she discovered her elbow caught in a firm grip as Fredrick wrenched open the door to a narrow linen closet. She gave a startled gasp as he shoved her inside and followed swiftly behind her. "Fredrick . . . what the devil are you doing?"

His only answer was to slam shut the door and haul her roughly against his chest. Even in the thick darkness his mouth managed to find her own, claiming her lips in a stark, near brutal kiss.

For long moments, Portia simply allowed herself to enjoy the heat and magic of his touch. After being alone for so long, she would never take the pleasure of Fredrick's touch for granted. And much to her astonishment, she found being in the dark, cramped confines of the linen closet, while the servants passed just a few yards away, oddly erotic.

Then, as his fingers brushed tenderly over her flushed cheeks she forced herself to pull back.

She did not trust this strange mood of his. "Fredrick?"

"I hate this," he muttered as he rested his forehead against hers.

"Kissing me?"

"God, no." His hands lightly framed her face, his warm breath brushing over her skin. "I hate that we must hide in a linen closet just so I can kiss you."

"You knew that I could not risk a scandal . . ."

"I hate those idiots who ruined a perfectly wonderful morning," he continued in a low, fierce voice.

Her heart gave a painful jerk. "Yes."

"I hate that no matter what I achieve in my life I will always be a bastard who is scorned by society." His fingers tightened on her countenance. "And that just by being at the Queen's Arms you have been tainted as well."

She reached up to grasp his forearms, wishing that he could see her frown. "Balderdash," she snapped in annoyance.

"Balderdash?"

"Yes. I think that I would know if I had been *tainted.*"

He made a frustrated sound deep in his throat. "God, I just wish we were far away from here, poppet. Somewhere that we could forget everything but being together."

A poignant longing touched her own heart. Oh yes. To be alone with Fredrick—far from the inn and those who knew either one of them—it would be paradise.

It was also an impossible dream.

"I . . ."

"I am certain she came this way." The intrusive sound of Molly's voice floated through the door, followed by the thud of footsteps. "Maybe she went to the kitchens."

Portia heaved a sigh. Paradise seemed very far away.

"I must go."

Fredrick's fingers briefly tightened before they abruptly dropped away. "Of course you must."

Feeling oddly chilled as he stepped away, Portia instinctively reached out in the dark to clutch at his arm.

"Fredrick?"

"What?"

"Are you . . ." She was forced to halt and swallow the lump in her throat. "Are you leaving with your friend?"

"Ian is traveling with me today to Winchester."

"You will return tonight, will you not?"

There was a short pause before he heaved a deep sigh. "I will keep my rooms here, but I think it would be best if I remain in Winchester for the next few days."

"No, Fredrick . . ."

"Portia, I am doing this for you," he said, the certainty in his tone warning Portia that he had made his decision and nothing would alter his mind.

Her lingering annoyance deepened. Damnation. There were times when this gentleman could be just as thick-skulled, illogical, and downright idiotic as any other man.

Wishing she was large enough to give him a good shaking, Portia was forced to content herself with brushing past his stiff form and yanking open the door to the closet.

"Because I, of course, cannot possibly know what is best for me?" she accused as she stepped into the hall and headed directly for the kitchen.

"It is not that . . . damn you, Portia."

"Have a safe journey, Mr. Smith."

The scenery about Winchester was hardly the most famous, or the most dramatic in England. There was little more to boast of than quiet streams that ran through thick forests and heaths. As well as an occasional village spread across a pretty parkland.

The more whimsical might take to heart the stories of Arthur's Roundtable that was once believed to be hidden at Winchester's Great Hall and consider the area somewhat magical, but most were wise enough to accept (and some to even appreciate) that its days of glory were nicely in the past.

Despite its lack of spectacular mountains or cliffs or looming castles, however, it did have a placid beauty that was quite undeserving of the fierce scowl that Fredrick Smith was currently bestowing upon it.

Riding at his side, Ian at last flashed him an aggravated glance, weary of the brooding silence and deep sighs worthy of a Shakespearean tragedy.

"I must warn you, Fredrick, that you are not the most scintillating companion under the best of circumstances," he drawled. "When you are in this surly mood you are downright tedious."

With a small jerk, Fredrick pulled himself from his brown-study to meet his friend's sardonic smile.

"Forgive me, Ian. Would you prefer that I sing a jig or do a bit of juggling to keep you entertained?" he demanded, his nerves still raw. It had been one hell of a day thus far. And not likely to improve if he were to spend the next few nights in Winchester rather than in the arms of Mrs. Portia Walker.

"You could tell me of your Portia," Ian said, his gaze absently lingering upon a buxom dairy maid who leaned against a nearby fence.

Fredrick smiled wryly. His friend's gaze was always lingering upon one female or another. His gaze, however, like his attention, rarely lingered for long.

"Unfortunately she is not mine," he muttered, his own gaze staring aimlessly down the narrow road that led toward Winchester. It was a beautiful morning for a ride. The sun shining, the breeze still cool, but not unpleasant, and the crocuses just coming into bloom.

With a last smile that sent the dairy maid to her knees, Ian turned his head to stab his companion with a searching gaze.

"Do you want her to be?"

"I think . . ." Fredrick sucked in a deep breath, forcing himself to acknowledge the truth that had been fermenting in the back of his mind. "Yes, I think I do."

"Good God."

He gave a lift of his brows as Ian nearly tumbled from his saddle. "Why is that so shocking? Even you must admit that she is uncommonly beautiful."

"Without a doubt," Ian readily agreed. Too readily. "She is one of the most beautiful women that I have ever laid eyes upon."

Fredrick resisted the urge to warn his companion. For all his faults Ian would never poach on a friend's territory. It was an unspoken rule that the three of them had upheld no matter what the temptation.

Which was no doubt one of the prime reasons the three were still friends after all these years, he acknowledged with a faint flare of amusement.

"Then why your surprise, Ian?"

The dark-haired gentleman shrugged, his expression pensive. "When you spoke of your perfect woman I always supposed that she would be a meek and biddable sort of female who would provide you with a mob of brats and keep your house in order. I did not suspect you had a taste for exotic angels with a dictatorial nature."

Fredrick's smile widened. "It is even worse than you know, my friend."

"Indeed?"

"Oh yes, she not only demands to be in charge of everything and everyone about her, but she has a habit of collecting unsavory strays, from smugglers to prostitutes." He gave a resigned shake of his head. "Anyone foolish enough to take her on will be stuck with an endless parade of worthy causes."

Ian gave a sudden laugh. "Actually, she is probably just the female for you, now that I think upon it. She will fuss over your employees who, even you cannot deny, are odd, reclusive creatures. And hopefully make sure that you recall to eat your vegetables and to dress warmly when the wind is chill." He tilted his dark head to one side. "And there is no doubt that any children the two of you produce will be insufferably beautiful. Yes, it is obviously a good match. You have my blessing."

On the point of making a flippant retort, Fredrick abruptly halted his words, the memory of the ugly scene at the inn returning with a vengeance.

"Perhaps not that great a match," he admitted, his heart unpleasantly heavy. "At least not for her."

"Ah, I recognize that tone." Ian narrowed his gaze. "What is troubling you?"

"Portia has . . . suffered over the years."

"Who has not?"

"She has suffered more than any young woman should have," Fredrick insisted, knowing that there were still dark secrets Portia did not feel comfortable confessing. "I cannot help but wonder if she would not be better served if I were to walk away and leave her to enjoy her peaceful existence."

Ian's brows snapped together. "What the devil are you babbling about?"

Fredrick slowed his mount, carefully considering his

words. "Until this morning I never truly considered what my lack of pedigree would mean to my wife and family."

Ian made a rude sound. "Bloody hell, Fredrick, you cannot allow a herd of mincing jackasses to trouble you."

"Jackasses or not, they only said what others will always be thinking." He caught and held the golden gaze. "I *am* a bastard."

"A bastard who has acquired a fortune greater than half those grand aristocrats rattling around London. And a bastard with the ear of some of the most influential politicians in the country." Ian smiled with an expression of wicked satisfaction. "If you truly desired to wield your power I do not doubt you could force those three dandies to beg on their knees for your forgiveness."

Fredrick did not bother to argue. He could make them beg if he wished to go to the effort, he supposed. Over the years he had managed to acquire the sort of fortune and connections guaranteed to punish those foolish enough to treat him with less than respect.

Still, there was no amount of money or connections that could completely remove the stigma of his birth.

"And yet I shall never be able to move among respectable society," he muttered.

"Is that what Mrs. Walker desires? To be a member of the *ton*?"

"It is where she was born to be." The image of Portia swathed in silk dancing through an elegant ballroom flared through his mind. Good Lord, she would bring society to its knees. "It is where she *should* be."

"That does not answer my question."

Fredrick shrugged. "She claims that she has no interest in London society."

"And what of you?"

"Me?"

"Does she have an interest in you?"

A small smile touched his lips. "I believe there is a measure of interest."

"Then you have nothing to fret over."

Portia refused to pout as Fredrick collected his horse from the stables two hours later and rode off without so much as a good-bye.

She could not expect that he would always be reasonable. He was a man, after all. And his encounter with the hateful noblemen had obviously rattled his usual good sense. Perhaps it would be for the best that he had time in Winchester with his friend.

And if there was a deep, aching fear that he truly might not return to the Queen's Arms, Portia firmly refused to dwell upon it. Or at least she refused to dwell upon it after she had snuck into his rooms and assured herself that he had left behind the greatest share of his belongings.

She was just slipping from his rooms when she noticed Quinn working at the end of the hallway. Curious, she strolled down to stand at his side, a rueful smile touching her lips as she realized that he had replaced the pulley that was attached to the small lift the servants used to haul water and dinner trays from the kitchen below with a much more complicated design. One of Fredrick's designs.

"There we are," Quinn at last muttered, stepping

back to give Portia room to study his handiwork. "Give it a go and see if it works."

"Really, Quinn . . ."

"Give it a go, luv," he insisted.

Knowing she was only wasting her breath in chastising the older man for having once again made alterations without her permission, Portia reached out her hand and gave a tug on the thick rope that was attached to the wooden shelf. Her eyes widened in shock as the light touch sent the shelf flying upward without the slightest hitch.

"Good heavens."

"Easier to pull, is it not?" Quinn demanded smugly.

"Much easier." She gave a wondering shake of her head. She did not understand the various wheels and pulleys, but she did know that it was a vast improvement to the old system. "Molly will be delighted."

"Aye, she will. That Mr. Smith is rather a clever chap." Quinn flashed a knowing grin. "Just like a magpie, always fussing and fixing at his nest."

"Actually it happens to be my nest he continues to fuss and fix," she pointed out dryly.

"A sight better, eh?"

Well, of course it was a sight better, she wryly acknowledged. Mr. Fredrick Smith possessed an uncanny genius for seeing beyond the mundane to the magical.

A visionary, a voice whispered in the back of her mind. A dream-maker.

"Yes, I suppose it is."

"As are ye."

She turned to regard her old friend with a lift of her brows. "I beg your pardon?"

"I have never seen ye smile so much as ye have the

past few days." He gently patted her shoulder. "Perhaps Mr. Smith has a talent for fixing more than gadgets."

Her heart flopped in her chest as she gave an instinctive shake of her head. Fredrick had brought a brief, unexpected joy to her life that she would never forget. But she was not foolish enough to believe it was anything but a passing interlude.

She had endured too many disappointments to set herself up for another.

"Quinn . . ."

"Mrs. Walker."

The sound of Molly's voice floated from the bottom of the stairs and with a faint grimace at the disturbance, Portia moved to peer down at the young maid.

"Yes, Molly, what is it?"

"Ye have a gent wanting to speak with you."

"Very well. Take him to the back salon. I will be down in just a moment."

Absently smoothing her hands down her plain grey skirt, Portia was on the point of heading down the stairs when Quinn reached out to grasp her arm.

"Wait until I can clean meself up a bit. I will be going with you."

She regarded Quinn in puzzlement until she at last realized the cause for his odd behavior.

Obviously he feared the gentleman wanting to speak with her had some connection to the elegant buffoons who had created a disturbance earlier in the day.

She resisted the urge to sigh in frustration. "That is not necessary."

His expression settled into lines that revealed he intended to be utterly unreasonable.

"I did not say it was necessary, I merely said that I

was going with ye," he growled in warning. "If ye do not wish to wait then I will go in all me dirt."

"Why is everyone suddenly so certain that I am incapable of caring for my own inn?"

"Ye are perfectly capable, as ye well know, but if there is to be trouble I will not have ye facing it alone." A sly smile touched his lips. "Mr. Smith would have me head on a platter."

"This is absurd, Quinn—"

"I will be no more than the shake of a peacock tail," the older man interrupted as he stomped down the stairs.

"In the shake of a what?" Following in his trail, Portia gave a lift of her hands, wondering what the devil had happened to her unshakable authority. "Dammit. Mr. Fredrick Smith has a great deal to answer for."

Pacing the downstairs hall, Portia discovered that the shake of a peacock tail took approximately a quarter of an hour. That, at least, was the length of time it took for Quinn to return with his face washed and his hair combed. Offering him a sour glance, Portia thrust open the door to the back salon and stepped over the threshold.

Pausing to study the slender male form that was standing near the window, Portia instinctively pinned a smile to her lips. She possessed an experienced enough eye to recognize the expensive cut of the mulberry jacket and champagne gloss of his boots.

A gentleman of means. A great deal of means.

Stepping forward with a brisk professionalism, Portia was barely aware of Quinn halting at the door as her guest slowly turned to face her. Her breath tangled in her throat, her feet coming to an unconscious halt as she caught sight of the delicate features.

Good Lord. The man looked exactly like Fredrick.

Thankfully unaware of her shock, the gentleman moved toward the center of the room and regarded her with a quizzical expression.

"Mrs. Walker?"

"Yes." Portia struggled to gather her rattled composure. "Yes, I am Mrs. Walker. May I be of assistance?"

"I am Lord Graystone."

"Graystone. Fredrick's father . . ." she muttered before she could halt the words.

"Yes." A small, wistful smile touched his lips. "Your maid said that he had left for the day?"

"He went to Winchester, although I do expect him back."

"Ah."

"Is there a message that I can give to him?"

Lord Graystone turned away, but not before Portia managed to catch sight of the pain that flared in his pale eyes. A pain that wrenched at Portia's heart.

Good God, it was so deep, so terribly profound. As if it came from his very soul.

"I heard there was . . . trouble here this morning," he muttered, his slender body stiff with suppressed emotions.

Portia's smothered a rueful smile. She had learned never to be surprised by how swiftly gossip could travel through the neighborhood.

Of course, it was rather startling that Lord Graystone would have scurried to the inn after learning that Fredrick had been accosted. After all, the boorish aristocrats had deliberately sought out Fredrick because they were friends with Lord Graystone's legitimate son, Simon.

"There was a minor skirmish," she admitted cautiously. "Fredrick was not hurt, was he?"

There was no mistaking the edge of anxiety in his voice. "No," Portia reassured him. "I can safely assure you that he is in excellent health. Not so much as a blackened eye."

"Thank God," he breathed, the tension slowly easing from his stiff shoulders. "When I learned that Griffith and his friends had come in search of Fredrick I feared the worst."

"To be honest, my lord, your son and his friend managed to make mincemeat of the three gentlemen and I was forced to have them carried away by their servants."

The older gentleman gave a soft, almost bitter laugh. "I suppose I should have guessed that Fredrick could take care of himself. It is obvious that he has become quite skilled in overcoming any difficulty."

"No doubt because he has been forced to do so his entire life," Portia retorted, unaware she had said her thoughts out loud until the nobleman turned to regard her with that raw, haunting pain. Her annoyance faded beneath a surge of pity. Lord Graystone might possess one of the finest estates in the county, but he was a deeply unhappy man. "Forgive me," she said softly.

He gave a slow shake of his head. "No, you are quite right. Fredrick has not been given anything he did not have to earn himself. And the blame for that lies squarely upon my shoulders."

"He is a fine man, me lord," Quinn abruptly said from the doorway, causing Portia to turn and regard him with a startled glance. "One that any father can take pride in."

"Yes, yes he is. Perhaps a finer man without my interference," Lord Graystone said softly, that heart-rending smile tugging at his lips. "When he returns, will you tell him that I called for him, and that . . ."

"Yes?" Portia gently prompted.

"And that I would be pleased if he could join me for dinner on any night that is convenient for him."

"I will tell him."

"Thank you."

With a dip of his head, the nobleman walked stiffly out of the room, leaving behind the scent of expensive cologne and a lingering air of aching loneliness.

Chapter Fourteen

The narrow, brick structure with its white shutters, ruthlessly polished windows, and brass knocker possessed the depressing air of an aging matron who battled age and encroaching poverty with more pride than success.

Dismounting, Fredrick looped the reins of his horse around the hitch post and regarded the place with an unexpected flare of curiosity. If asked he would describe himself as a gentleman of the future. A man who not only believed in change, but actively sought to bring it about. But he could not deny an interest in Dunnington's past.

Had the tutor always been such a quiet, sober man or had he been a young rapscallion who had enjoyed the sort of high spirits he had encouraged in his students? Had he ever dreamed of finding a wife and having children or had he been content with his life of a bachelor? Had he been happy?

"This is the boarding house," he murmured as Ian dismounted to stand at his side.

"Dunnington lived here?" his friend demanded.

"For a time at least."

"Good God." Ian grimaced as he regarded the sagging roof and crumbling chimney. "I hope that it was in better condition when he was a resident."

"Most likely not. From what I could discover he was only a lowly assistant at the local college on a limited income," Fredrick retorted. "I doubt that he would have had much to pay for room and board."

Ian flashed him a bored glance. "And how does knowing where Dunnington lived assist in discovering the truth of your father?"

"Their paths must have crossed somewhere in Winchester." Fredrick gave a lift of his shoulder. "I hope that by following Dunnington's trail I will stumble across that of my father."

"Ah. A brilliant plan."

Fredrick smiled ruefully at his friend's obvious lack of confidence. "I am well aware that I am grasping at straws, Ian, but for the moment I am without the least notion of how to uncover my father's past."

Ian reached out to smack him on the back. "Then we shall grasp at straws together, Freddie boy."

Fredrick led the way through the gate and up the flagstone path, not missing the twitch of the white lace curtains as someone from within watched their approach. Giving the brass knocker a sharp rap, they waited in silence until the door was pulled open to reveal a large, middle-aged woman with thick features and fading brown hair pulled into a painful bun.

"Yes, may I be of assistance?"

Fredrick conjured a pleasant smile. "This is the Greaves Boarding House?"

The woman lowered her brows (unfortunately emphasizing her resemblance to a hound) as she openly surveyed Fredrick and then Ian, paying particular notice to the obvious expense of their attire.

"It is, but we only have one room open and it's in the attics. I doubt it would suit either one of you," she warned.

"Are you the proprietress, Mrs. Greaves?" Fredrick gamely pressed on.

"I am Miss Greaves. My mother still owns the house, but she is far too old to be taking care of the daily chores. What is it that you're wanting?"

"Forgive me, Miss Greaves, I am being unaccountably rude." Fredrick attempted another smile. "First allow me to introduce my companion, Mr. Breckford, and myself, Mr. Smith. We are both from London."

Realizing that Fredrick had yet to accomplish anything more than a deepening suspicion, Ian took matters into his own hands. Quite literally.

With a smile that had felled legions of women, Ian took the woman's thick hand and lifted the stubby fingers to his lips.

"A pleasure, my dear," he murmured. "A very great pleasure."

"Oh." Miss Greaves fluttered (a rather frightening sight) beneath the force of Ian's charm. "Thank you."

Fredrick resisted the urge to roll his eyes as he hurriedly took advantage of the woman's distraction.

"We are in Winchester searching for the family of an old friend of ours, a Mr. Dunnington, who we believe lived at this boarding house some twenty or thirty years ago."

Miss Greaves reluctantly returned her attention in his direction. "Dunnington?"

"He worked at the local college."

"Yes . . . it does seem as if we had someone of that

name here. My mother would remember better, of course."

Fredrick was careful to keep his expression composed. The woman could barely have been more than ten or so years old when Dunnington lived at the house. Hardly old enough to recall much of a temporary lodger.

"If it is not too much trouble, could we speak with her?"

"Actually, I am not at all certain that she should be bothered." The woman glanced over her shoulder, discreetly lowering her voice. "Her health, you know, is rather delicate and to be honest, her memory is not what it once was. It might only upset her to be pestered with your questions."

Fredrick attempted to appear properly sympathetic. "I assure you that I shall take great care not to upset her."

"Well, I do not know . . ."

Once again it was Ian who expertly diverted the woman from her natural caution.

"Perhaps, Miss Greaves, while my friend is visiting with your mother, you will take a turn with me in the garden?" Dazzling the poor woman with a practiced smile, Ian took her hand to lay it firmly upon his arm. "I will be staying some days in Winchester and I suspect that I shall need the advice of a woman such as yourself if I am to find rooms that are not flea-infested and the best pubs to discover a decent dinner."

Miss Greaves blinked, her expression one of dazed joy. A common enough expression when Ian was near a woman.

"You are staying in Winchester?"

"How could I resist when the scenery is so very charming?" Ian husked.

"Oh."

Fredrick delicately cleared his throat. "Your mother, Miss Greaves?"

"Yes . . . I . . ." Never allowing her gaze to stray from the man at her side, the spinster motioned toward a maid who hovered at the bottom of the stairs. "Janet, please show Mr. . . . ."

"Smith."

"Please show Mr. Smith to my mother's sitting room."

"Yes, mum." The young girl with a spotted face stepped forward, her blue eyes bulging with wonderment at the sight of her dull, petulant mistress fluttering like a common tart. "This way, sir."

Tossing Ian a grateful smile, Fredrick allowed himself to be led up the narrow stairs to a cramped drawing room that was stuffed with mismatched chairs, sofas, and tables that were nearly hidden beneath an appalling collection of china figurines.

"A Mr. Smith to see you, Ma'am," the maid croaked.

The woman with a puff of silver hair and a narrow countenance lined with age, glanced up to regard Fredrick with a startlingly perceptive gaze.

Unlike her unfortunate daughter, Mrs. Greaves had once claimed a measure of beauty. She was also far more eager to welcome Fredrick into her home.

"Bring us tea, Janet," she murmured, setting aside her needlework.

"Aye." With a bob the servant backed toward the door, knocking into a table and potted plant before at last scurrying away.

The elder woman heaved a resigned sigh. "Really, it is so difficult to find competent servants these days."

"I hope that I am not disturbing you?" Fredrick said gently.

"I suppose my daughter warned you that my health is delicate and I am not to have the least amount of enjoyment whatsoever?"

Fredrick gave a startled chuckle. "She did mention that you are not to be bothered."

"Such a dull, overbearing creature, poor thing. Always has been. It is no wonder she has never managed to marry. A gentleman prefers to hold the reins on occasion, am I right?"

"Perhaps upon occasion," Fredrick agreed, although he was not entirely averse to one particular overbearing woman.

"Well, you might as well have a seat." She motioned for Fredrick to take a seat on a chair near the window.

"Thank you."

Watching as Fredrick perched on the edge of the cushion, the elder woman gave a vague shake of her head.

"You look very familiar. Have we been introduced before?"

"I fear I have not had the pleasure, although I do hope you might know an old acquaintance of mine. A Homer Dunnington? I believe he rented rooms from you years ago."

A silence descended as the woman struggled to search through her various memories, her gnarled fingers tapping upon the arm of her chair. At last the pale eyes glittered with satisfaction.

"Ah . . . of course. He was a teacher."

Fredrick felt a surge of satisfaction. He was not entirely on the wrong path.

"Yes."

"He was one of my first borders," Mrs. Greaves murmured, her eyes misty as she dredged up the long ago days. "I had to begin taking in guests after my husband died. Quite a handsome young gentleman. And always so polite. I was very sorry when he decided to leave Winchester."

"So he did have rooms here?" he pressed.

"Oh yes. He stayed . . . oh . . . two years, perhaps a bit more." She gave a tinkling laugh, her hand rising to unconsciously pat her silver curls. "I will admit that I hoped he might have a bit of affection for a poor widow, but he was always so dedicated to his studies. I suppose he married in later years?"

Fredrick was careful to hide his amusement. Had Dunnington deliberately ignored the lures thrown out by a young widow, or had he truly been enwrapped in his studies?

Certainly when Fredrick had known the scholar he had preferred books to females.

"No, he remained a bachelor," he informed the curious woman.

A hopeful glint entered the blue eyes. "Did he now? Hmmm . . . still a bachelor."

Realizing the direction of her thoughts, Fredrick gave an awkward cough. Good Lord.

"Unfortunately he passed a few months ago."

"Ah. A pity." The blue eyes dimmed. "Of course, at my age one becomes accustomed to learning that friends and acquaintances have turned up their toes." Mrs. Greaves gave a small, philosophical shrug. "What is it you wanted?"

Bemused by the woman's tendency to flutter from one subject to another without warning, Fredrick gave a brief shake of his head.

"I have been searching for any family Mr. Dunnington might have possessed."

"Family, eh. Well, I can't say as I recall him mentioning any family. Certainly none of them lived in Winchester." Her gaze shifted toward the window. "Now that I think upon it, it could be that he said he had come from Surrey or maybe it was Essex . . . in any event, I do not believe he originally lived in this area."

"I see."

The blue eyes turned back to stab him with a curious gaze. "Is there a particular reason you are seeking his family?"

"I did not know who to contact after his death." Fredrick gave a lift of his hands. "And of course, he did leave behind a few personal effects that I wished to give to his loved ones."

"And you have traveled all this way? He must have meant a great deal to you."

"He did." Fredrick struggled to breathe as the familiar pain clenched his body. The loss of Dunnington would be an ache he would carry the rest of his life. "He was a teacher and a mentor to me, as well as several other young lads who had no one else."

"That does sound like the Mr. Dunnington I knew." A reminiscent smile touched her lips. "Always rattling on about the urchins who littered the streets. He claimed that it was only education that separated the lower orders from the aristocrats. Something of a radical."

"Yes, that he was."

"I recall that he was always arguing with the other gentleman who had taken rooms here. Now what was his name . . . ?" Her words broke off as her eyes widened. "Good heavens, that's it."

"What is it?"

She leaned forward, pointing a finger in his direction. "Now I know why you appear so familiar. You are the spitting image of that gentleman lodger."

Fredrick struggled to keep his expression composed, not wanting to terrify the poor old woman by leaping from his chair and shouting his relief.

"Do I? Who . . ."

"Here we are, Ma'am." The maid entered the room, knocking over a silver candelabrum and two statuettes on her way to the sofa.

"Good God, girl, set down the tray and leave the room before you manage to destroy what few belongings I have left," the older woman groused, waiting until the girl had managed to turn and flee before returning her attention to the impatient Fredrick. "Now, Mr. Smith, how do you take your tea?"

He bit his lip and managed a tight smile. "Two spoons of sugar, thank you."

"A sweet tooth, eh?"

"Yes, I fear so." He leaned forward to accept the delicate china cup. "You said that I remind you of a lodger?"

"Mmmm. It is rather uncanny, really," she muttered in distracted tones, filling a small plate with thin slices of seed cake. "Ham or cucumber sandwich?"

"Ham," Fredrick muttered, silently damning the entire tea tray to the netherworld. "Do you recall his name?"

"His name?"

"The name of your lodger." Fredrick gritted his teeth. She handed Fredrick the plate that he promptly set aside. Ham and seed cake was the last thing he desired at the moment.

"Oh yes . . . now what was it?" Settling back in the cushions, the older woman knit her brows in concentration. "My dratted memory. It is not at all what it once used to be. Mr. . . . Clayton . . . Coleman . . . Colstone. Yes, that was it. A Mr. Colstone."

"Fredrick Colstone?" he demanded.

"Yes, such a handsome young man," the woman twittered. "Just like you."

Fredrick smiled, inwardly dwelling upon his amazing stroke of fortune. To actually have stumbled across the place his father had resided while he was in Winchester . . . it was almost uncanny.

"Thank you."

"No need to blush, my boy." Mrs. Greaves wagged her finger in Fredrick's direction, mistaking his high color for that of embarrassment. "I may be old, but I am not blind. I know quality when I see it. And Mr. Colstone was most certainly quality. Related to some nobleman not far from here."

"Lord Graystone."

"Was that the family?"

"Yes."

"Ah." She nibbled on the edge of a sandwich. "He never spoke much about them. I always suspected there must have been some rift with his family."

"Yes, I believe there was." Fredrick attempted to sort through the hundreds of questions that clamored through his mind.

"Did he live here alone?"

"Mercy, no. He had his young wife with him."

Fredrick winced, feeling as if he had taken a physical blow at her unwitting words. She had to be speaking of his mother since his father had not wed his current wife until after he had inherited his title and returned to Oak Manor.

"His . . . wife?"

"Oh, yes." She gave a brisk nod. "Such a sweet, lovely young lady. She was with child when they came to stay here. She died giving birth, poor dear."

Fredrick could not halt his rather bitter smile. "And Mr. Colstone claimed that they were wed?"

Surprisingly, the woman regarded him with a chiding frown. "Now really, sir, there is no need to stir up such an old scandal. It is true enough that the two came to live here without the blessings of the church, but they soon enough shared their vows. All right and proper it was and in plenty of time to give the babe a respectable birth." She gave a choked gasp as Fredrick surged to his feet, knocking his chair backward. "Good heavens."

Fredrick tipped the chair upright, his movements heavy and uncoordinated. Hardly a surprise. He had just endured the greatest shock of his life.

"Forgive me," he muttered.

"Is anything the matter?"

"I . . ." Fredrick was forced to halt and clear the lump from his throat. "You are certain that the two of them were wed?"

The older woman stiffened, her expression faintly offended that he dared to doubt her word.

"I should be sure enough, I attended the ceremony, along with Mr. Dunnington," she said tartly. "They, after all, did need witnesses to make it all legal."

For the first time in his life Fredrick came perilously close to falling into a swoon. What else could explain the light-headed dizziness and sensation that he was tumbling into a deep tunnel?

Sheer pride allowed him to battle through the encroaching darkness, his hand reaching out to steady himself against the window frame.

"Where? Where was the ceremony?" he rasped.

"At the small church just around the corner, St. Mary's," the elder woman retorted absently, her gaze trained on Fredrick's pale countenance. "Really, Mr. Smith, I think you should sit down. You do not look at all well."

"I am fine." Knowing that he was incapable of conducting a reasonable conversation, Fredrick instead moved to take one of the older woman's hands and performed a stiff bow. Later he would no doubt return and question Mrs. Greaves more thoroughly, but for the moment he needed time to adjust to the shock he had just received. "I must thank you, Mrs. Greaves."

"Whatever for?"

"For agreeing to meet with me and being so patient to answer my questions." He reached beneath his jacket to withdraw a handful of coins that he pressed into her hand. "You have been of great assistance."

"I do not know what I have done, but I will happily accept your gratitude." The blue eyes abruptly twinkled as she hastily tucked the coins into her pocket. "Oh, if you do not mind, you might keep this between the two of us. My daughter is a fine woman, but she has a distressing lack of imagination. She would no doubt insist that this little windfall be used for something quite tedious."

"My lips are sealed," he promised as he headed for the door.

"Bless you, lad."

Leaving behind the woman who was happily plotting the secret treat she intended to purchase with her coins, Fredrick managed to make his way down the stairs to the front foyer without falling and breaking his neck. He even managed to fumble open the door and was headed down the walk when Ian abruptly darted from the side of the house and grasped his arm in a painful grip.

"Good Lord, it is about time," he hissed directly into his ear. "I thought you meant to leave me with that rabid spinster . . ." He broke off his words and conjured a smooth smile as Miss Greaves grimly charged in his wake. "My dear, I cannot tell you how much I have enjoyed our brief stroll. Now, I fear, we must be on our way."

"You will remember that the Boar's Head is not at all suitable for a gentleman," the woman puffed, out of breath as she attempted to prevent Ian from slipping away without a proper farewell.

Covertly, Ian inched Fredrick closer to the gate. "Yes, indeed, and I will be sure to have my luncheon at the Royal Oak."

"And, of course, I do have a tidy tea tray prepared every afternoon at precisely five o'clock." The broad face was faintly flushed and the pale eyes glowing with an unmistakable enchantment. "You and Mr. Smith are always welcome."

"Ah . . . yes," Ian muttered. "We will most certainly keep that in mind. Good day."

Fredrick would have found the entire encounter stunningly amusing at any other time.

The hardened spinster, batting her lashes like a

dewy-eyed chit. Ian, the Casanova, awkwardly retreating from the frontal attack like a skittish greenhorn.

Fredrick, however, felt inexplicably numb as he allowed Ian to hustle him through the gate to gather their horses. Even when he was mounted and headed down the cobblestone street, he could manage no more than a vague sense of unreality.

Swaying in his saddle, Fredrick managed to make it out of the neighborhood when Ian abruptly reached out to grasp the reins he held loosely in his fingers, pulling them both to a halt.

"Holy hell, Fredrick, you look as if you have seen a ghost. What the devil did that old lady say to you?" The golden gaze searched Fredrick's countenance that was bathed in a thin coating of perspiration. "What you need is a drink, Freddie boy."

Fredrick managed a short nod. Perhaps a few pints would help to clear the fog in his brain.

"Here, boy, see to our horses." Tossing the reins to a nearby lad, Ian helped Fredrick dismount.

The urchin caught the reins with a practiced ease. "Aye, sir."

"Do not get any foolish notions unless you wish to be strung from the nearest tree. Understood?" Ian growled as he pulled Fredrick firmly toward the nearby pub.

The lad swallowed heavily. "Aye."

"This way," Ian commanded his silent friend, managing to maneuver Fredrick down the worn steps that led to the dark, open-beamed room with a handful of tables scattered across the planked floor. "You, there," Ian called toward the man standing behind the heavy bar at the back. "Two pints of your finest."

Fredrick discovered himself settled at a small table

in a shadowed corner as the barkeep hurried to place two mugs of ale in front of them.

"Here you are, sir," the round-faced man said, expertly pocketing the shilling that Ian tossed in his direction before bowing back toward the bar.

A silence descended as Ian studied Fredrick with a discomfited expression. "You are not intending to cast up your accounts, are you?"

Fredrick smiled wryly, knowing just how difficult it was for Ian to remain at his side. He was the sort who preferred to solve troubles with his fists, not dole out comfort over mugs of ale.

"Not at the moment, no."

"Good. I do not play nursemaid, not even for my brother," he muttered.

"You never fail to touch my heart, Ian."

Watching as Fredrick drained his mug, Ian at last leaned forward with a frown.

"Can you tell me what you have discovered, or would you prefer to keep it to yourself?"

Fredrick battled back the hysterical urge to laugh.

Good Lord. He had been so stunned by the mere possibility that his parents had been wed that he had not considered what the truth might mean to others.

Rather ridiculous since there was a great deal more at stake than the fact that he was not a mere bastard.

Did he reveal the extraordinary truth and change the future of the entire Graystone clan, or allow the lie to continue?

"Fredrick?" Ian prompted, his expression hard with concern. "What the devil is the matter?"

Scrubbing his hands over his face, Fredrick made a determined effort to gather his shattered wits.

"Mrs. Greaves confirmed that Dunnington was a tenant at her boarding house," he at last admitted.

Ian took a sip of his ale as he made an effort to disguise his puzzlement. "That is what you suspected, was it not?"

"Yes."

"And?"

"And my father was a tenant as well."

"I'll be damned." Ian sat down his mug with a short laugh. "It was a brilliant plan after all."

"So it would seem."

"Whatever your father's secret, it must have occurred while he lived in the boarding house. That would explain how Dunnington came to know of it."

"Oh, yes," Fredrick muttered. "It did indeed occur while he was at the boarding house."

The golden eyes narrowed. "Did you discover what the secret is?"

"I . . ." Fredrick sucked in a steadying breath. "I at least discovered a secret he has been harboring for the past twenty-eight years."

"Bloody hell." Ian reached out to slap him on the shoulder. "You have done it."

"Yes."

Sensing Fredrick's seething turmoil, Ian slowly leaned back in his seat and folded his arms over his chest.

"You know what, Freddie boy, it does not matter what the damnable secret might be," he said firmly. "We might have been burdened with worthless wastrels for fathers, but we have managed to do quite well." He paused, a determined smile curving his lips. "No, you have done better than well, Fredrick. As difficult as it might be for me to admit, those ridiculous gadgets of yours have managed to make you one of the most influential men in all of England. Whatever your jackass of a father did twenty-some-odd years ago cannot change all you have accomplished."

Fredrick smiled at his friend's obvious attempt to distract him from his troubles. "Actually, Ian, it might very well change everything."

"Not unless you allow it to."

"True . . ." Fredrick shuddered at the thought of the turmoil and tumultuous pain the truth would cause. "I suppose it is now my decision whether to go forward or let well enough alone."

"Come, let us forget our troubles in a barrel of ale," Ian commanded gruffly, his golden eyes dark with worry. "Troubles are always best left for tomorrow."

"Ian Breckford's philosophy of life?" Fredrick demanded wryly.

Ian shrugged. "'Tis not a bad one, even you must admit."

"No, not a bad one." Fredrick gave a sharp, bitter laugh as he abruptly rose to his feet. "Oh God, Ian, what am I to do?"

"Damn, Fredrick . . . tell me what it is." Ian was swiftly standing at his side, his hands clenched in frustration as he helplessly studied his friend's tortured expression. "Tell me what it is so that I can hunt down your father and beat the bloody hell out of him."

"They were wed."

The words tumbled from Fredrick's lips before he had ever realized he intended to confess the truth to his friend. Not surprisingly, Ian's brow wrinkled in confusion.

"What?"

"My mother and father, they were wed before I was

born," Fredrick rasped, shoving his hands roughly through his hair. "I am not a bastard."

Ian appeared nearly as stunned as Fredrick felt, his golden eyes wide with shock and his mouth opening and closing a half a dozen times before he could speak.

"Holy hell, Fredrick. If you are not a bastard, then . . ."

"Then I am the legal, legitimate heir of the Graystone family."

"Holy hell."

Chapter Fifteen

Casting a glance about the taproom that was slowly beginning to fill with the local tradesmen, Ian gave a slow, disbelieving shake of his head.

"Are you certain?"

"Mrs. Greaves claims that she attended the wedding at St. Mary's," Fredrick muttered. "It should be a simple matter to search the church records and discover the truth."

"Then why the hell are we at this shoddy pub instead of at the church?"

For a moment Fredrick struggled to sort through his tangled emotions. He could not deny a reluctance to charge off to the church and find the proof of his legitimacy.

It was not so much fear, he slowly accepted. Or at least not precisely fear.

No, it was more a sickening sensation at the thought of discovering the truth of his birth written upon some crumbling piece of parchment.

Surely any man deserved better than that?

Fredrick forced himself to meet the searching

golden gaze. "Because as ridiculous as it might seem, I want the truth from my father's lips."

Ian made a sound of disgust deep in his throat. He had always been a man who held a simple, if rather cynical approach to life.

Always believe the worst in others and one is never disappointed.

"You believe the old man will tell the truth after all these years?"

"Since I do not know why he felt compelled to hide the marriage in the first place, I do not know what he will do." His heart gave a painful squeeze even as his thoughts shied from the staggering implications. "Of course, it is rather difficult to deny a wedding that was attended by Mrs. Greaves and Dunnington."

"Dunnington was at the wedding?" Ian sucked in a sharp breath, his brows jerking together. "No, I do not believe it."

"That is what the old lady claims."

"Then she must be batty. I mean . . ." Ian gave an angry shake of his head. "Surely to God Dunnington would not have allowed you to be tossed aside as a bastard if he knew for a fact that you were the legitimate heir to the Graystone estate?"

Fredrick gave a sharp jerk at the blunt question. Gads, he had not yet given thought to Dunnington's culpability in keeping such a secret. It seemed bad enough that his father had spent eight and twenty years lying to him.

Dunnington's seeming betrayal would have to be pondered and mourned later.

"Perhaps my father managed to convince him to keep his silence," he muttered. "Dunnington did, after all, manage to extort a fortune from the old miser."

"You think Dunnington sold your legitimacy for twenty thousand pounds?"

"It is a possibility."

Ian muttered a foul curse. "If it is true then it's a bloody sin. It is one thing to keep a secret, it is quite another to steal a man's name." Reaching out, Ian grasped Fredrick's arm and gave him an impatient shake. "By God, Fredrick, you have been cheated of your very destiny."

Fredrick swallowed a choked laugh as Ian's furious words rang through the room with enough force to turn the heads of the half a dozen patrons. His own anger was still rigidly contained behind a thick layer of shock.

Given time he would no doubt be ranting and raving like a lunatic. For now, however, he was uncannily calm.

"Come, we are attracting attention," he said, taking Ian's arm and firmly steering him out of the pub. Once on the street he loosened his grip and halted in the shadows of the building.

Ian studied his tight expression with undisguised concern. "What are you going to do?"

"The first thing I must do is speak with my father."

"Do you desire me to accompany you?"

Fredrick debated for a silent moment. A part of him wanted Ian to travel to Oak Manor with him. Despite the man's sharp tongue and sardonic wit, he possessed an unwavering loyalty and would readily commit murder if he thought it would make Fredrick happy.

"No," he reluctantly muttered. "I believe it would be best if I confront him alone."

"Are you certain?" The dark, elegant features hardened. "It might take some . . . effort to make him amenable to confessing the truth. I happen to have a talent in making unwilling gentlemen amenable."

Fredrick gave a short laugh. There were few in London who did not know the dangers of stirring Ian Breckford's ready temper.

"So I have heard."

"If nothing else I can help you bury the corpse."

"A most generous offer."

"What are friends for?"

Fredrick stilled as he regarded the man who had been such an essential part of his life for so many years. The bond between them went far beyond the ties of blood. Whatever happened, whatever he learned from his father, he would never be alone. Ian and Raoul would always be at his side.

It was a knowledge that offered a deep, unshakable comfort that nothing could touch.

Not even his father's treachery.

Reaching out, Fredrick placed his hand on his friend's shoulder. "Ian, I do not know what stroke of fortune brought you to my side just when I needed you, but I am grateful."

Ian shifted, his expression revealing his discomfort. "Good Lord, you need not become maudlin, Freddie boy. I am here because it suits me to be here, and the moment I decide otherwise I shall disappear without a care as to whether or not you have need of me."

"Oh, yes," Fredrick drawled in tones of patent disbelief. "Of course you will."

Ian gave him a small shove toward his waiting horse. "Hell and damnation, would you be on your way already? I intend to devote the rest of the evening to becoming corned, pickled, and salted. And after that . . ."

A wicked smile curved his lips. "After that I intend to find a beautiful, willing woman to ease my loneliness."

Fredrick reluctantly accepted the reins to his horse from the waiting urchin. He could not deny a hint of envy.

A few drinks and the night spent in the arms of a beautiful woman (so long as that woman happened to be Portia Walker) sounded far preferable to the upcoming confrontation with his father.

Unfortunately he knew that until he had settled matters with Lord Graystone he would be unable to concentrate upon anything else.

With a smooth motion he was in the saddle, and with a brief wave in Ian's direction, he was headed down the street.

Before this night was through he intended to have the truth.

After that . . .

He gave a shake of his head.

He would worry about "after thats," well . . . after that.

Fredrick pulled his mount to a halt as he turned onto the lane that led to the manor house.

Before this moment the towering oaks and sprawling parkland had meant nothing to him. At least nothing more than the fact that he had arrived at his father's estate for another tedious, painful visit.

There was no sense of homecoming, no innate pride of ownership, no pondering of how he would alter this or that once his father came to his timely end.

Now he forced himself to truly study the estate. The sculpted gardens with their fountains and Greek statuary. The untamed woodlands. The refurbished conservatory. The rich farmlands that offered an endless source of income for a proper and diligent owner.

It was truly beautiful.

A graceful, elegant testament to the rich tradition and power of the Graystone family.

A tradition that could very well belong to him once he forced his father to confess the truth.

Fredrick abruptly urged his horse forward as an unpleasant shiver raced down his spine. He had never been a mercenary gentleman. The wealth he had accumulated over the years had been nothing more than an unintended result of the success of his business.

Certainly he had never eyed a statue or tidy outbuilding and considered the worth when the lord of the manor was dead.

Gads, it was little wonder that Simon had become such a pathetic twit if that had been the manner he had passed his days rather than pursuing a decent career. Could there be anything more disgustingly morbid than waiting for your own father to die?

At last reaching the house, Fredrick readily handed his horse over to the waiting groom and climbed the stairs. He had barely managed to make the top step when the door was yanked open, and Morgan was regarding him with an expression that lacked its usual impassiveness. Indeed, there was very nearly relief etched on the long, stoic countenance.

"Oh, sir, it is good to see you," he murmured, showing Fredrick into the foyer and shutting the door behind them. "The master feared you might not return from Winchester in time to share dinner with him."

Fredrick set aside his hat and gloves, his brows lifting at Morgan's low words.

"Lord Graystone knew I was in Winchester?"

Morgan gave a discreet cough as he led Fredrick down the Staircase Gallery. "I believe the master visited the Queen's Arms and was informed you had gone to Winchester." His steps slowed as he realized that Fredrick had halted before the large portrait of Simon. "Will Mr. Breckford be joining us?"

"No, he is remaining in Winchester."

"Very good. If you will come this way, the master is in the library." The elder servant cleared his throat as Fredrick continued to stare at Simon's round pudding face. "Sir?"

"Do you know, I have never so much as exchanged greetings with my own brother," Fredrick muttered, his fingers lifting to touch the solid wood frame. "Indeed, if it were not for these portraits I should be able to pass him on the street and never even recognize him. It is odd, is it not?"

"I believe that Lady Graystone was quite insistent that the two of you not cross paths," Morgan was forced to reveal in strained tones.

Fredrick gave a sharp laugh. "No doubt she feared that I might contaminate her precious offspring with my tainted blood?"

"More likely she is a jealous cat who has always harbored a nasty belief that your father preferred you to that tallow-faced son of hers," a female voice retorted from the end of the hall.

Morgan gave a strangled sound as the cook's large bulk bore down upon them. "Mrs. Shaw, it is not your place to—"

"'Tis true enough, and you know it, Morgan," the

woman interrupted with a hint of impatience. "How many dinners has the master endured listening to that woman lecture him upon his 'unnatural disinterest in her beloved Simon' ? As if any gentleman wouldn't prefer to read of his son's business success in the newspapers rather than what foolish prank the boy has been committing, or what color his coat might have been when he attended the Petersons' Ball."

"What is said between the lord and lady are none of our concern, Mrs. Shaw." Morgan managed to glare down the length of his pointed nose despite the fact the woman had a good inch on him. "We are here to serve, not to judge."

Mrs. Shaw offered a disdainful sniff. "I serve as well as any other, but that does not mean I do not have eyes and ears." She turned to offer Fredrick a knowing smile. "And I know true quality from the rabble."

Sensing the onslaught of a full blown squabble, Fredrick stepped away from the portrait and lightly patted his staunch defender upon the shoulder.

"Thank you, Mrs. Shaw, but I will not have you risking your position in such a manner." He managed a strained smile. "It would be a sin against nature for Oak Manor to lose your magical touch in the kitchen."

A misty smile touched her lips as she preened beneath his fulsome flattery.

"There, that is what I mean. . . . Quality. It always shows."

"Magical touch," Morgan muttered beneath his breath, turning on his heel to march toward the nearby stairs. "The master is waiting, sir."

Following the bristling butler up the staircase, Fredrick briefly considered the cook's unwitting words.

Quality.

What the devil did it mean?

Did the fact that his mother was the daughter of a doctor rather than a common farmer make him quality? Did the fact that his parents had exchanged a handful of vows before a vicar purify his tainted blood? Did the . . .

Damnation. He was precisely the same man as he had been before arriving in Wessex, and yet . . . everything was different. One piece of paper and the entire world would soon see him as much, much more than Fredrick Smith.

It was as confusing as it was unnerving.

At last reaching the library, Fredrick waited for Morgan to announce him and silently disappear down the hall before he stepped into the long, shadowed room.

Abruptly turning from the window where he had been standing, Lord Graystone regarded his son with a restrained pleasure.

"Fredrick, you are here. I feared . . ." He halted and cleared his throat. "I was not certain that you would be able to join me."

"It was something of a last-minute decision."

"Ah." The blue eyes warily regarded Fredrick's pale countenance, perhaps sensing the tension that held him in a fierce grip. "Come near the fire. Will you have a sherry?"

Fredrick instinctively moved toward the cheery flames despite the knowledge that the chill gripping him would not eased by the heat from a fire.

"Actually, I think the evening calls for a brandy," he said, leaning against the mantle as his father carefully poured the amber spirit and carried the glass back across the room to press it into his fingers.

"My grandfather laid this down the year my father was born. I think you will enjoy it."

"Thank you." Fredrick drained the fiery brandy and set aside the glass. At the moment he had no desire to savor the well-aged spirit. "Morgan mentioned that you visited the Queen's Arms."

"Yes." The pale blue gaze flickered toward the fire. "I was concerned."

"Concerned?" Fredrick gave a short laugh. This man had devoted a lifetime to proving his absolute lack of concern for his eldest son. "Why?"

The faintest hint of color stole along the chiseled line of his cheekbones. "The country is not much different from London when it comes to gossip. The rumors of your scuffle with Griffith reached me before I sat down to luncheon."

"And you rushed to the inn to make sure I was unharmed?"

Lord Graystone's brows drew together at the edge of mockery in his son's voice. "Mrs. Walker assured me that you held your own."

"It was hardly a difficult task. I have encountered chimney sweeps who could offer a greater threat."

"And no doubt could offer a great deal more sense," the older man muttered. "Griffith and his friends are decidedly stupid young men who have been ruined by too much wealth and too few responsibilities."

Although there was no mention of Simon, his name hung in the air with a silent rebuke.

"They are like most dandies that litter London."

"Which is one of the many reasons I prefer the quiet of this estate. I cannot abide frivolous fools who have nothing better to do than bother decent citizens who actually contribute to society."

"Decent citizens?" Fredrick gave a lift of his brows as he deliberately caught and held his father's gaze. "Well, there are not many who consider me decent. I am, after all, a bastard, am I not?"

If Fredrick had not been watching his father so closely he would easily have missed his small jerk.

"You are a gentleman who has claimed a position of respect."

"Perhaps among some, but society will always hold me in contempt for my shameful birth."

Lord Graystone's expression settled in the cool, wary lines that were so familiar to Fredrick.

"I realize it must be difficult for you, Fredrick," he said, his tone warning that he was not pleased with the direction of the conversation.

For eight and twenty years Fredrick had instinctively obeyed that unspoken command. Even as a child he had understood that his father would tolerate his presence only so long as he did not step beyond the boundaries. Today, however, he did not hesitate to challenge the man who had deliberately stolen his birthright.

"No, Father, I do not believe that you could possibly realize just what it means to be a bastard," he grated.

The older nobleman stiffened, no doubt considering his usual habit of simply abandoning his son when he decided the conversation did not suit him.

"Perhaps not entirely, but I was a younger son without prospects until my brother's unexpected death," he retorted, his voice edged with ice. "I always expected to make my own way in the world."

Fredrick gave a sharp, disbelieving laugh. "God

almighty, you desire to compare being a younger son to that of bastard?" Pushing away from the mantle he paced restlessly across the room. "Tell me, Father, just how many society matrons have given you the cut direct when you meet on the street? And how many noblemen seek you out to invest in your business at the same moment they are discreetly warning their daughters to have nothing to do with you? On how many occasions have you walked past gentlemen clubs with the certain knowledge that the members would more readily welcome a leper than you within their hallowed grounds?" Coming to a halt he glared into the pale, grimly impassive features. "No, Father, you have no notion of what I have endured."

Astonishingly, a hint of genuine anger flashed in the pale blue eyes. Lord Graystone was always so careful to keep his emotions hidden it was nearly as shocking as if he had sprouted wings and flown about the room.

"Your lot was not as bad as it could have been, Fredrick. You at least were given an education and the opportunity to succeed."

Just a few hours before, Fredrick might have agreed. There were any number of bastards who never managed to crawl out of the gutters they were tossed in. He, at least, had been given into the care of Dunnington, who had given him the skills he needed to survive.

And, more importantly, the affection that a young, unwanted boy was starved for.

Now, however, he was painfully aware of all that had been stolen from him.

"Hardly the same as being offered a grand estate and respectable place in society, is it?" he gritted.

The older man's expression hardened with a soul-deep bitterness. "And you believe that being Baron is such a wondrous destiny?" His short laugh rasped through the room. "Believe me, there has not been a day that has passed when I have not paid dearly for my position as Lord Graystone. It . . . it is a yoke that has cost me everything."

Fredrick refused to be swayed by his father's obvious pain. Whatever the old man believed he had suffered, it could be nothing to what Fredrick had been forced to endure his entire life.

"And what has it cost you, Father?" he demanded with a deliberate lack of sympathy. "The discomfort of living with a constant lie? The fear that Dunnington might one day expose the truth and destroy your precious family?"

Lord Graystone froze, his annoyance fading as an unmistakable wariness flickered over his countenance at Fredrick's unexpected words.

"What did you say?"

Turning his back on his father's uneasy regard, Fredrick paced toward the window. "Do you wish to know the true reason I came to Wessex?"

"I . . . I think perhaps dinner should . . ."

Fredrick abruptly turned. "I came here to solve a mystery."

"Did you?" Still clutching his glass, Lord Graystone made his way toward the door. "I believe that dinner is waiting. Mrs. Shaw will be disappointed if we are late."

With a speed that caught his father off-guard, Fredrick moved to stand directly in his path, forcing the older man to halt or run him over.

"You see, when Dunnington died he left behind a

peculiar legacy," he ruthlessly continued. "A legacy of twenty thousand pounds."

He had to give his father credit, Fredrick grimly acknowledged. There was barely more than a whisper of fear before he was coolly smoothing the superfine fabric of his pearl grey jacket.

"Congratulations, my son. It is a most generous gift."

"Yes, it was," Fredrick drawled. "A gift that Dunnington claimed was given to him by you."

"I, of course, paid for your schooling . . ."

"No, Father, this was not my tuition. This was extortion money. A bribe to keep your dark secret just that." He leaned deliberately forward. "A secret."

"That is absurd."

"Is it?"

"Of course." He gave a dismissive lift of his hands. "I have no secrets, dark or otherwise."

Fredrick curled his lips in a cold smile. "If that is true then perhaps you will join me tomorrow at St. Mary's in Winchester as I search the records for proof of your marriage to my mother? A marriage that Mrs. Greaves is prepared to swear took place before my birth."

Chapter Sixteen

A shocked silence blanketed the room, at last broken by the shattering crystal as Lord Graystone's glass slid from his fingers and landed on the floor.

"You . . . You spoke with Mrs. Greaves?" the older man rasped, his countenance ashen.

"Yes, a most charming widow who runs a boarding house," Fredrick drawled. "She remembered a young teacher by the name of Dunnington, as well as you and my mother. Indeed, she remembered you in particular with remarkable clarity. She commented several times on how much we resemble one another."

The cool, aloof composure was torn aside to reveal an aging, uncertain gentleman who was clearly disturbed to have his sins uncovered.

"Did Dunnington tell you of Mrs. Greaves?"

"Dunnington kept his promise of silence, Father," Fredrick retorted, a pain clutching at his heart. "It was not until he died and left me his legacy that I became curious as to what dark secret could possibly be worth twenty thousand pounds. Now I know."

The older man futilely struggled to find some

means of denying the truth when he was interrupted by the entrance of the butler.

"My lord, dinner is . . ."

"Not now, Morgan," Lord Graystone snapped, his wary gaze never leaving Fredrick's stark expression.

The servant stiffened, something that might have been disappointment flaring over the lined countenance before he was bowing his way out of the room.

"Very good, sir."

Waiting until the door closed, Lord Graystone drew in a deep breath and squared his shoulders.

"And what is it that you believe you know, Fredrick?"

"I know that my mother was no common tart who made a habit of littering the streets with bastards." Fredrick folded his arms over his chest. "She was a lady, was she not?"

The older man hissed in surprise before he turned to offer Fredrick his tense profile. "Of course she was a lady."

"Why do you seem shocked that I wouldn't have assumed my mother was Covent Garden ware? You certainly never gave the impression she held the least amount of respect, let alone affection, in your heart. You cannot imagine my amazement when I discovered that she was my grandmother's companion who resided in this very house."

"Adeline," Lord Graystone muttered.

"What?"

"That was her name," he clarified, slowly turning to meet Fredrick's hard gaze. "Adeline. She was so beautiful. You have her eyes. And her smile."

Adeline. Fredrick tucked the name away, anxious to know everything possible about the woman who had given birth to him.

"She was the daughter of a doctor?"

"Yes." The older man heaved a sigh that spoke of his inner defeat. He clearly realized that Fredrick would no longer settle for anything but the truth. A pity it was eight and twenty years too late. "She kept house for him and occasionally assisted in his surgery until he was killed in a carriage accident. After his death she was forced to seek a means to support herself."

"How old was she?"

The pale blue eyes narrowed, as if he sensed Fredrick's disdain for those gentlemen who took advantage of defenseless women.

"She had just turned twenty. A mere fortnight younger than myself."

Well, at least she had not been a mere child, Fredrick acknowledged. Although she clearly had no experience with noblemen.

"And naïve enough to be seduced by the first rake to cross her path, eh?"

"I was no rake, Fredrick," his father denied, his hand lifting to rub over his face in a weary motion. "Far from it, in fact. Adeline was the first woman, the only woman, I have ever loved. I knew from the moment I caught sight of her that I would marry her."

Fredrick refused to be swayed by the thick sincerity in his father's voice. "And when you caught sight of her did you also make the decision you would deny her as your wife and brand your son as a bastard?"

"I never denied . . ." Lord Graystone broke off his words with a sharp shake of his head. "Dammit, Fredrick, this is not nearly so simple as you would wish to believe."

"No, I do not believe for a moment that it was in any way simple," Fredrick agreed dryly. "I should think keeping a legitimate marriage a secret for eight and twenty years a very difficult task. How did you accomplish such a feat?"

With an abrupt motion, the older man paced across the room, halting at the window that overlooked the dark garden.

"I never intended to keep it a secret. It was Adeline who desired secrecy."

Fredrick gave a disbelieving laugh. "Ah . . . of course she did."

"It is true enough." Lord Graystone gave a restless lift of his shoulder, his expression revealing he was lost in the past. "She possessed a remarkably soft heart and even after my mother tossed her from this estate and insisted that I be cut off without a quid, she feared the announcement of our wedding would put the old tartar in the grave."

"Why would my grandmother be so opposed to the marriage? My mother might not have been of the highest social standing, but she was obviously respectable enough."

"I thought at the time she was simply being her usual arrogant self. After all, she had managed to convince herself that being the wife of a baron was quite equal to possessing royal blood. She ruled over this neighborhood like a queen for over forty years, long after my father was cold in his grave," he said slowly. "It was not until later that I realized she was desperate for her sons to wed for wealth. She understood just how close to ruin we were treading."

Fredrick frowned. In truth it was rather easy to believe his mother might wish to avoid dealing with Lady Graystone. The old dragon would have terrified a young girl who was unaccustomed to dealing with temperamental aristocrats.

"So you never told any of your family of the wedding?"

"No, I revealed the truth only to my old groom who had been forced to remain at Oak Manor when I traveled to Winchester. I was closer to him than either my mother or brother."

Fredrick sucked in a sharp breath, recalling Mrs. Shaw's confession that the entire staff at Oak Manor had been hired from Winchester when his father came into the title.

"Ah, so that was why you pensioned off the old staff," he accused in chiding tones. "You feared that your groom had shared the news with the other servants and one of them might whisper the truth in the ear of your new bride."

Lord Graystone shifted beneath the accusation, his gaze never wavering from the window. "It was Wilhelmina's desire to pension off the staff. She thought it would be less . . . awkward for all if she were to choose her own servants rather than training those who were loyal to the previous mistress."

Fredrick didn't doubt his words. The current Lady Graystone was the sort of woman who would always be conscious of her lack of noble birth and be swift to take offense to any hint she was being treated with anything less than utter deference. Still, Fredrick did not accept for a moment that his father would have allowed the loyal staff to be dismissed without his own selfish reason.

"And you did nothing to halt her?" he demanded.

A hint of color touched the pallor of his skin. "No,

I did nothing to halt her. As you say, I did not wish ancient gossip to create difficulties."

"Why?" Fredrick moved toward the older man, determined to have the answers that had been denied him for far too long. "You cannot convince me that this elaborate deception has been to spare Grandmother's pride."

"No, it . . ." Lord Graystone slowly turned and regarded Fredrick with grim determination. "Sit down, Fredrick, and I will attempt to explain what occurred."

With a shrug Fredrick grabbed a bottle of brandy from the nearby side-table. "I think I shall have need of this," he muttered before he lowered himself into a leather wing chair and met his father's gaze with a taunting smile. "Very well, Father, explain to me why you stole my birthright."

The older man recoiled, his hands clenching and unclenching at his side as he struggled to find the words to adequately justify his cruel betrayal.

"As you have already discovered, Adeline came to Oak Manor as a companion. My mother was bedridden and her health was considered precarious. Adeline's experience with various medicines was invaluable." The blue eyes became misty as Lord Graystone recalled happier days. "She was here only a few weeks when I knew beyond a doubt that we were meant to be together."

Fredrick's fingers tightened on the brandy bottle. He knew something of having a special, utterly perfect woman tumble into his life without warning.

"And did she feel the same?"

"She loved me, although she was more sensitive to the differences in our social positions than I. She understood the difficulties we would be forced to confront from the very beginning."

"With good reason," Fredrick was swift to point out. "She was the one who suffered from your relationship."

His father frowned with a flare of annoyance. "That is not entirely fair, Fredrick. It is true that my mother dismissed Adeline when she discovered our relationship, but I stood by her side. When she was forced to leave the estate I went with her, even though it cost me my home, my family, and what little allowance I possessed." His chin tilted as if daring Fredrick to challenge his devotion to his beloved Adeline. "I would have done anything to be at her side."

There was an unmistakable earnestness in his father's countenance, but Fredrick was not overly impressed. If Lord Graystone had truly loved his wife he would have honored her memory, not allowed others to believe she had given birth to an illegitimate brat.

"That is when you went to the boarding house in Winchester?" he demanded.

"Yes, I had some notion that I could find a teaching position at the college." The older man gave a wave of his slender hands. "It was not as if I was trained to pursue a career, and I had to have some means of supporting my family. While I was pleading for a position with the headmaster I encountered Dunnington and he suggested that I rent rooms at Mrs. Greaves' boarding house."

Once again the mention of Dunnington brought a pain to Fredrick's heart. Dammit, the tutor had been more a father than this man standing before him. How could he . . .

With an effort, Fredrick forced himself to concentrate upon his father's unfolding story.

"And he also attended your wedding?"

"Yes. Adeline demanded that we have a quiet ceremony at the local church. Only Dunnington and Mrs. Greaves attended." A small, profoundly sad smile curved his lips. "Still, it was the happiest day of my life. I had the woman I loved and a child soon to be born. If only . . ."

"If only what?"

The nobleman gave a shake of his head. "You will never believe me, but I wish that those days had never come to an end. We were happy in those cramped rooms with nothing to concern ourselves other than making ends meet."

Fredrick battled back the instinctive flare of sympathy. By God, Lord Graystone deserved many things, but pity was not among them.

"Oh, I am certain it was all quite romantic," he drawled.

The blue eyes flashed. "It was."

"So what happened?"

His father struggled against his natural instinct to retreat behind his aloof composure. For nearly three decades he had refused to answer the questions that must have been upon the lips of many. Now it was clearly a painful process to speak the truth he had hidden for so long.

"First my mother died and I was forced to return to Oak Manor for the funeral." He gave a faint grimace. "No matter what the rift was between us, she was my mother and I owed her my respect."

"You did not bring your wife?"

The delicate features abruptly tightened with an ancient grief. "By the gods, I wish I had," he rasped, his hand reaching out to clutch at a nearby shelf, as if his knees were no longer to be trusted. "While I was gone,

Adeline fell down the stairs and was grievously injured. She regained consciousness only long enough to give birth to you. She died a few hours later."

Fredrick took a long swig of the brandy, feeling oddly discomfited by the undisguised agony in his father's eyes. Whatever had happened all those years ago, Fredrick was being forced to accept that his father truly cared for his mother.

"I . . . I am sorry. It must have been a very difficult time for you," he grudgingly conceded.

"For weeks I was numb." Lord Graystone grimaced. "I could not accept that my beloved Adeline had been stolen from me. It was simply inconceivable. And then I received word that my brother had been shot in a hunting accident." He met Fredrick's gaze squarely. "Within a matter of a month I had lost my mother, my wife, and my brother. Even worse, I was thrust into the position of Lord Graystone and burdened with the debacle my brother had made of the estate."

"And what of me?" he demanded.

"I left you in the care of Mrs. Griffin while I returned to Oak Manor."

Fredrick slowly stood, thrusting aside his brief feelings of pity.

"And while you were there you simply forgot that you were married and had a son?"

"Of course not." His father thrust an unsteady hand through his silver hair. "I . . . it was . . ."

"What?"

With a frustrated growl, Lord Graystone paced across the carpet, his movements sharp and uneven as he struggled with the flood of emotions.

"You must understand that the estate was on the brink of ruin," he rasped. "My brother had managed to squander his inheritance and strip the estate of everything that might hold value. There was no principal, no assets, and no capital to attempt to retrieve the fallow fields. Even the manor house was beginning to tumble into shambles." His hand lifted to wave around the library that was now the envy of the neighborhood. "I had to find some means of staving off disaster."

Fredrick narrowed his gaze. "You have offered a great number of excuses, Father, and far fewer explanations."

His father hunched his shoulders, his steps slowing as he regarded Fredrick with a resigned expression.

"I just wish you to comprehend my situation. I had family and servants and tenants all depending upon me. I could not fail them, no matter what the cost to myself." His lips twisted. "Even if it meant selling my soul to the devil."

"What devil?"

There was a brief pause before Lord Graystone heaved a sigh. "My father-in-law, Jacob Burke."

"The gentleman who handed you a fortune?" Fredrick gave a humorless laugh. "We should all have such devils."

Ignoring Fredrick's mocking response, Lord Graystone resumed his pacing.

"He came to Oak Manor," the older man said. "He had heard the rumors of my desperate straits." A hint of bitterness glittered in his pale eyes. "Not surprising. It seemed at the time that everyone knew that the current Baron could not so much as pay his butcher bill."

"What did he want?"

"He wished to offer me his only daughter and her considerable dowry in holy matrimony."

"How considerable a dowry?"

Coming to a halt behind one of the wing chairs, Lord Graystone clutched the high back.

"One hundred thousand pounds."

Fredrick gave a choked cough. He had always suspected that his father had been handsomely rewarded for taking Lady Graystone as his bride, but not even he had imagined just how handsome the reward had been.

No wonder he was willing to hand over a miserly twenty thousand pounds to keep Dunnington's lips sealed.

"God almighty."

"Yes," his father softly agreed with his shock. "Like you, he was a self-made man, although his fortune came from his vast shipping empire. And to be frank, he did not have the benefit of being educated. His manners were . . . less than what one might desire. In truth, he was loud and coarse and inclined to be an embarrassment."

Fredrick gave a lift of his brows. "No doubt one hundred thousand pounds allowed you to overlook his lack of manners?"

"I will not lie to you, Fredrick, his offer seemed to be the answer to all my troubles." His glance strayed toward the shelves that were now filled with endless rows of leather-bound books. "With such resources I could sow the fields, I could repair the tenants' cottages, I could halt the encroaching ruin upon Oak Manor. There was only one difficulty."

"And what difficulty was that?"

"When Jacob came to me he assumed that he was

bargaining his fortune for a grandson who would someday possess the title he coveted. He did not realize that I already had a son." The pale eyes held Fredrick's gaze. "A son who was now the legitimate heir to the title."

"Ah." A ridiculous pain flared through Fredrick as he imagined that moment when his father made the irrevocable decision to trade his only child for the funds he needed. Had he hesitated for even a moment? Had he considered what it would mean to Fredrick's future or had he been too blinded by the vast wealth to even give thought to the baby he had created with the woman he loved? "What an inconvenient bother I must have been," he taunted, his voice thick with disappointment. "One hundred thousand pounds yours for the taking if only you could be rid of me. I suppose I should be relieved that you merely bartered off my inheritance rather than smothering me in my cradle."

His father gave a lift of his hands, his countenance becoming an odd shade of grey as he licked his lips.

"What would you have me do, Fredrick?" he pleaded in a harsh voice. "Watch as my tenants starved? Huddle with my aging servants in the cellars as Oak Manor rotted to a hollow shell?"

Fredrick smiled with a cold amusement. His father was not the first to travel the path to hell that had been paved with good intentions.

"So your motives were completely altruistic?" he mocked, his gaze deliberately traveling over the furnishings that were obviously of the finest craftsmanship. "You thought nothing of yourself or the notion that being Lord Graystone with a grand and prosperous estate was far preferable to living in genteel poverty?"

The pale gaze dropped at the accusation. "I certainly told myself my decision was entirely for the benefit of others. I was abandoning the child of my beloved Adeline and marrying a woman I could barely tolerate to salvage the estate. It seemed a rather harsh payment for a destiny I never desired."

Fredrick widened his eyes. His father thought *he* had paid a harsh price?

"And what of my destiny?"

"What destiny?" His father made an impatient sound. "Your inheritance would have been nothing more than a ramshackle home and mountain of debt."

Fredrick's hands curled as a savage blast of anger shook his body. Good God. Even now his father would not admit his selfishness. At least not without comforting himself with the thought it had been his only choice.

"Oh yes, far better to be a bastard." He stabbed the older man with a malevolent glare. "My God, you abandoned me to a horrid woman who beat me with her cane when I did not polish the silver to her satisfaction."

"No, no." His father rounded the wing chair, his eyes troubled. "I swear that I did not know, Fredrick. When I gave you into the care of Mrs. Griffin she promised to raise you as her own. I sent money each month to see to your care and education. I did not dream that she would prove to be so treacherous."

Just for a moment Fredrick continued to glare at the man who had betrayed him, and then with a sharp shake of his head he was turning away.

"Do you know, Father, I am not at all surprised that you would abandon me to a stranger and never bother to ensure that I was not being ill-treated. You have proven you are willing to sacrifice me for the greater good. But I find it impossible to imagine Dunnington being nearly so indifferent. He . . ." Fredrick was forced to halt and clear his throat. "I thought he truly cared for me, but he is just as guilty as you in stealing all that should have been mine. My name, my position, my inheritance."

"No, Fredrick. Blame me, but not Dunnington." With a jerky motion, Lord Graystone was at Fredrick's side, his hand reaching out to grasp his shoulder. "He left Winchester just days after you were born. He knew nothing of your fate until he was passing through the neighborhood near eight years later."

"He came here?"

"Yes." The older man's fingers unwittingly dug into Fredrick's muscles. "I assure you that the moment he realized that you were missing from Oak Manor he had every intention of announcing to the world that you were my legitimate son, especially once he traveled to Winchester and discovered the manner you were being treated by Mrs. Griffin."

Fredrick narrowed his gaze. "What halted him?"

"Simon." Slowly Lord Graystone released his grip on Fredrick's shoulder. "He realized that by returning you to your rightful place he would be destroying Simon's future."

The brief flare of relief at the knowledge Dunnington had not deliberately abandoned him was swiftly muted by the realization that his father had deliberately used Dunnington's instinctive desire to protect children against him.

"Of course." Fredrick made a sound of disgust deep in his throat. "How very wise of you to hide your sins behind a child. Did you dangle little Simon on

Dunnington's knee while you pointed out the evils of revealing the sordid truth?"

A guilty heat touched his father's pale cheeks. "What does it matter?" he demanded, not willing to admit that he had deliberately used one child to betray another. "We agreed that once Dunnington was settled in London he would send for you and that I would offer him a substantial sum to see to your welfare and education."

Fredrick gave a slow shake of his head. He could not blame his poor tutor. Dunnington would have been horrified at being put in the position of choosing one child's future over another. He obviously did the best his conscience would allow for.

Turning on his heel, Fredrick paced toward the fireplace, staring blindly at the dancing flames.

"Did he also force a promise that you would bring me to Oak Manor each year and endure my unwelcome presence?"

He heard his father's pained hiss at his stark accusation. "No, Fredrick, I was the one to insist that you be returned to me at least a few weeks out of the year."

"Why? It was obvious that I made you miserable while I was here."

"It was my own shame that made me miserable, Fredrick," Lord Graystone confessed. "I could not look at you and not know just how deeply I betrayed you. With every passing year the burden of my guilt has weighed more heavily upon my conscience. Still, I discovered . . ."

Against his will Fredrick turned to meet his father's darkened gaze. "Discovered what?"

"I discovered that no matter how painful, I needed to have you near." The lean features held a measure of sorrow as the older man regarded his son. "The past few years have been almost unbearable while I waited and hoped for some word from you."

Fredrick stiffened against the unwelcome flare of remorse. By God, he owed this man nothing. Certainly not guilt at having spared them both the awkward pain of his yearly visits.

"And now you no doubt wish that I had chosen to remain in London rather than returning to Oak Manor," he sneered.

"No." His father gave a shake of his head. "You may not believe me, Fredrick, but a part of me is relieved that you have discovered the truth."

Fredrick gave a humorless laugh. "You are right, Father, I do not believe you." He took a step toward the slender gentleman who seemed to have aged a decade in the past minutes. "Not when you had eight and twenty years to do the honorable thing."

Lord Graystone tilted his chin, his eyes hardening with some inner determination.

"I was too much a coward to face the consequences. Now that they are taken out of my hands I am prepared to face whatever may come."

Fredrick arched a brow. "Even if I choose to claim my birthright and destroy your family?"

There was not the faintest pause. "Yes."

"And what of Simon?"

"Simon has no genuine interest in Oak Manor or his responsibilities as a baron. To be honest, he would be far happier with a large allowance and the knowledge that he need never lift a finger to earn his keep." Lord Graystone's lips twisted. "And there is no denying that the estate would be better served in your hands. You have proven you possess the skill and intelligence necessary to keep the lands profitable, while the tenants would more readily respect a man of sense rather than an overdressed buffoon. I cannot tell you how often I have rued the knowledge that it was Simon who would follow in my footsteps rather than you."

Fredrick briefly recalled the strange sensations that had assaulted him as he had ridden toward the estate. There had been an undeniable moment when he had viewed the manor house and grounds with a measure of . . . rightness. As if he suddenly realized that Oak Manor should belong to him.

With an unconscious shake of his head at his ridiculous thoughts, Fredrick sternly reminded himself that nothing had truly changed.

At least not yet.

"You are not so foolish as to believe that Simon will accept me as your heir, Father," he retorted harshly.

Lord Graystone merely shrugged. "You have the means to force him to accept."

Well, that was true enough, Fredrick acknowledged. Once he searched the church records there would be no one who could refuse his position as heir. Still, he could not deny a measure of surprise at his father's lack of fear in having his lies exposed.

"And your wife?"

"She will be . . ." The older man searched for the proper word. "Displeased."

"I should say that she would be a good deal more than merely displeased. She might very well demand that her considerable dowry be returned since you failed to uphold your end of the bargain."

"Perhaps," he murmured, his lean features unreadable. "Although with Jacob long dead there is little she could truly do beyond sue me for perjury, always presuming any judge would be willing to hear her case. Highly doubtful."

Fredrick regarded his father with a disbelieving frown. "You do not seem particularly bothered at the thought of causing your wife such distress," he accused.

Lord Graystone heaved a deep sigh. "I know that you consider me a man without a heart, Fredrick, but Wilhelmina has devoted every day of our marriage to reminding me that I have been bought and paid for by her ill-bred father." His expression hardened with an age-old bitterness. "Even worse, she has indulged Simon past all bearing."

Fredrick shrugged. "In my experience most young bucks have been indulged beyond all bearing."

"Bah. She has spoiled the boy. And over the past few years I have come to the unshakable conclusion that the moment I am in my grave he will swiftly bring to ruin all that I have sacrificed to salvage." His father gave a sharp bark of laughter. "Ironic, is it not? I bartered one son to save an estate that will be destroyed by another son."

Fredrick was not yet in a humor to appreciate the irony of the situation.

"So if I choose to claim my rightful place you will not stand in my way?" he demanded.

"Stand in your way?" His father met his gaze squarely. "No, Fredrick, I will not stand in your way. Indeed, I shall willingly stand at your side."

Chapter Seventeen

The treacherous spring weather had taken a turn for the worse when Portia awoke the next morning. Huddled beneath her blankets she could hear the sound of rain lashing against her windows.

Just for a moment she considered the notion of remaining in the cocooned warmth of her bed rather than braving the inhospitable rain and wind.

She was tired, she acknowledged with a deep sigh. The night had been long and restless as she had fretted over Fredrick's abrupt departure.

What if his friend convinced him to remain in Winchester? Or worse, what if his friend convinced him to return to London? Despite leaving his belongings at the inn, it would be a simple matter to send a servant to collect them.

She might never see him again. And that would be . . .

With a groan Portia forced herself out of the bed and dressed in a heavy woolen gown. She covered it with an equally heavy woolen cape before she made her way through the stirring inn.

No matter how uninviting the weather it was preferable to her dark, brooding thoughts.

Intent upon slipping through the side door, Portia nearly missed the slender form that was pacing the shadows in the back parlor. With a sharp flare of relief she stepped through the open door and regarded the gentleman with a wide gaze.

"Fredrick?" she breathed. "I thought you were staying in Winchester?"

For a moment she thought he might actually ignore her as he continued his restless pacing then, halting beside the window, he at last turned to face her. Portia caught her breath at the sight of his ashen countenance and the deep shadows that lay like bruises beneath his eyes.

"I returned last eve," he said, his voice thick and raspy as if his throat were raw.

She instinctively stepped forward, uncertain if he were ill or simply suffering from the aftereffects of a night of overindulgence.

Goodness knew that her father often enough had come home in such a sickly condition.

"It must have been very late," she said, her tone instinctively softening. Her father disliked any loud noise after such a night.

His hand lifted to scrub through his already tousled curls. "I suppose it was."

"You look weary."

"No doubt because I have yet to sleep."

She frowned, her concern deepening. He looked more than merely exhausted. He looked . . . cold. As if his emotions had been drained from him.

"Why do you not return to your rooms and I shall have a tray sent up to you?"

His eyes slowly narrowed, his gaze lowering to take in her heavy cloak.

"Where are you going?"

Despite her fierce relief at his return, Portia was swift to retreat behind her guarded composure. It was a hard-earned habit she did without thought.

"I enjoy an early morning stroll," she murmured.

The smoky grey gaze shifted deliberately toward the window that rattled beneath the force of the wind.

"It is hardly the sort of weather for a stroll."

"A little rain does not trouble me."

Not surprisingly his brows arched in disbelief. "It is more than a little rain, it is a bloody gale. You will be soaked through."

"My cloak will protect me from the worst of the rain."

"For Christ's sake, Portia, what could possibly be so important to risk a lung infection?"

Her practiced smile never faltered. Damn him, what right did he have to press her with these unwanted questions? Was she pestering him with details of his obviously eventful night?

"I am never ill." She pulled the cloak tighter. "If you will excuse me, I must return before breakfast."

She was turning away when Fredrick took a jerky step forward, his expression impossible to read.

"Where are you going, Portia?"

"I have told you—"

"Lies," he interrupted harshly. "You have told me lies. Just as everyone else in my life has done."

She sucked in a sharp breath, caught off-guard by his unmistakable anger.

"Fredrick, what has happened?"

He offered a mocking laugh that flared painfully

over her skin. "Oh no, poppet, you horde your secrets like some rare treasure. I shall do the same. Enjoy your stroll, Mrs. Walker."

With a deliberate motion he turned his back to her and glared out the rain-slick window. Portia did her own share of glaring, fiercely telling herself to walk away.

He was behaving like a sulky child who was determined to pout if he could not have his way. The only mature way to respond was to ignore his tantrum.

But Portia discovered her feet refusing to budge as her hands clutched the thick material of her cloak. This was not just about a male behaving in an unreasonable manner. After all, that was a common enough thing. Most men were unreasonable.

This was about a lover who kept demanding more and more despite her obvious desire to keep him at a distance.

"I do not have to share all my secrets with you," she ridiculously charged.

"Certainly not," he drawled. "You have made it painfully clear that you are willing to share your passion, your body, and even a measure of your heart, but not your soul."

"And why would you care about my soul?"

"I care about all of you." He turned to regard her with a humorless smile, his eyes dark and haunted. "Foolish of me, eh, poppet?"

Her teeth clenched as a shaft of guilt pierced her heart. A guilt that she had not earned, she told herself with a flare of annoyance.

Why should she be expected to bare her soul to this man? He could claim to care all he wanted for her; in the end he would be leaving the Queen's Arms.

"I have asked nothing of you," she charged.

"Of course not." He stabbed her with a narrow-eyed glare. "You ask for nothing because you have no wish to offer anything. You are impervious to the needs that plague us lesser mortals."

Her brows snapped together. Blast it all, how dare he lecture and chastise her in this fashion?

"And what is that supposed to mean?"

He regarded her defensive expression for a long moment, and then with a slow shake of his head, he folded his arms across his chest and turned back to the window.

"It means nothing," he muttered. "Nothing at all."

"Fredrick . . ." She heaved a loud sigh. "Damn you."

"Be on your way, Portia. My mood is far too foul to share with anyone."

She *should* be on her way. Mr. Fredrick Smith might have ample leisure time to pout in back parlors, but she was a busy woman with far too many responsibilities. Even now she could hear Mrs. Cornell commanding the kitchen staff to stoke the fires and gather the eggs.

Once the guests began heading down for breakfast she would not have a moment to spare for herself.

She did not go on her way, however. Instead she squared her shoulders and marched across the room to stand at the annoying man's side.

"Well, you have now managed to ruin my own mood, so we might as well be foul together," she said in grim tones. "Come along."

With a wary frown, he slowly turned to meet her fierce glare. "I beg your pardon?"

"If you wish to know my secrets then come with me," she said, marching back across the carpet to await him at the door.

Still he hesitated, clearly wise enough to sense her dangerous mood.

"Portia . . ."

She pointed a finger toward his pale countenance. "Fredrick, you desired the truth and you shall have it. Are you coming or not?"

"Very well," he slowly agreed, crossing the room to join her.

In silence, Portia led her suspicious companion from the inn, pulling the hood of her cloak over her head as the heavy rain hit them with startling force. A part of her could not believe that she was doing anything so foolish. She had carefully harbored her secret for years.

And with good reason.

Why would she share it with this gentleman who would soon be leaving Wessex and her behind?

A larger part of her, however, was content with the thought of sharing her deepest self. At least with Fredrick. He was the one man who would understand. The one man who would never judge or condemn her for her choices.

The silence remained until they entered the protection of the copse of trees that surrounded the inn. In the same moment they both slowed their steps and Fredrick gave a shake of his head to rid his curls of the clinging dampness.

"This land is connected to the inn?" he inquired.

Portia flashed him a surprised glance. It was not what she had been expecting.

"Yes." She turned toward a barely discernable path that led toward a nearby stream. "When Thomas was younger he was able to provide enough meat and fish for most of the kitchen's needs." She gave a faint grimace. "Unfortunately Quinn and Spenser are now too old to hunt, which means that the game is left for the poachers and I am forced to wrangle with a butcher who is convinced that it is perfectly acceptable to take advantage of a woman who dares to be in charge of her own business."

A hint of his customary humor glittered in the grey eyes. A welcome relief to Portia.

"Do you know, poppet, I feel sympathy for that ridiculous butcher," he teased. "I do not doubt that you have managed to harangue the poor man until he is practically giving you his meat."

"I do not harangue," she protested.

"No?"

"No, I . . ." She briefly considered the best word to describe her rather forcible bargaining skills. "Barter."

His lips twitched, but there was a strange expression on his handsome features as he studied her damp features.

"As you will," he murmured.

"Why are you looking at me so oddly?"

"I was just struck with the absurdity of you bartering with the local butcher. You were born for a life far different from this, Portia." His voice deepened, that edge of bitterness returning. "Your father ruined your prospects and forced you to travel a path that was far beneath you."

She frowned, not at all certain what the devil was the matter with the man. Something had clearly happened last eve. Something that was troubling him intensely.

"My path is what it is, Fredrick," she said with a shrug. "No amount of wishing can make it otherwise."

Without warning he reached out to grasp her arm, swinging her about to meet the hectic glitter of his gaze.

"What if you could have what was stolen from you? What if you could have your place as a leader of society?"

She gave a shake of her head. Why was he so determined to dwell in the past? They had both managed to overcome the obstacles in their lives. Surely it was best to concentrate on the future?

"It is an impossible dream, Fredrick."

"Indulge me, poppet." His hand shifted to grasp her fingers in a tight grip. "What if you could be whisked to London and offered entrée into the most exclusive drawing rooms?"

When she had been seventeen nothing had seemed more rewarding than dancing about the ballroom in the arms of a handsome partner. Now she merely gave a shake of her head at such foolish dreams.

"We both know that will never happen."

"But what if it could?"

She swallowed her flippant retort. For whatever reason, her response was important to Fredrick.

Profoundly important.

"Do you mean if I had a fairy godmother complete with a magical wand?" she asked, choosing her words with care.

"Something of the sort."

Ignoring the danger to her cloak, Portia leaned against a moss-slick tree and regarded her companion with a searching gaze. As always her heart gave a small flip at the astonishing beauty of his pale features. Surely even the gods must envy such perfection? But it was the troubled shadows that lurked in the depths of his eyes that forced her to answer his question.

"I might occasionally wish that I possessed enough wealth that I need never again worry about my finances and, of course, that I could hire all those who come to me in need of employment, but overall I would not change my life." She tilted her chin with a measure of pride. And why not? She had earned it. "If I had not endured the hardships life has given me, then I should never have realized just how much strength and courage I possess. I would have been no more than another bored matron, at the utter mercy of my husband and in constant fear of fickle society."

He leaned forward, studying her features as if attempting to determine the depth of her sincerity.

"You truly prefer the life as an innkeeper to that of a wife of a nobleman?"

"Why does that shock you?"

"I should think anyone would prefer a life of leisure to toiling day and night to see to the comfort of others," he said, his tone almost accusing.

She paused, beginning to suspect whatever was troubling Fredrick had something to do with his past.

Had his father said or done something? Or had he endured another unpleasant confrontation with those stupid dandies who were determined to punish him for being a bastard?

"And what of you, Fredrick?"

He shivered as a sharp breeze managed to slip between the protective boundary of trees.

"Me?"

She tilted her head to one side. "Would you truly give up the business you have created to devote your life to mincing through London society?"

He gave a lift of his shoulder. "If I were a nobleman then I should have an estate to keep me occupied."

"And you would be content to tend to your fields and settle the petty complaints of your tenants?"

"I will admit that it hardly sounds appealing in such terms," he said dryly.

Realizing just how revealing her words had been, Portia offered a small grimace.

"I suppose my opinion of noblemen and their positions has been tarnished by my past."

"Tarnished by your father?"

She paused before forcing herself from the tree and continuing down the narrow path. She did not know how to lay Fredrick's demons to rest. All she could do was be honest with her own.

"No," she muttered. "Not just my father."

Fredrick fell into step at her side. "Your fiancé?"

"Yes."

"Tell me of him."

A shudder of ancient disgust raced through her body. It seemed almost impossible to believe that she had ever been so utterly stupid as to be deceived by a common rogue.

Granted, she had been young and naïve. But even that was hardly a suitable excuse not to have seen through such shallow, immature charm.

"I . . ." She was forced to halt and clear her throat. "I met Edward at one of the local assemblies. For a young maiden who had rarely been beyond the nearest village he seemed more like a fantasy than a flesh and blood gentleman."

She sensed Fredrick stiffen at her soft words. "He was handsome, I suppose?"

Portia heaved a disgusted sigh. "Handsome and sophisticated and well-skilled in seducing any woman who might stray across his path. Had I not been such a bumbling innocent I would have spotted him as a rake the moment he approached me."

Fredrick lifted his hand to stroke his fingers over her chilled cheek. "Obviously he was not entirely a rake. He did offer you marriage, after all."

Despite her best efforts, Portia could not entirely repress the memory of her giddy happiness when Edward had gone to his knee and pleaded for her to become his wife. In that moment she had felt that all her dreams had come true.

She still blamed that giddiness for the disastrous mistakes that were yet to come.

"He only proposed because he was laboring beneath the mistaken belief that my rather large dowry was still intact." She shivered beneath the heavy cloak. As easily as she remembered the romantic proposal she also remembered the frightening fury when Edward realized that he had wasted near six months in his pursuit of her. "Once he discovered that my father had already managed to plunder my fortune he could not abandon me quickly enough."

Reaching out to brush a dripping branch out of her path, Fredrick slanted her a small frown. "How did he learn the truth?"

"He approached my father the day before our wedding with the intention of collecting my dowry before we left on our honeymoon trip. Imagine his horror when he discovered that instead of the money he had been anticipating my father greeted him with a stack of bills he hoped his soon to be son-in-law would settle for him." She gave a short laugh. "Can you truly blame him from bolting?"

"Yes, I can," Fredrick gritted, a startling color flaring

along his cheekbones. "I can also blame him for destroying a young maiden's heart."

Coming to a halt at a small clearing, Portia flashed Fredrick a sad smile.

"He did not destroy my heart, Fredrick. Do you believe that I would be so weak-spirited as to mourn the loss of a rank fortune-hunter?"

"Portia, you may not wish acknowledge the wounds that you still carry, but it is obvious that you have never truly healed from Edward's betrayal."

"No, Fredrick." With a slow motion, Portia settled on a low marble bench and pointed to the small wooden cross that was nearly hidden beneath a pile of dead leaves. "This is the reason I still mourn."

With a startled frown, Fredrick bent down to read the name roughly carved into the wood.

"Rosalind?" He turned his head to regard her with open puzzlement. "Who was Rosalind?"

"My daughter."

Chapter Eighteen

Fredrick's eyes widened at her whispered words. "You and Thomas had a child?"

There was a tense moment before she gave a shake of her head. "No. Not Thomas."

Barely aware of her tightening muscles, Portia steeled herself for Fredrick's reaction. How could he not be shocked? Even horrified?

Proper maidens did not allow themselves to get with child without the benefit of a husband. Not even if she happened to be engaged at the time.

It was not shock, however, that settled upon the fine, elegantly chiseled features. Instead she would have sworn that it was a slow, swiftly hidden comprehension.

"Edward was the father?" he said, his tone making it more a statement than question.

"Yes." She absently reached down to brush the leaves from the tiny grave. "As I said, I was very young and very stupid. It took little effort for Edward to seduce me."

"Did he know that you carried his child when he left?"

"Yes," she admitted softly.

He muttered a string of foul curses as he settled on the bench beside her, and firmly gathered her hands in his.

"What of your father?"

She flinched as the memory of her father's disgusted face flashed through her thoughts. He could happily behave with a complete lack of morals, but the mere hint of a scandal being attached to his daughter was unbearable.

"I . . . I confessed the truth when I realized that I had been jilted. I believe that is one the reasons for his hasty flight to India."

His breath hissed between his teeth as Fredrick gave a shake of his head.

"It is no wonder that you lost faith in men, poppet. You must have been terrified to have been abandoned when you were at your most vulnerable."

Dear God, she had been beyond terrified at the disappearance of her father. For the first few days she had been in a state of near panic, pacing the empty rooms with mindless shock.

She shivered, not even noticing that the rain had halted and the wind trailed to a mere breeze.

"I did not know where to turn," she admitted, her gaze lowering to where her hands lay in Fredrick's comforting fingers. "I had no close family to take me in and while I could live at my father's estate I had no income to pay the servants or even to put food on the table. There was also the knowledge that soon enough my neighbors would discover I was with child and I would be ostracized by those few friends I had left."

His thumbs absently rubbed the sensitive skin of her wrists. "What did you do?"

"I wish I could claim that I awoke one morning and took matters in hand. That is what a woman of genuine courage would do." She gave a faint shrug. "But in truth, I was still cowering at my father's estate when Thomas came to my rescue."

"What do you mean, came to your rescue?"

A portion of her tension eased as the thought of Thomas Walker chased away the more unpleasant memories. Unlike Edward, he had made no effort at sophistication. He had been a large, barrel-chested man with shabby coats, a shock of grey hair, and an expression of kindness that had been desperately needed by a young, frightened maiden.

"At first I did not even realize he was visiting the estate. Not until my sparse meals began to include fresh fish and venison. Quinn at last confessed the bounty was a gift from Thomas Walker, the local innkeeper." She smiled wryly. "Naturally, I was rather suspicious of his unexpected generosity and I sought him out to discover what it was he desired of me."

An unexpected anger darkened Fredrick's eyes. "I believe I can guess what he desired."

"You could guess, but you would be wrong," she said tartly.

He arched a honey brow. "Would I?"

"Thomas had once been in love with my mother, despite the fact she was well above his touch, and even after she had been compelled to wed my father he had continued to care for her."

"Your mother." His short, scoffing laugh revealed his disbelief. Not entirely surprising. At first Portia had not been entirely certain it was not merely a ploy by the older gentleman. Time had proven the depths of his sincerity. "That is what he told you?"

"Yes."

"He weds the daughter of the woman he once loved. Rather Shakespearean of him, was it not?"

She tugged her hands from his grasp as she offered him a fierce glare.

"No, it was not, and I will not endure that tone of voice when you speak of Thomas," she warned. "He was the one person in my world who offered me friendship with no ulterior motives. Never once did he attempt to manipulate me or gain anything from me."

"Good God, he gained you as his wife," he rasped.

"It was *never* his intention to have me as his wife, Fredrick," she said. "He looked upon me as the daughter he might have had if his social standing had been different. But then he discovered . . ."

There was a brief pause as Fredrick sorted through her words and then understanding dawned.

"Ah," he breathed, the brittle expression softening. "He discovered that you were with child."

"Yes." Portia rose to her feet as her stomach twisted with emotion. Those terrifying days would be branded into her mind for an eternity. "He was so kind. He offered to send me away so that I could have the child in secret and return without anyone ever knowing the truth. He even offered to foster the child for me."

Fredrick rose to his feet, careful to move slowly as if sensing that she might bolt at any unexpected movement. And perhaps she would, she ruefully acknowledged. She felt as if she was wound as tightly as a child's top.

"That seems as if it were a reasonable offer. Why did you not accept?"

"No doubt I would have if I possessed any sense whatsoever, but I could not bear the thought of giving up my child." She wrapped her arms about her waist. Despite the heavy cloak she felt chilled to the very bone. "I cannot rationally explain my feelings, but I knew in my heart that I would do anything, sacrifice anything, to hold that baby in my arms."

"And so Walker married you so that you could keep your child?"

"Yes."

He lightly touched her shoulder. "You would have made a wonderful mother, Portia."

"I like to think I should have, but it was not to be. I had been married only a few weeks when . . ."

Portia was caught off-guard when her voice broke and a sudden flood of tears filled her eyes. The swell of sadness seemed to come out of nowhere and as Fredrick gathered her into his arms she was incapable of denying the need to snuggle against his warmth and welcome the silent sympathy he offered.

Mercy, it had been so long since she had lowered her guard enough to take comfort from another.

So long since she had not been battling the world all alone. . . .

Fredrick briefly closed his eyes as he held Portia's trembling body close.

For a moment he regretted having forced her to reveal such painful memories. She had surely suffered enough without him stirring up the loss and betrayal she had endured. And nothing could be altered by confessing her secrets.

But as Portia's tears began to lessen, he could not

deny a fierce flare of pleasure at her display of trust. At last she had lowered her walls and allowed him to see into her heart.

Whatever the future might bring he would ensure that she never regretted her faith in him.

"Shhh. I have you, poppet," he whispered, his lips lightly brushing over her temple.

"I do not know what is the matter," she muttered. "I never cry."

Fredrick readily believed her. While many females might use tears as a potent weapon, Portia would view them only as a weakness.

"Why did you keep the child a secret?" he demanded, more baffled than shocked.

Pulling back she blotted her cheeks with her handkerchief and gave a loud sniff. Fredrick felt his heart melt at the sight of her tangled lashes and reddened nose. She looked young and vulnerable and delectably sweet.

"I was ill for a very long time and when I at last felt well enough to leave my bed I realized that no one in the neighborhood realized that I had ever carried a child," she admitted in thick tones. "At least no one beyond Thomas and Quinn."

"And they were too loyal to spread gossip?"

"Precisely. Thomas thought it was best not to mention the baby since our marriage had already been a rushed affair that had raised more than a few brows." She gave another sniff as her gaze strayed to the wooden cross. "He buried Rosalind here so I could visit her."

He tightened his arms around her slender body, wishing that he could somehow ease the grief that continued to plague her.

"Do you come every morning?"

"Most mornings," she admitted. "It is peaceful here and I can prepare for the day without interruption."

"And that is all?" he pressed.

"What do you mean?"

"This grave seems almost a . . . shrine," he said softly. "A reminder that you are no longer a young, vulnerable girl who is forced to depend upon others."

She stiffened at his words, wrestling away from his clinging arms to regard him with a wary frown.

"I can easily look in the mirror if I wish to be reminded I am no longer a young girl, Fredrick," she retorted, the edge in her voice warning that she had revealed all that she intended to on this cold, grey morning.

"Come." Firmly regaining her arm, Fredrick turned his companion toward the inn. "It is too cold on this morning to linger."

They traveled the narrow path with only the whistle of the wind to break the silence. Fredrick kept her close to his side, but he hesitated to break into her broodings. She would share her thoughts when she was prepared to speak, he told himself sternly. And he had demanded enough of her on this day.

At last she sucked in a deep breath and turned her head to meet his concerned gaze.

"You do not seem to be particularly shocked by my confession."

He gave a lift of his brows at her unexpected words. "Did you believe I might be?"

"Most gentlemen would condemn me if they knew the truth."

"I am not most gentlemen."

Her lips reluctantly twitched. "True enough."

"Surely, Portia, you have not forgotten that my own mother conceived me without the benefit of marriage vows?" he reminded her gently. "From all I have discovered she was a warm, loving woman who I would be proud to have as my mother. Just as you are a warm and loving woman who Rosalind would have been proud to call mother."

She stumbled, her breath rasping through the air as Fredrick tightened his hold to keep her upright.

"Gads, you are amazing," she breathed.

He gave a startled chuckle. Even with all that was upon his mind he could not help but be pleased by her words. What man did not desire to be amazing in the eyes of a beautiful woman?

"Am I?"

"You always seem to have the perfect words to make me feel better."

"They are not just words, Portia," he said, catching and holding her gaze. "If I could take away the pain you were forced to suffer, I would, but as you have so eloquently informed me, it is your past that has molded you into the woman you are today." He reached up his free hand to lightly outline her lips. "You are like a fine sword that has been perfectly tempered."

A hint of color touched her pale cheeks before she was offering a small laugh.

"Quinn says that I am like a mule that plods behind a carrot of the wrong color."

"That certainly sounds like something your groom would say, although I will admit I do not know what the devil it means."

"Actually, neither do I." She gave a faint shrug. "I assume that it has something to do with my being set in my ways."

"Or blindly stubborn."

Her eyes flashed with a dangerous fire. "I beg your pardon?"

Fredrick smiled, happy to note her usual spirits returning. "Astonishingly, beautifully stubborn?"

She hid her amusement behind a mock frown. "Why is it that any gentleman who refuses to bend to the will of another is considered firm in his resolve, while a woman is readily chastised as being stubborn?"

"Being a gentleman of firm resolve I have no intention of answering such a question," he wisely retorted, slowing his steps as they left the woods and entered the stable yard. Although it was still early, he knew that once at the inn Portia would be swiftly consumed by the heavy responsibilities that she shouldered. He was not yet prepared to bring an end to their time together. "Portia?"

"Yes?"

"Will you come to my rooms?"

Portia caught her breath at his blunt request, her entire body tingling with the thought of those slender fingers stripping away the damp wool of her gown.

It was a temptation that she found nearly impossible to resist. Only the knowledge that her entire staff would notice her absence kept her from leaping at his offer.

"I should see to my guests," she murmured. "Perhaps later we could . . ."

"Portia, I would not ask if it were not important," he interrupted softly, his expression oddly somber. "I assure you that I only wish to converse."

She studied him for a long moment, accepting that there was more to his offer than a mere desire to seduce her. A knowledge she was not sure pleased or disappointed her.

"Very well," she agreed with a small nod of her head.

"Thank you."

Keeping her arm in his grasp, Fredrick was careful to enter the inn from a side door and used the servants' staircase to reach the upper floor. She had no need to remind him of her reluctance to be seen sneaking to his rooms. Fredrick always sensed what she desired without having to say the words.

It was only one of the things that made him so extraordinary.

Once in the privacy of his chambers, Fredrick closed the door and headed directly for a side table. Tossing aside his great coat he poured himself a large measure of brandy and tossed it down his throat.

With a frown, Portia slipped off her cloak and regarded her companion with a growing concern. The tension that smoldered about his slender form was nearly tangible.

"You really should have something to eat, Fredrick," she murmured, her gaze lingering on the shadows beneath his beautiful eyes.

Setting aside the empty glass, Fredrick gave a small shrug and began to pace the cramped room.

"Perhaps later."

Portia watched his pacing in silence, waiting for him to confess what was troubling him. It was only when she feared that he might actually wear a hole in the carpet that she at last cleared her throat.

"Fredrick?"

Coming to a halt beside the window, Fredrick stared blindly at the stable yard where Quinn was diligently spreading the mixture that Fredrick insisted would combat the mud.

"You were not mistaken in your suspicion that there was more to my arrival at the Queen's Arms than just business," he admitted in abrupt tones. "I traveled to Wessex because I discovered my father was harboring a dark secret that I was determined to uncover."

Portia slowly perched on the edge of the bed, folding her hands in her lap as she studied his profile.

"What sort of secret?"

"A part of his past that he wished to keep hidden."

She smiled wryly. There were few who did not possess at least a few skeletons they desired to keep buried.

Of course, she was fortunate that Fredrick had accepted her past with such ready sympathy. She was wise enough to know that it was a rare man who would be capable of such understanding.

Which made his obvious anger with his father all the more unexpected.

"If it is your father's past then why are you so disturbed?" She considered a long moment. "Does it somehow concern you?"

"Oh, it most certainly concerns me." Portia winced at his sharp laugh. "You see, I am not quite the bastard I have always been told that I am."

She blinked, her brows drawing together in confusion at his abrupt words.

"I beg your pardon?"

"My father stood before a vicar and shared his wedding vows with my mother before I entered the world."

Not even aware she was moving, Portia rose to her feet, a strange dread lodging in the pit of her stomach.

"You . . . you are the legitimate son of Lord Gray-stone?"

He turned to reveal his bitter expression. "Not only legitimate son, but legitimate heir."

"Oh my God." She gave a slow shake of her head. It was like something out of a children's story, she thought in bemusement. The handsome prince who has his birthright stolen by an evil stepmother. "Are you certain? I mean, absolutely certain?"

The grey eyes were as dark as storm clouds with suppressed emotion. "Beyond a shadow of a doubt."

"But why? Why would your father claim that you were a bastard?"

"It is a rather long and tedious story, but the end result was that my father was in need of a large fortune and Jacob Burke was in search of a title," he drawled sardonically. "I was the only thing that stood in the path of each of them getting what they desired."

Portia pressed her hands to her stomach, knowing that she should be delighted for Fredrick. For God's sake, he had just been given a new life. A life that would offer him everything that had been denied as a bastard.

He could move among society, wed a proper debutante, and perhaps most importantly, he would never again have to endure the mocking contempt of frivolous dandies.

Stupidly, however, all she could feel was an emptiness that was spreading through her heart.

Almost as if she were losing something that she never truly possessed.

"This is unbelievable." She grimly battled back the urge to cry. Her stupid feelings did not matter. In this moment the only thing important was Fredrick and how his father's betrayal had clearly hurt him. "How did you learn the truth?"

With jerky motions, Fredrick moved to pour himself another shot of brandy. "It was Dunnington, the man who raised me, who set me on the path." He swallowed the spirits in one gulp. "But the truth is to be found in a church in Winchester."

"That is where your parents were wed?"

"Yes."

His voice was low and clipped, but it did not disguise the edge of pain. Portia moved forward to lay her hand on his arm, offering an unspoken comfort.

"Do you intend to tell your father you have discovered the truth?" she asked softly.

The elegant features hardened at her question. "I have already confronted him."

"So swiftly?"

"There seemed little point in delaying."

"I suppose not." She licked her dry lips, regarding him with a searching gaze. "And what did he say?"

The pale features were impossible to read. "He is prepared to admit to the world that I am not the bastard he has always claimed me to be. Indeed, he made it clear that he will do whatever necessary to make me his heir."

Portia gave a shocked sound as she dropped her fingers and stepped from his lean form. Good God, he was a . . . nobleman. A dreaded beast she had sworn to hate.

Her smile felt stiff as she attempted to appear pleased at his astonishing elevation from bastard to heir.

"Congratulations, Fredrick. You must be very pleased."

He did not return her smile. Instead, he regarded her with a brooding intensity.

"In truth, I do not know if I am pleased or not, poppet."

"How could you not be? You are to become the heir of a title and a great estate."

His lips twisted. It was not a smile of pleasure, but rather one of cynicism.

"Did you not just assure me that you would have no interest in having your destiny altered so you could take your rightful position in society?" he demanded.

"Yes, but you are a gentleman."

His brows lifted at her obscure response. "That much I am certain of, although I do not entirely comprehend what it has to do with your argument."

With a frustrated sigh, she wrapped her arms about her waist. Why did gentlemen never realize just how difficult it was to be a woman?

"As a female I would be expected to give up my freedom and put my fate into the hands of some man if I were to return to society," she pointed out, her expression revealing what she thought of such a hideous fate. "You are a gentleman and therefore you have no need to give up anything, not even your business, when you become Lord Graystone."

"I would, however, be burdened with responsibilities that I was never trained to shoulder. I haven't the least notion of what it might entail to be in charge of a vast estate," he said, his brows drawing together as Portia gave a sudden laugh. "Why do you find that amusing?"

She gave a shake of her head, unable to believe that

he could doubt his overwhelming ability to master whatever task might be required of him.

"For God's sake, Fredrick, you were not at this inn but a few moments before you were fussing and fretting and fixing everything in your path," she said.

His lips twitched. "Tinkering with pulley systems and drainage ditches can hardly compare to being groomed from birth to become a nobleman."

"It is far better," she insisted, her expression unwittingly fierce with the pride she felt in this gentleman's astonishing skills. "Any estate that you take under your wing will be the most profitable, the most well-run estate in all of England. It does not surprise me at all that your father would be anxious to make you his heir. Indeed, it only proves that he has at last come to his senses."

The silver eyes darkened as Fredrick slowly stepped forward, his arms encircling her waist as he lowered his head and stroked his lips down the line of her nose.

"Do you know, Portia Walker, I suddenly have little interest in estates and inheritances."

Portia gave a small squeak as she was swept off her feet and carried toward the nearby bed.

"Good heavens, Fredrick, what are you about?" she demanded.

He smiled tenderly as he lowered her onto the middle of the mattress and covered her with the welcome weight of his body.

"I have thought the truth would strike me like a bolt of lightning, poppet," he murmured, his head lowering to bury his face in the curve of her neck. "But it was actually more a slow, relentless tidal wave."

Portia shivered as he gave her skin a light nip, her

blood already shimmering with heat. Somewhere in the back of her mind she was aware of the faint noises that revealed the inn was stirring to life, but her usual sense of responsibility was being rapidly undermined by the gentle kisses he was pressing along the line of her bodice.

Besides, there was a tiny voice in the back of her mind whispering that this might be the very last occasion she would ever be held in Fredrick's arms.

Once he was acknowledged as Lord Graystone's heir he would be far beyond the touch of an aging innkeeper.

"The truth of your father?" she muttered, her thoughts already clouding with passion as her hands instinctively lifted to wrap around his neck.

He pulled back to smile deep into her eyes. "The truth of you."

"Me?" She frowned. "And what truth is that?"

"That you are the woman I have been waiting for," he said, his breath warm on her cheek. "The woman I was meant to love and keep at my side for all eternity."

Chapter Nineteen

Hiding his decidedly smug smile at Portia's shock, Fredrick returned his attention to spreading kisses down the curve of her neck even as his hands tugged at the fastenings of her thick gown.

Oddly, he did not feel nearly so disturbed as he perhaps should at the knowledge he had just pledged his undying love. It was, after all, nothing short of a declaration of his intention to make her his wife. Something no gentleman would offer lightly.

But as he tasted of her satin skin he felt nothing but absolute satisfaction. No doubt because he had accepted the truth of his feelings in his heart days ago, he acknowledged wryly.

"Fredrick?" Portia breathed, her fingers digging into his shoulders as he discovered the tender pulse at the base of her throat.

"Hmmm?"

"What did you say?"

Fredrick stripped away the heavy wool of her gown, revealing the lacy chemise beneath. He smiled as he outlined the pretty rose that had been embroidered upon the thin bodice. How could he not adore this woman?

So strong and commanding on the surface, and yet so soft and feminine beneath all that wool and starch.

A perfect combination that would fascinate him for all of eternity.

"I believe you heard me," he said as he efficiently unraveled the satin ribbons and laid bare her beautiful breasts.

"But . . ." Portia sucked in a sharp breath as Fredrick teased the tip of her nipple to a hard bud. "Fredrick, halt that. I cannot think clearly when you are touching me."

"We can think clearly later," he breathed, stroking his hands over the pure silk of her skin. "Much, much later."

She made a sound deep in her throat as his fingers skimmed through her lower curls.

"Yes, perhaps you are right," she husked.

"You will discover that I am always right, poppet," he teased. A groan wrenched from his throat as she awkwardly tugged off his cravat and struggled with the buttons of his jacket.

He had not been lying when he had assured Portia he only wished to converse when he invited her to his rooms. At the time his only thought had been confessing what he had discovered from his father and seeking her comfort.

But as she stood there fiercely defending his ability to become a nobleman, he had been overwhelmed with the need to prove to her just how much she had come to mean to him. How much he needed her in his life.

No matter what that life might be.

Adding his efforts to hers, they managed to divest him of his clothing, their movements growing ever more hasty as his mouth shifted to capture her lips in a searing kiss.

His troubled thoughts were drowned as bare skin encountered bare skin. A wave of heat and need and breathless pleasure charged through him and his hand trembled as he sought the dampness between her legs.

He sensed it would take very little to tumble him over the edge and he wanted to make certain that he managed to give Portia pleasure before he was utterly lost.

A moan rumbled deep in his chest as his fingers sank deep into her honey-sweetness. Her desire flamed and within moments her hips were lifting to meet the thrust of his hand.

Pressing his erection against the curve of her hip, Fredrick was unprepared when Portia gave a sharp tug on his hair.

"Wait, Fredrick," she muttered.

Wait? Fredrick swallowed a pained laugh at her innocence. She clearly did not realize that there came a point where it was no longer possible to wait.

"What is it, poppet?" he whispered in a strained voice.

"I want to have you within me."

Fredrick pulled back to regard her with a wary gaze even as his body shuddered with an aching need to bury himself deep within her.

"You are certain, Portia?"

As if to prove her determination, the vixen reached down to grasp his arousal. "I am certain."

"Christ . . ."

His breath was wrenched from his body as she firmly guided him between her legs and he at long last slid into the delectable heat of her body.

It was far from the first time he had made love to a woman, but as his climax clenched his body, Fredrick cried out, shaken by the sheer intensity of his pleasure.

Portia's own release occurred a heartbeat later, and keeping her tightly wrapped in his arms, Fredrick settled at her side to keep from crushing her.

"I love you, poppet," he whispered as he pressed his lips to the soft skin of her temple. "I will always love you."

Surprisingly Portia lifted her hand and pressed her fingers to his mouth, her expression troubled.

"No, Fredrick, do not say such a thing," she warned. "Not now."

Fredrick frowned as his gaze skimmed over her flushed, slightly damp countenance. She looked like a woman who had just been well-satisfied by a man who adored her. So why would she flinch from his confession of love?

"Why not now?" he demanded.

Reaching down she tugged a blanket over their entwined bodies, whether out of modesty or the desire to gain a moment to consider her answer, he could not determine.

"You have enough upon your mind," she at last said, settling her head upon his shoulder. "For now it is important that you consider what you have discovered of your birth and what it means for your future."

Fredrick absently buried his face in her rose scented curls, only vaguely conscious of just how right she felt in his arms as he pondered her stilted words.

"What if I prefer to consider what *you* mean to my future?"

She stiffened, almost as if afraid of his soft words. "Please, Fredrick," she pleaded huskily.

Fredrick frowned, puzzled by her wary reaction. Was she attempting to warn him that she could not return his feelings? Or was she protecting her own heart? Did she fear that he would prove to be as fickle and unreliable as her fiancé?

A glance at her stubborn expression was enough to assure him that whatever her reason for retreat, he was not about to discover the truth. At least not in this moment.

"I will agree to postpone our discussion, poppet," he grudgingly conceded. "But do not believe for a moment that it is at an end."

Her eyes narrowed but she was wise enough not to argue. Instead she smoothly turned the conversation in the one direction certain to distract him.

"What will you do with the information you have discovered?"

Fredrick absently ran his fingers down the bare skin of her arm, taking comfort in the warm feel of her snuggled so close.

"I am not entirely certain."

"Do you wish to be acknowledged as your father's legitimate son?"

He gave a short, strained laugh. "That is the question, is it not?"

She tilted back her head to regard him with undisguised confusion. "I should think that you would be anxious to claim your rightful place."

Fredrick did not blame Portia for her confusion. What gentleman with the smallest measure of sense would not be anxious to shed the ugly embarrassment of being a bastard to become a respected nobleman?

He, however, had long ago discovered that nothing came without a sacrifice. Especially something that would so drastically alter his life. He would make no decisions until he was convinced that he was ready to make that sacrifice.

"Certainly, it is tempting to demand my birthright," he slowly admitted. "After all, my mother deserves to have her reputation restored, even if I am the only one to appreciate the gesture. She . . ." He was startled to discover his voice becoming thick with emotion. "I believe she would have wanted that."

The beautiful blue eyes darkened with a shared understanding. "I think she would have as well."

His arms tightened. "And there is no doubt that becoming a legitimate nobleman as opposed to a bastard would open doors that have long been closed to me."

"They would be more than opened," she retorted with a dry smile. "A handsome, intelligent gentleman who also happens to be fabulously wealthy? Lud, society would trip over themselves in a rush to welcome you. Especially those matrons with debutantes they hope to wed this Season."

Fredrick did not bother to deny her charge. It was not that he considered himself such a fine catch. Quite the opposite. But there was no denying that the wealth he had managed to accumulate over the years would impress even the highest sticklers. Soon enough any memory that he had once been branded a bastard would be conveniently forgotten.

"There is also something very enticing at the thought of knowing Oak Manor could someday be mine," he continued, his lips twisting at the peculiar warmth that entered his heart at the thought of the rambling old manor house. "Rather strange considering I have spent my entire life in London and have no practical experience with the responsibilities that come with farming and tenants and cows."

"You do realize that there are more livestock upon the estate than just cows, do you not?" she teased.

"Ah, that would explain the eggs."

"Yes." The brief amusement drained away as she regarded him with a searching gaze. "Fredrick?" Her hand lifted to press against his chest, as if something upon his countenance troubled her. "Tell me what is upon your mind."

Damnation. She was as annoyingly perceptive as Ian and Raoul, he ruefully acknowledged.

"I have a townhouse, but it has never truly been more than a place to sleep when I am in London. It certainly has never offered a sense of . . . home."

"Oak Manor has been in your family for some time?"

"For centuries, I believe, although I know little of the actual history beyond the fact that a distant Graystone did a favor for one king or another." He gave a small shake of his head. "I suppose it never seemed necessary for my father to reveal the history of his ancestors to his bastard son, and, to be honest, I never questioned him. I always assumed that they were a scurrilous lot who were best left shrouded in mystery."

"We all possess one or two scurrilous ancestors," she muttered, her expression revealing that her thoughts had turned to her father. Hardly surprising. It would be difficult to discover a more scurrilous relative. "They are all part of having a family."

A home.

A family.

The breath was jerked from his lungs. To his mind, Dunnington would always be the father he had never had, and Ian and Raoul his brothers. But what would it be to know he could trace his blood back through the centuries? To possess an absolute sense of belonging at Oak Manor? To be assured that his own son would follow in his footsteps, and his son's son . . .

"Yes, I suppose they would be," he muttered absently, his thoughts consumed with the lingering image of Oak Manor slumbering beneath the spring sunlight.

Able to sense the longing he had never allowed himself to acknowledge, Portia lifted herself to a seated position, careful to keep the blanket tucked around her as she glanced down at him with a faint frown.

"So why do you hesitate, Fredrick?"

He grimaced as the cold air struck his naked skin, and with a sigh he slid from the bed and wrapped a robe about his chilled body.

"Because the decision I make will affect more than just my own life."

"You speak of your brother?"

"I have never truly thought of Simon as my brother, but yes . . ." With a shrug he moved to pour himself a shot of brandy. Speaking of Simon nearly always called for a large amount of spirits. "If I claim my place as the eldest son, then he will have his own inheritance stolen from him. It hardly seems an honorable path to choose."

"It was never his inheritance, Fredrick. It has always been yours," she countered, shocking him with her vehemence. "And if your brother is anything like those buffoons who came to the inn, Oak Manor will be in far better hands if you are to become the next Lord Graystone."

Fredrick slowly smiled, his heart filled with love. "You know, poppet, if I do accept my position as heir . . ." A sharp knock interrupted his words, and with a glance toward the suddenly pale Portia he moved to stand next to the door. "Yes?"

"There is a gent here to see you, Mr. Smith," Molly called through the heavy wood. "A Lord Graystone."

Fredrick's teeth snapped together. Damnation. What the blazes was his father doing here?

Did he think to pressure Fredrick into accepting his place as his legitimate heir? Or worse, had he reconsidered and come to plead for Fredrick to remain the bastard he had named him?

Just for a moment, he considered the notion of refusing to see the elder nobleman.

This entire mess was Lord Graystone's fault, by God. And now that Fredrick was forced to confront the crossroads that lay before him, he was not about to be bullied or cajoled.

Then, grudgingly, common sense came to his rescue.

It was only natural that his father would be anxious to know what decision Fredrick intended to make. It did, after all, affect him deeply.

"Tell him I shall join him in a few moments," he commanded.

"Aye, sir."

Listening to the maid's footsteps echo down the corridor, Fredrick at last turned to meet Portia's worried gaze.

"One of these days, poppet, I intend to sweep you off to a place where no one will dare to interrupt us."

With a faint smile she shoved aside the blankets, and, catching Fredrick off-guard, she rose from the bed and strolled across the floor, completely and gloriously naked.

"One of these days I might just agree to go with you."

It took Fredrick less than a quarter of an hour to attire himself in casual buff breeches, a blue jacket, and a loosely tied cravat that was more comfortable than fashionable.

A glance in the mirror revealed a golden stubble on his chin and shadows beneath his eyes, but with a shrug he left his chambers and forced his feet to carry him down the narrow staircase. What did he care if he appeared like he had slept in the hedgerow?

The only opinion he truly cared about was Portia's, and she had already seen him at his worst.

At the thought of Portia a bittersweet ache clutched at his stomach. Christ, he was a fool not to still be in bed, holding her slender form in his arms. It was only the suspicion that she would continue to evade his discussion of their future together until his own future was settled that had made him reluctantly loosen his hold upon her so that she could flee to her chambers.

Perhaps he could not blame Portia for her wariness.

If he were not yet certain of his desires regarding his father, how could he be certain of his desires regarding her?

His words alone could not convince her that his

love for her was indisputable, without question. And that it was for all eternity.

He would have to deal with his father and then return to Portia and persuade her to share his life.

Whatever that life might bring.

Giving a faint shake of his head, Fredrick reached the bottom of the staircase and was nearly knocked from his feet as his father rushed from the foyer and grasped his hands in a tight grip.

"Fredrick." The older gentleman swallowed heavily as he regarded his son with an oddly frantic gaze. "Thank you for agreeing to meet with me. I feared—"

"I think it would be best if we spoke in private," he interrupted, although his tone was kinder than he had intended. Whatever his feelings toward his father, he was not impervious to the sight of the lined, weary expression upon his countenance. Clearly, Fredrick was not the only one to have spent a sleepless night. Annoyed at his weakness, Fredrick lifted an impatient hand toward the lad who was sweeping the dirt on the flagstones with more enthusiasm than skill. "Tolly, would you request Mrs. Cornell to send a breakfast tray to the back parlor?"

The boy dropped the broom and gave a hasty bow. "Aye, sir. At once, sir."

Tossing Tolly a small coin, Fredrick returned his attention to his father.

"This way."

With an obvious effort Lord Graystone held his tongue as the two of them made their way to the back of the inn and Fredrick motioned him into the private parlor.

It was not until the door had been closed and Fredrick moved to stare blindly out the damp window that he at last cleared his throat and broke the tense silence.

"Forgive me for intruding at such an early hour, Fredrick, but I feared you might leave the neighborhood before I could speak with you."

Fredrick smiled wryly. His father was not wrong to fear that he might bolt. More than once during the long night he had battled the instinctive urge to return to London. Or even to travel to Winchester and join Ian in his drunken revelry.

It was only his fierce need to remain close to Portia that had kept him at the Queen's Arms.

"Is there something in particular you wish to say to me?" he demanded.

"Actually, there is something I wish to give to you."

Reaching beneath his caped driving coat, Lord Graystone pulled out a leather packet and pressed it into Fredrick's reluctant fingers.

"What is this?" Fredrick pulled open the packet to reveal a stack of documents that had been sealed with his father's insignia.

"They are papers . . ." Lord Graystone halted, his expression vulnerable and uncertain beneath Fredrick's steady gaze. "Legal documents that begin the process of publicly acknowledging you as my heir."

Fredrick sucked in a sharp breath, stunned by his father's audacity. "Where the devil did they come from?"

"I called upon my lawyer last eve." The slender fingers trembled as Lord Graystone tugged off his hat and tossed it aside. "Needless to say, he was shocked by my confession. But once I had thoroughly explained the situation, he was quite willing to assist me."

"Why would you do this?" Fredrick waved the

papers in an angry motion. "I have not yet decided whether or not I want to become your heir. I will not be forced—"

"No, Fredrick," his father harshly interrupted. "I spoke with Charles in the strictest confidence, I assure you. He will say nothing unless I give him leave to do so." He reached out his hand, but as Fredrick instinctively flinched from his touch he allowed it to drop with a sad sigh. "I just wanted you to know that my desire to return you to your proper birthright is genuine. I will do whatever you need me to do to make matters right."

That uninvited surge of pity threatened to stir deep in Fredrick's heart as he studied the pale, near fragile features of his father's face.

Damn it all.

Why should he have sympathy for this man? Why should he care that he suddenly appeared far older than his years? Or that he seemed to be suffering untold pain as he tried to make amends for his past?

"And what if my decision is to deny my inheritance and never see you again?" Fredrick forced himself to ask, not willing to acknowledge that his words might be some long festering need to punish the man who had hurt him over and over during the long years of his childhood. "Will you let me go?"

There was a long pause before his father gave a slow, grudging nod of his head.

"If that is your wish, Fredrick, then yes, I will allow you to walk away without a fight."

"You will tell no one that I am your legitimate son or try and make me heir to Oak Manor?"

"If that is your wish." The nobleman pressed his hand to his chest, as if to ease a painful tightness. "But

Fredrick, I will not allow you to leave here without knowing that I love you. I have always loved you. Even when I was distant and cold to you . . ." He gave a shake of his head, his regret nearly palpable in the air. "I loved you so much that it made me ache."

"Father . . ."

Fredrick was not at all certain what he intended to say. Whether he intended to offer the forgiveness that Lord Graystone ached to receive, or whether he intended to turn away the man who had so nearly ruined his life.

In the end, it did not matter as a loud, slurred voice echoed through the inn.

"I know that bastard is here. Tell him to show himself or be branded a coward."

"Good God." With an unsteady movement, Lord Graystone moved to pull open the door to the parlor. "What the devil is he doing here?"

"Who?"

His father rubbed his neck in a gesture of utter weariness. "It is Simon."

Fredrick lifted his brows in surprise. "Simon? I thought he was in London?"

"He was." His father shrugged. "Do not fret, I will send him on his way."

Fredrick took a step forward and laid a restraining hand on his father's arm. "No."

"Fredrick?"

"He came to visit me. I think perhaps it is time that the two of us at last meet."

"Not now, Fredrick," his father urged. "I know Simon well enough to recognize that he is cast to the wind."

"At this hour?"

"Yes."

"Is he often bosky before breakfast?"

"Too often as of late. His friends . . ." The ashen features tightened with disappointment. "No, I cannot blame others for his weakness. I had hoped that he would eventually mature and put aside his childish behavior, but I begin to fear that he shall forever be a ridiculous fop with no consideration beyond the cut of his coat and his own selfish pleasures."

Fredrick wavered as he met his father's troubled gaze. Maybe it would be best to postpone any meeting with his half-brother until his brain was not fogged with spirits. It was bound to be fraught with difficulties without the addition of the younger man being foxed.

But then the sound of his shrill voice once again reverberated through the halls.

"Smith! Where the bloody hell are you?"

Fredrick firmly stepped past his father and headed down the short hall. He was no longer concerned with his father or half-brother.

All that mattered in this moment was ridding Portia of a drunken oaf who was disturbing her inn.

Simon was glaring at the empty staircase when Fredrick stepped beside him. For a moment, he silently studied the brother he had never known. Perhaps he was prejudiced, he silently acknowledged, but to his mind there was no mistaking the obvious signs of dissipation.

At the age of three and twenty Simon's body was already soft with a growing paunch that not even his girdle could disguise. There was also an unhealthy cast to his round face that spoke of endless nights devoted to too much food and too much wine.

Fredrick had known too many gentlemen who were overly fond of the bottle not to recognize the weakness that was etched into Simon's petulant features.

With a shake of his head he moved to stand directly before the swaying gentleman.

"There is no need to screech like a fishmonger, dear brother," he drawled softly. "I am here."

"You." Stiffening in outrage, Simon held up a threatening fist. Or at least a fist that might have been threatening if it were not plump and nearly hidden beneath gem-crusted rings. "Do not call me that."

"Call you what?" Fredrick demanded. "A fishmonger or my brother?"

"Do you dare to mock me?"

Fredrick might have felt a measure of sympathy for the ridiculous dandy if he had not noticed the ugly hatred that twisted his features.

This weak, foolish boy had been given everything. A secure childhood, the love of his parents, the respect of his peers and yet he dared to hate his only brother?

For what?

For having the audacity to simply be born?

Dark, seething anger rushed through Fredrick. By God, he was not about to endure any further insults. Especially not when they came from a pasty-faced drunk who wasted every opportunity that he had been given.

With a deliberate gesture, Fredrick allowed his gaze to roam over Simon's lace-trimmed jacket with a scornful smile.

"I would mock anyone doltish enough to wear a coat in that particular shade of yellow."

A flush stained the heavy cheeks before Simon was thrusting out his weak chin.

"And what would a bastard know of fashion?"

Fredrick's lips twisted. He did not doubt that his own London tailor was far more expensive, not to mention more exclusive, than any Simon could claim.

"I have no need to be a fashion connoisseur to realize you look like a wilted buttercup rather than a dashing gentleman."

"You will regret speaking to me in that manner."

"Will I?"

The short, pudgy gentleman quivered with rage, but wisely he restrained his response to a frustrated glare.

"You are fortunate that I do not intend to teach you a lesson in how to treat your betters with the respect that they deserve," he bluffed.

Fredrick gave a short laugh, suddenly realizing that the three buffoons must have rushed to London to warn Simon that his half-brother was lurking about the neighborhood.

Idiots.

"The same lesson your friends attempted to teach me before they were lying senseless upon the floor?" he demanded.

A small amount of spittle gathered at the corners of Simon's mouth as he struggled to contain his fury.

"Oh yes, they told me of how you attacked them with a gang of ruffians."

"A gang of ruffians?" Fredrick tilted back his head as he laughed with genuine amusement. Clearly the dandies were so embarrassed by their thumping they had to invent wild tales to explain their ignominious defeat. "I could have dealt with those namby-pamby idiots with a gang of schoolgirls. And if you truly desire to share their sad fate, then by all means, let us have a proper mill."

Fredrick made a movement to shed his jacket, not at all surprised when Simon nearly tumbled on his backside as he hastily backed away. He might be all sorts of a fool, but he at least realized that he was bound to lose in any physical battle with Fredrick.

"Why are you here?" he charged, his thick features twisted into a scowl.

"At the Queen's Arms?"

"In this neighborhood."

Fredrick gave a lift of his brows. "That is really none of your concern."

The round countenance hardened with determination. "It is if you think to try and bamboozle money from the old man with some hard-luck story."

"You think I came here for money?"

"Why else would you be here?" Simon scoffed, clearly unaware of the fortune Fredrick had managed to amass. "I will hand you over to the local magistrate if I discover you have been given so much as a quid."

Fredrick gave a slow shake of his head. "You would begrudge your own brother a mere quid?"

"Oak Manor would be a pile of rubbish if not for my mother's dowry, and now that the place is finally making a profit I will not have you sniffing around in the hopes of picking at the crumbs." His eyes glittered with a frustrated greed. "'Tis bad enough that my inheritance is forever being wasted upon those ignorant tenants my father dotes upon. Things will be a good deal different once I am Lord Graystone."

Fredrick's stomach twisted at the utter indifference his brother displayed in speaking of their father's eventual death, and even worse, his lack of concern for those vulnerable tenants who depended upon his goodwill.

"I suppose you intend to use the profits from Oak Manor for your own amusement?"

"Well, I most certainly do not intend to bury myself in this God-forsaken place and play the role of gentleman farmer."

"And yet, someday that is precisely what you will be . . . a gentleman farmer."

Simon offered a mocking laugh at the mere thought. "Not bloody likely."

Fredrick gave a shake of his head. Gads, it was little wonder Lord Graystone was so desperate to coax him into becoming his heir. No doubt he was beginning to realize that the village idiot would be preferable to Simon, he ruefully acknowledged. And Fredrick had to agree.

If this weak-willed, stunningly selfish twit gained command of Oak Manor, it would take only a few months before the coffers were bled dry and the tenants once again suffering.

"Do you know, dear brother, I am beginning to suspect that you are absolutely correct." The words were leaving his lips before Fredrick had even thought them through. "There is no need for you to ever concern yourself with becoming the next baron."

Simon narrowed his beady eyes. "What the hell is that supposed to mean?"

"It means that you have convinced me that Oak Manor will never survive if it is so unfortunate as to fall into your hands."

There was a choked sound from behind him, and

Fredrick slowly turned to meet his father's desperate gaze.

"Fredrick, are you saying . . ."

Drawing in a deep, steadying breath, Fredrick gave a nod of his head.

"Yes, Father, I will accept the inheritance that is mine," he said, his voice astonishingly steady considering he was about to alter his life completely and irrevocably. "I will allow you to name me as your legal heir."

Neither man noticed the pasty-faced Simon as he tottered forward and then, without warning, charged wildly at Fredrick's exposed back.

"Nooooo . . ."

Chapter Twenty

By the time Portia returned to her chambers to replace her damp clothing with a dry gown of dark grey wool, the rain had given way to a sullen fog. Still, as she headed down to the main floor, she discovered that despite the inhospitable weather, many of the guests were eager to be upon their way before the threatening rain returned.

For once, however, Portia did not rush to take command of the guests who were gathered near the foyer. Instead she paused long enough to watch Molly efficiently settling their accounts before she slipped from the inn and into the damp kitchen garden.

She had trained the maids, as well as Mrs. Cornell, on the necessary details in dealing with arriving and departing guests the previous year. The staff took shifts to ensure that there was always someone about to assist the guests if Portia was busy or asleep.

It was not until today, however, that she had willingly given over her duties during the bustling morning hours, and astonishingly, it felt . . . liberating to know that she could depend upon another.

An odd reaction, considering she had always assumed she would be terrified at the mere notion of sharing her control of the inn with anyone.

A tribute to Fredrick Smith, she acknowledged as she paced the damp garden. If he had not arrived at this tiny inn, she would still be clinging to her comfortable routines and refusing to acknowledge that there might be something missing from her life.

Now . . .

She gave a near hysterical laugh. Now everything was different. Everything from the manner in which she awoke in the morning, eager to face the day, to the vivid dreams that kept her warm during the long nights.

She felt alive, as if she had been slumbering for years and had been suddenly revived.

And he claimed to love her.

Violent, astonishing shivers of excitement raced through her body, nearly bringing her to her knees. Edward had once said those words. He had showered her in compliments and promised a life filled with everlasting happiness. But even as a giddy, naïve child, she had not felt those shivers.

In truth, there was nothing about her tepid feelings for her previous fiancé that could compare to those for Fredrick.

Still, the years had taught her a measure of caution. Love, even the everlasting sort of love, was not without its share of peril. There was far less danger in simply ignoring her emotions and remaining tidily settled in her safe and secure routine.

A sharp bark from Puck warned Portia that she was no longer alone, and, turning toward the nearby gate, she watched as Quinn crossed the muddy path to stand at her side.

"Tolly told me that I could find ye here." He tilted his head to the side. "What is troubling you, luv?"

She smiled wryly. Quinn knew her far too well at times. "Why do you think something is troubling me?"

"There were half a dozen guests ready to depart and ye have allowed Molly to see to them all."

"Did she need my assistance?"

"Nay, she has dealt with them just as ye taught her, but it is not like ye to leave yer business to others. So . . ." He lowered his shaggy brows in a warning gesture. "What is troubling ye?"

"Perhaps I have decided that it is time to give others more responsibilities," Portia replied with a shrug. "You have chided me often enough that I should hand over my duties to the staff."

Quinn gave a snort of disbelief. "And I might as well have been talking to me own foot for all the good it has ever done me. So why this morning?"

Wrapping her arms about her waist, Portia turned to regard the weathered but sturdy building that had been the center of her world for so long.

"Do you know, Quinn, after I married Thomas, I never considered a life beyond this place," she said softly. "It seemed quite enough to have found a sanctuary where I would feel safe."

She sensed as Quinn stepped behind her. "Feeling safe can be a fine thing, especially for a lass who has known little of it."

"Yes." She drew in a deep breath, for the first time in years considering the possibility of a different path. "So long as I felt I could rule over my small domain then nothing else mattered."

"Until Mr. Fredrick Smith arrived at the inn?"

"Precisely." An unwitting smile touched her lips. It was a tender, whimsical smile that thoughts of Fredrick Smith always managed to produce. "He has made me remember that I am still a young woman who once had dreams far beyond Wessex and the Queen's Arms."

"Thank the good Lord," Quinn muttered, his hand reaching up to grasp her shoulder in a comforting grasp. "Ye have buried yerself here long enough. It is time that ye remember ye are a gentleman's daughter and yer place is among society, not drudging like a common servant."

She laughed at his fierce words. "You well know that I do not drudge, Quinn," she chided, heaving a deep sigh as she turned to meet his hopeful gaze. "And I have yet to decide if I wish to return to society."

"Ye needn't fear they won't accept ye, luv. Yer birth demands yer place among the upper orders."

Her expression hardened with remembered betrayal. "You cannot have forgotten how easily they turned their backs upon me, Quinn? It was only Thomas who cared enough to rescue me from utter destitution."

Quinn gave a click of his tongue. "Ye are not the same innocent maid as ye were then, luv."

Portia slowly nodded her head. "That is true enough."

"Ye have grown into a lady who need never again fear others and their opinions," Quinn continued to press. "Ye are more than strong enough to take on society and bend it to yer will."

"A fine notion," Portia said with a rueful chuckle.

"You know it is true, luv."

She shivered again, rubbing her hands up and down her arms. "At the moment all I know for certain is that I suddenly feel restless and not at all myself. It is a disturbing sensation that I blame entirely upon Mr. Smith."

Quinn frowned as he glanced about the empty garden. "Where is the boy? I have not clapped eyes upon him the entire morning."

Portia's heart gave a sharp squeeze. Damn Lord Graystone and his black heart. As far as she was concerned, he should be rotting in hell, not standing in her inn causing his son even more pain and grief.

"His father arrived a short time ago wanting to speak with him," she said, her clipped voice revealing her displeasure. "I presume that they are closeted in one of the parlors."

"Ah." Quinn scratched the stubble on his chin. "I thought I recognized the gent who came charging into the stable yard as if the devil were upon his heels. He seemed quite disturbed."

"As well he should," Portia retorted, her entire body rigid with disgust. "He destroyed Fredrick's life and now seeks to gain his favor."

Quinn gave a startled cough, his gaze straying toward the stables where Lord Graystone's magnificent stallion was enjoying his morning oats.

"Did he now? Odd. I always thought Lord Graystone to be a decent sort of chap."

Portia rolled her eyes at Quinn's astonishment. The groom too often judged others by the care that they gave to their horses.

"It just proves that appearances are too often deceitful," she muttered.

"Lordy, lass, you are too young and beautiful to be

so cynical. I remember the days . . ." Quinn's words broke off as the sound of breaking furniture echoed from the inn. "What the devil?"

Portia did not pause to wonder what could be causing such a disturbance. Her only thought was discovering the trouble and bringing it to a swift end.

"Go fetch Spenser," she commanded as she hiked her skirts and dashed toward the nearby door.

"Aye, and me shotgun," Quinn muttered as he turned toward the gate.

"No."

"Just for protection."

"No. No guns," she warned, knowing that Quinn was quite capable of shooting anyone he thought a threat. "Lord have mercy," she muttered as she continued through the door and into the kitchen.

Not surprisingly, Mrs. Cornell was stationed in the center of the room, her grim expression ensuring that her staff did not so much as hesitate in their duties despite the shouts and curses that filled the air. The forbidding woman would stand as guardian while the inn burned down around her.

At last reaching the foyer, Portia skidded to a halt as she watched Fredrick pull back his arm and with one efficient swing knock the short, rather plump gentleman onto the flagstones.

With a low groan the unknown man rolled onto his side and rubbed his battered chin, whimpering curses and ridiculous threats beneath his breath as Lord Graystone moved to kneel beside him.

With a frown of concern, Portia placed her hand on Fredrick's stiff arm.

"What has happened?" she demanded softly.

With a wry smile, Fredrick covered her hand with his slender fingers.

"I fear that I have once again been involved in an ugly brawl at your fine establishment, poppet."

Her gaze briefly flicked over the crumbled gentleman before returning to Fredrick's beautiful countenance. There was a flush on his cheekbones and a hectic glitter in his eyes that made her heart skip a beat.

This was more than just another skirmish.

"Yes, well . . . you do seem to make a habit of it," she said carefully. "Who is he?"

"My brother, Simon."

"Oh." She thinned her lips, just barely squashing the childish urge to give the pudgy backside a firm kick. "What is he doing here?"

Fredrick shrugged. "I believe he came to remind me that Lord Graystone owes nothing to a mere bastard. Imagine his surprise when he discovered that he is no longer the heir apparent."

She sucked in a startled breath at his bland confession that he intended to take his rightful place. She had not been certain what he intended to do with his future. And in truth it did not matter to her.

The love that she felt for this man had nothing to do with his position in the world, or any estate he might or might not inherit.

She loved him because he was quite simply the finest man ever born.

A rather wonderful reason to love someone, she acknowledged as a warm glow flowed through her veins.

"I see." A frown touched her brows as her gaze caught sight of his bloody knuckles. "Are you harmed?"

His hand lifted to trace over her cheek, the grey eyes darkening with a familiar heat.

"Nothing that a kiss will not cure," he murmured, his husky voice bringing a blush to her cheeks.

"Fredrick, people are watching us," she chided, vividly aware of Lord Graystone's curious gaze.

Indifferent to his father and even his brother, who had rolled onto his back to glare at the two of them with a feral hatred, Fredrick wrapped his arm around her shoulders.

"You do know that once you are my wife I will no longer give a damn who might watch me kissing you?" he warned.

Her heart skipped several beats before rushing into a frantic pace.

Wife.

Good heavens, she had never thought to wed again. Certainly not to a nobleman who was destined to thrust her back into the society she had once fled. But just meeting that steady silver gaze was enough to melt away any doubts that might have lingered.

Of course, she had no intention of making matters too easy. She rather enjoyed the thought of being seduced into wedded bliss. So long as it were Fredrick doing the seducing.

"I have not yet agreed to wed you, you know," she teased with a small smile.

"Not yet, but you will." His fingers shifted to outline her lips. "I may not be the most intelligent or most skilled gentleman, but I am by far the most patient. There is not a goal that I have desired that I did not eventually conquer with enough hard work and patience."

She lifted her brows at his deliberately arrogant tone. "I am now a goal to be conquered?"

His expression softened with a love that Portia could feel to her very soul.

"One that I desire above all others, poppet," he husked. "Whatever my future might hold, the only thing that truly matters is whether or not you are standing at my side."

"But your future does hold Oak Manor in it as well, does it not?" Lord Graystone demanded anxiously, still kneeling beside his youngest son.

Fredrick gave a slow nod. "In the distant future. The very distant future, I hope." Turning back to Portia, Fredrick missed the profound relief that eased the older gentleman's lean countenance. Instead, he gently cupped Portia's face in his hands. "Does that trouble you, my love?"

"Not nearly so much as I thought it would," she admitted with a smile. "You know, Fredrick, I have loved this inn and the independence that it has offered me, but in some ways it has too easily allowed me to hide from the world."

"You were a mere child when you were betrayed by everyone you depended upon, Portia. No one would blame you for wishing to find a safe haven to heal your wounds."

She heaved a faint sigh. "My wounds healed some time ago, it was my fear that kept me here."

"Actually, I prefer to think of it as fate," he breathed, his head lowering to brush a light kiss over her lips. "Just as the rainstorm was fate. We were destined to meet, poppet."

She shuddered as a swift, potent desire clutched at her body. Mercy, just having Fredrick near was enough to make her tremble with need.

"Do you truly believe that?"

"With all my heart." He folded her tightly in his arms, his lips moving against her temple. "Say you will marry me."

Breathing deeply of his delicious scent, Portia lifted her arms and wrapped them about his neck.

"Have you not had enough excitement for one day, Fredrick Smith?"

With a low chuckle he abruptly scooped her off her feet and brazenly headed for the nearby stairs, utterly indifferent to the gathering crowd that watched them with wide eyes.

"Actually, Portia Walker, I predict that the excitement is just about to begin . . ."

Epilogue

The wedding took place two weeks later in the formal drawing room of Oak Manor.

It was a simple ceremony with only a handful of guests, but any of those fortunate enough to receive an invitation could not help but be moved by the unmistakable love that shimmered between the bride and groom.

Even the cynical Ian Breckford could not deny a secret pang of envy as he watched Fredrick bend his head to place a tender kiss upon Portia's willing lips.

It was not the typical jealousy at seeing a beautiful woman in the arms of another man. That was familiar enough. He was an undoubted connoisseur of the fairer sex, and Portia Walker was a fine specimen. Instead, it was a disturbing ache that had more to do with the unfettered joy that glowed upon Fredrick's countenance.

Bloody hell. It was enough to make the most jaded of men believe in love.

Giving a small snort of disgust at his maudlin

thoughts, Ian swiftly made his way to the wide balcony and lit a slender cheroot.

A bit of fresh air and some fine tobacco, and he would be back to his usual sardonic self.

Leaning against the balustrade, Ian listened to the approaching footsteps, not at all surprised that Raoul had followed him from the house. The elegant gentleman had been hovering about him like a mother hen since he had arrived in Wessex the previous evening.

Not that Ian disliked Raoul's fussing nearly as much as he pretended to. There was something comforting in Fredrick's gentle teasing and Raoul's incessant chiding.

Without the two of them . . .

Instinctively, Ian reached beneath his jacket to retrieve his silver flask filled with the finest whiskey to be bought outside Ireland.

Prepared for Raoul's stern warning at drinking at such an early hour, Ian was caught off-guard when the handsome actor instead leaned against the railing and regarded the sun-drenched garden with a thoughtful expression.

"It was a beautiful service."

Ian gave a bark of laughter. "Yes, so long as you ignored Lady Graystone, who sobbed and moaned loud enough to rattle the windows, and that drunken jackass Simon who passed out in the midst of the ceremony."

Raoul shrugged, ignoring the giggling maids who leaned out the kitchen door in an obvious attempt to capture their attention.

"Lady Graystone is intelligent enough to keep her opinions to herself, and I sense that beneath all his bluster, Simon is relieved to hand over his responsibilities as baron to Fredrick." The thin lips twisted with distaste at the overdressed peacock. "Now he need do nothing more than prance about London and be an embarrassment to the Graystone name."

"Poor Fredrick." Ian tossed aside his cheroot and took a swig of the whiskey. "Saddled not only with a wife, but a family who will no doubt be nothing more than blood-sucking leeches. That is not even to mention his tedious business ventures and now an aging inn with a staff of reformed rapscallions."

"He does not appear concerned." Raoul's smile softened. "In fact, I have never seen a gentleman appear quite so content with his lot in life."

Ian deliberately refused to dwell upon his friend's obvious satisfaction with his new life.

"Ah, well, better him than me."

"And what of you, Ian?"

"What the devil is that supposed to mean?"

"Were you not determined to travel to Surrey and discover your own father's secret?"

Ian took another draw on the flask. Clearly the expected lecture was in the offing.

"I will get there." He grimaced at the mere thought of encountering his arrogant, disdainful father. "Eventually."

He sensed Raoul move, then the warmth of his hand as it gently squeezed his shoulder.

"Ian, there is nothing to force you to seek out your father. You are content with your life as it is. Return to London and enjoy it."

Ian gave a sharp, bitter laugh. As much as he disliked the thought of stepping beneath his father's roof it was preferable to returning to London and the cold, empty rooms that awaited him there.

It was nothing short of pathetic.

"Oh yes, quite content," he muttered.

Raoul's fingers tightened, his expression concerned. "Ian?"

"What of you, Raoul?" Smoothly stepping from his friend's grasp before he confessed the haunting restlessness that would not leave him in peace, Ian managed a bland smile. "When do you begin your own search for the truth?"

Raoul arched one pale, perfect brow. "I cannot leave London until the end of the theatre season."

"Ah, yes. The irresistible Romeo who slays the ladies of the *ton* with his honey voice and come-hither glance."

"Actually, it has been years since I played Romeo," Raoul retorted dryly. "My current role is that of King Lear."

Ian shrugged, knowing full well what role his friend was performing. He had attended the production on opening night and on a half a dozen evenings after that. Like most of London, he remained in awe of Raoul's extraordinary skill.

Not that he would ever admit his admiration, he wryly acknowledged. Not without the threat of a hot poker.

"No doubt it is your own royal blood that makes you such a convincing king," he drawled.

Raoul shrugged aside the noble blood that ran in his veins. "Hardly royal."

"No?" Ian lifted his flask in a mocking toast. "Unlike Fredrick, our lives are still shrouded in mystery. Who is to say what we might discover?"

* * *

The sleek black carriage pulled away from Oak Manor at a sharp pace, urged on by Fredrick's muttered command to flee the lingering guests with all possible speed.

He had waited a fortnight for this moment, he acknowledged, as he reached out to tug Portia firmly onto his lap. Or perhaps a lifetime.

Gazing down at the beauty of her upturned countenance, Fredrick found his breath tangling in his throat. When he had first seen this woman standing in the shadowed foyer of the inn he had known that she was different from any other woman he had ever encountered.

Wonderfully and spectacularly different.

"Alone at last," he murmured, his hand absently stroking her shoulder that was left bare by the daring satin bodice. No one had been more shocked than him when Portia had arrived at Oak Manor attired in an ivory gown that was designed to set a man's blood on fire. He had been slowly burning throughout the brief ceremony and wedding breakfast his father had insisted upon. "Thank God."

She offered a slow, tantalizing smile that did nothing to ease the tightness of his groin.

"You do realize that I still have no notion of where we are going?"

He growled low in his throat as his gaze drifted to the ripe swell of her breasts blatantly revealed by the low cut of her neckline.

"I promised myself that I would whisk you somewhere that we would not be interrupted once I had you as my wife." His frustration was thick in his voice. Although Portia had willingly allowed Mrs. Cornell to take command of the inn, she remained living in the attic until they were wed. Which, of course, had meant that they could not find a moment alone. "I want to walk through the gardens without concern that some disaster is looming in the kitchens, and hold you in my arms with the knowledge that there will be no one knocking upon your door at some inconvenient moment."

Her breath caught at his soft caresses. "And where would this magical place be located?"

"My father has offered us the use of his hunting lodge. He promises that there are no more than a handful of servants who are all quite discreet and not one neighbor within twenty miles at this time of year."

"Good heavens, we shall be terribly isolated." She gave a tormenting bat of her lashes. "Whatever shall we do with ourselves?"

He shivered, his fingers continuing to explore the silken heat of her skin.

"Do you desire a description, or would you prefer a demonstration?"

She stilled as she gazed deep into his eyes, her expression sending a wave of golden pleasure through his body.

"I love you, Fredrick Colstone," she said softly, her hand lifting to touch his cheek as he gave a small jerk of surprise. "What is the matter?"

He gave a rueful shake of his head. Even after two weeks he found it difficult to think of himself as anything other than Fredrick Smith. And no doubt a part of him would always be the shy, determined young lad that Dunnington had molded into a man.

"That name still seems . . . odd," he admitted.

"You shall have to accustom yourself to it," she warned, her eyes darkening with concern. "By the time we return from our honeymoon everyone will know that you are Lord Graystone's legitimate heir."

He gave a pretend shudder. "Then perhaps we should remain hidden at the hunting lodge."

"Oh, no," she swiftly countered, her expression resolute. "No more hiding. From now on we will confront the world with our chins held high."

Fredrick wrapped her more tightly in his arms, his heart overwhelmed with the love she had stirred to life. He had come to Wessex to dig through the past and instead discovered his future.

"An easy task, so long as I have you at my side," he whispered, his head lowering toward her waiting lips.

"At your side is where I shall always be, my wicked baron."

And for a taste of something different
Please turn the page for a sneak peek of
Alexandra Ivy's
EMBRACE THE DARKNESS,
now on sale at bookstores everywhere!

The auction house on the outskirts of Chicago didn't look like a cesspit.

Behind the iron fences the elegant brick structure sprawled over the landscape with a visible arrogance. The rooms were large with vaulted ceilings that boasted beautiful murals and elegant chandeliers. And on the advice of a professional, they had been decorated with thick ivory carpets, glossy dark paneling, and hand-carved furniture.

The overall atmosphere was the sort of quiet hush that only money could buy. Lots and lots of money.

It was the sort of swanky place that should be peddling rare paintings, priceless jewels, and museum artifacts.

Instead it was no more than a flesh market. A sewer where demons were sold like so much meat.

There was nothing pleasant about the slave trade. Not even when the trade was demons rather than humans. It was a sordid business that attracted every decadent, demented slimeball in the country.

They came for all sorts of pathetic reasons.

Those who bought demons for mercenaries or bodyguards. Those who lusted after the more exotic sex slaves. Those who believed the blood of demons could bring them magic or eternal life. And those who purchased demons to be released into their private lands and hunted like wild animals.

The bidders were men and women without conscience or morals. Only enough money to sate their twisted pleasures.

And at the top of the dung heap was the owner of the auction house, Evor. He was one of the lesser trolls who made his living upon the misery of others with a smile on his face.

Someday Shay intended to kill Evor.

Unfortunately it would not be today.

Or rather tonight.

Attired in ridiculous harem pants and a tiny sequined top that revealed far more than it concealed, she paced the cramped cell behind the auction rooms. Her long raven-black hair had been pulled to a braid that hung nearly to her waist. Better to reveal her slanted golden eyes, the delicate cast to her features, and the bronzed skin that marked her as something other than human.

Less than two months before, she had been a slave to a coven of witches who intended to bring Armageddon to all demons. At the time she had thought anything was preferable to being their toady as she helplessly watched their evil plotting.

Hell, it's tough to top genocide.

It was only when she had been forced back to the power of Evor that she understood that death was not always the worst fate.

The grave was really nothing compared to what waited for her beyond the door.

Without thinking Shay struck out with her foot, sending the lone table sailing through the air to crash against the iron bars with astonishing force.

From behind her came a heavy sigh that had her spinning to regard the small gargoyle hiding behind a chair in the far corner.

Levet wasn't much of a gargoyle.

Oh, he had the traditional grotesque features. Thick grey skin, reptilian eyes, horns, and cloven hoofs. He even possessed a long tail he polished and pampered with great pride. Unfortunately, despite his frightening appearance, he was barely three feet tall. And worse, as far as he was concerned, he possessed a pair of delicate, gossamer wings that would have been more fitting on a sprite or a fairy than a lethal creature of the dark.

To add to his humiliation, his powers were unpredictable under the best of circumstances, and his courage more often than not missing in action.

It was little wonder he had been voted out of the Gargoyle Guild and forced to fend for himself. They claimed he was an embarrassment to the entire community, and not one had stepped forward when he had been captured and made a slave by Evor.

Shay had taken the pathetic creature under her protection the moment she had been forced back to the auction house. Not only because she had a regrettable tendency to leap to the defense of anyone weaker than herself, but also because she knew that it aggravated Evor to have his favorite whipping boy taken away.

The troll might hold the curse that bound her, but

if he pressed her far enough she would be willing to kill him, even if it meant an end to her own life.

"*Cherie,* did the table do something I did not see, or were you just attempting to teach it a lesson?" Levet demanded, his voice low and laced with a lilting French accent.

Not at all the sort of thing to improve his status among the gargoyles.

Shay smiled wryly. "I was imagining it was Evor."

"Strange, they do not greatly resemble one another."

"I have a good imagination."

"Ah." He gave a ridiculous wiggle of his thick brow. "In that case, I do not suppose you are imagining I'm Brad Pitt?"

Shay smiled wryly. "I'm good, but not that good, gargoyle."

"A pity."

Her brief amusement faded. "No, the pity is that it was a table and not Evor smashed to pieces."

"A delightful notion, but a mere dream." The gray eyes slowly narrowed. "Unless you intend to be stupid?"

Shay deliberately widened her eyes. "Who me?"

"*Mon dieu,*" the demon growled. "You intend to fight him."

"I can't fight him. Not as long as I remain held by the curse."

"As if that has ever halted you." Levet tossed aside the pillow to reveal his tail furiously twitching about his hoofs. A sure sign of distress. "You can't kill him, but that never keeps you from trying to kick his fat troll ass."

"It passes the time."

"And leaves you screaming in agony for hours." He

abruptly shuddered. "*Cherie,* I can't bear seeing you like that. Not again. It's insane to battle against fate."

Shay grimaced. As part of the curse, she was punished for any attempt to harm her master. The searing pain that gripped her body could leave her gasping on the ground or even passed out for hours. Lately, however, the punishment had become so brutal she feared that each time she pressed her luck it might be the last time.

She gave a tug on her braid. A gesture that revealed the frustration that smoldered just below the surface.

"You think I should just give in? Accept defeat?"

"What choice do you have? What choice do any of us have? Not all the fighting in the world can change the fact we belong—" Levet rubbed one of his stunted horns. "How do you say . . . lock, stock, and jug . . ."

"Barrel."

"Ah, yes, barrel to Evor. And that he can do whatever he wants with us."

Shay gritted her teeth as she turned to glare at the iron bars that held her captive. "Shit. I hate this. I hate Evor. I hate this cell. I hate those pathetic demons up there waiting to bid on me. I almost wish I had let those witches bring an end to all of us."

"You will get no arguments from me, my sweet Shay," Levet agreed with a sigh.

Shay closed her eyes. Dammit. She hadn't meant the words. She was tired and frustrated, but she was no coward. Just the fact she had survived the past century proved that.

"No," she muttered. "No."

Levet gave a flap of his wings. "And why not? We are trapped here like rats in a maze until we can be sold to the highest bidder. What could be worse?"

Shay smiled without humor. "Allowing fate to win."

"What?"

"So far, fate or destiny or fortune or whatever the hell you want to call it has done nothing but crap on us," Shay growled. "I'm not going to just give in and allow it to thumb its nose at me as I slink into my grave. One of these days I'm going to have an opportunity to spit fate in its face. That's what keeps me fighting."

There was a long silence before the gargoyle moved to stand near enough so that he could rub his head on her leg. It was an unconscious gesture. A quest for reassurance that he would rather die than admit.

"I am uncertain I have ever heard such an inelegant speech, but I believe you. If anyone can get away from Evor, it's you."

Absently, Shay shifted the horn poking into her thigh. "I'll come back for you, Levet, that much I promise."

"Well, well, isn't this touching?" Abruptly appearing before the iron bars of the cell, Evor smiled to reveal his pointed teeth. "Beauty and the Beast."

With a smooth motion, Shay had pressed Levet behind her and turned to regard her captor.

A sneer touched her face as the troll stepped into the cell and locked the door behind him. Evor easily passed for human. An incredibly ugly human.

He was a short, pudgy man with a round, squishy face and heavy jowls. His hair was little more than tufts of stray strands that he carefully combed over his head. And his small black eyes had a tendency to flash red when he was annoyed.

The eyes he hid behind black-framed glasses.

The thickly fleshed body he hid behind an obscenely expensive tailored suit.

Only the teeth marked him for the troll he was.

That and his utter lack of morals.

"Screw you, Evor," Shay muttered.

The nasty smile widened. "You wish."

Shay narrowed her gaze. The troll had been trying to get into her bed since gaining control of her curse. The only thing that had halted him from forcing her had been the knowledge she was quite willing to kill the both of them to prevent such a horror.

"I'll walk through the fires of hell before I let you touch me."

Fury rippled over the pudgy features before the oily smile returned. "Someday, my beauty, you'll be happy to be spread beneath me. We all have our breaking point. Eventually you'll reach yours."

"Not in this lifetime."

His tongue flicked out in an obscene motion. "So proud. So powerful. I shall enjoy pouring my seed into you. But not yet. There is still money to be made from you. And money always comes first." Lifting his hand he revealed the heavy iron shackles that he had hid behind his body. "Will you put these on or do I need to call for the boys?"

Shay crossed her arms over her chest. She might only be half Shalott, but she possessed all of the strength and agility of her ancestors. They were not the favorite assassins of the demon world without cause.

"After all these years you still think those goons can hurt me?"

"Oh, I have no intention of having them hurt you. I should hate to have you damaged before the bidding." Very deliberately his gaze shifted to where

Levet was cowering behind her legs. "I merely wish them to encourage your good behavior."

The gargoyle gave a low moan. "Shay?"

Shit.

She battled back the instinctive urge to punch the pointed teeth down Evor's throat. It would only put her on the ground in agony. Worse, it would leave Levet at the mercy of the hulking mountain trolls Evor used as protection.

They would take great delight in torturing the poor gargoyle.

As far as she knew their only pleasure was giving pain to others.

Freaking trolls.

"Fine." She held out her arms with a furious scowl.

"A wise choice." Keeping a wary eye on her, Evor pressed the shackles over her wrists and locked them shut. "I knew you would understand the situation once it was properly explained."

Shay hissed as the iron bit into her skin. She could feel her power draining and her flesh chafing beneath the iron. It was her one certain Achilles' heel.

"All I understand is that someday I'm going to kill you."

He gave a jerk on the chain that draped between the shackles. "Behave yourself, bitch, or your little friend pays the consequences. Got it?"

Shay battled back the sickness that clutched at her stomach.

Once again she was going to be placed on the stage and sold to the highest bidder. She would be utterly at the mercy of some stranger who could do whatever he pleased with her.

And there wasn't a damn thing she could do to stop it.

"Yeah, I got it. Let's just get this over with."

Evor opened his mouth as if to make a smart-ass comment, only to snap the fish lips shut when he caught sight of her expression. Obviously he could sense she was close to the edge.

Which only proved that he wasn't quite as stupid as he looked.

In silence they left the cell and climbed the narrow stairs to the back of the stage. Evor paused only long enough to lock her shackles to a pole anchored in the floor before moving toward the closed curtains and slipping through them to face the crowd.

Alone in the darkness, Shay sucked in a deep breath and tried to ignore the rumblings of the crowd just beyond the curtain.

Even without being able to see the potential bidders she could feel the presence of the gathering demons and humans. She could smell the stench of their sweat. Feel the smoldering impatience. Taste the depraved lust in the air.

She abruptly frowned. There was something else. Something that was subtly laced through it all.

A sense of decaying evil that sent a chill of horror over her skin.

It was vague. As if the being was not truly in the room in full form. More like a looming, intangible presence. An echo of foulness that made her stomach clench in fear.

Swallowing back her instinctive scream she closed her eyes and forced herself to take a deep, steadying breath. In the distance she heard Evor loudly clear his throat to command attention.

"And now, ladies and gentlemen, demons and fairies, dead and undead . . . it is time for our main attraction. Our *pièce de résistance*. An item so rare, so extraordinary that only those who possess a golden token may remain," he dramatically announced. "The rest may retire to our reception rooms where you will be offered your choice of refreshment."

Despite the lingering certainty that she had just been brushed by some malignant gaze, Shay managed a disgusted grimace. Evor was always a pompous blowhard. Tonight, however, he put even the cheesiest ringmaster to shame.

"Gather close, my friends," Evor commanded as the dregs of the bidders were forced to leave the room. To be granted a golden token, a person or demon had to carry at least $50,000 in cash on them. The slave trade rarely accepted checks or credit cards. Go figure. "You will not wish to miss your first glimpse of my precious treasure. Do not fear, I have ensured that she is properly chained. She will offer no danger. No danger beyond her perilous charm. She will not rip your heart from your chest, but I do not promise she will not steal it with her beauty."

"Shut your mouth and open the curtain," a voice growled.

"You are impatient?" Evor demanded, his tone edged with anger. He didn't like his well-practiced act interrupted.

"I don't have all night. Get on with it."

"Ah, a premature . . . bidder, a pity. Let us hope for your sake that it is not an affliction that taints your performance in other areas," Evor sneered, pausing to allow the roar of coarse laughter to fade. "Now where was I? Oh, yes. My prize. My most beloved slave.

Demons and ghouls, allow me to introduce you to Lady Shay . . . the last Shalott to walk our world."

With a dramatic motion the curtain disappeared in a puff of smoke, leaving Shay exposed to the near two dozen men and demons.

Deliberately she lowered her gaze as she heard the gasps echo through the room. It was humiliating enough to smell their rabid hunger. She didn't need to see it written on their faces.

"Is this a trick?" a dark voice demanded in disbelief. Hardly surprising. As far as Shay knew, she truly was the last Shalott remaining in the world.

"No trick, no illusion."

"As if I'd take your word for it, troll. I want proof."

"Proof? Very well." There was a momentary pause as Evor searched the crowd. "You there, come forward," he commanded.

Shay tensed as she felt the cold chill that warned her it was a vampire approaching. Her blood was more precious than gold to the undead. An aphrodisiac that they would kill to procure.

With her attention focused on the tall, gaunt vampire, Shay barely noticed when Evor grabbed her arm and used a knife to slice through the skin of her forearm. Hissing softly, the vamp leaned downward to lick the welling blood. His entire body shivered as he lifted his head to regard her with stark hunger.

"There is human blood, but she is genuine Shalott," he rasped.

With a smooth motion, Evor had placed his pudgy form between the vamp and Shay, shooing the predator away with a wave of his hand. Reluctantly, the undead creature left the stage, no doubt sensing the impending riot if he were to give in to his impulse to sink his teeth into her and drain her dry.

Evor waited until the stage was cleared before moving to stand behind his podium. He grasped his gavel and lifted it over his head. Ridiculous twit.

"Satisfied? Good." Evor smacked the gavel onto the podium. "The bidding starts at fifty thousand dollars. Remember, gentlemen, cash only."

"Fifty-five thouand."

"Sixty thousand."

"Sixty-one thousand."

Shay's gaze once again dropped to her feet as the voices called out their bids. Soon enough she would be forced to confront her new master. She didn't want to watch as they wrangled over her like a pack of dogs slavering over a juicy bone.

"One hundred thousand dollars," a shrill voice shouted from the back of the room.

A sly smile touched Evor's thin lips. "A most generous bid, my good sir. Anyone else? No? Going once . . . Going twice . . ."

"Five hundred thousand."

A sharp silence filled the room. Without even realizing what she was doing, Shay lifted her head to stare into the crowd jamming the auction floor.

There was something about that silky dark voice. Something . . . familiar.

"Step forward," Evor demanded, his eyes shimmering red. "Step forward and offer your name."

There was a stir as the crowd parted. From the back shadows, a tall, elegant form glided forward.

A hushed whisper spread through the room as the muted light revealed the hauntingly beautiful face and satin curtain of silver hair that fell down his back.

It took only a glance to realize he was a vampire.

No human could so closely resemble an angel that had fallen from heaven. And fallen recently. Or move with such liquid grace. Or cause the demons to back away in wary fear.

Shay's breath caught in her throat. Not at his stunning beauty, or powerful presence, or even the flamboyant velvet cloak that shrouded his slender form.

It was the fact that she knew this vampire.

He had been at her side when they had battled the coven of witches weeks ago. And, more importantly, he had been at her side when she had saved his life.

And now he was here bidding on her like she was no more than a piece of property.

Damn his rotten soul to hell.

Viper had been in the world for centuries. He had witnessed the rise and fall of empires. He had seduced the most beautiful women in the world. He had taken the blood of kings, czars, and pharaohs.

He had even changed the course of history at times.

Now he was sated, jaded, and magnificently bored.

He no longer struggled to broaden his power base. He didn't involve himself in battles with demons or humans. He didn't form alliances or interfere in politics.

His only concern was ensuring the safety of his clan and keeping his business profitable enough to allow him the luxurious lifestyle he had grown accustomed to.

But somehow the Shalott demon had managed the impossible.

She had managed to linger in his thoughts long after she had disappeared.

For weeks she had haunted his memories and even invaded his dreams. She was like a thorn that had lodged beneath his skin and refused to be removed.

A realization that he wasn't sure pleased or annoyed him as he had scoured the streets of Chicago in search of the woman.

Glancing at his latest acquisition, he didn't have to wonder if Shay was pleased or annoyed. Even in the muted light it was obvious her glorious golden eyes were flashing with fury.

Clearly she failed to fully appreciate the honor he was bestowing upon her.

His lips twitched with amusement as he was returning his attention to the troll standing behind the podium.

"You may call me Viper," he informed the lesser demon with cold dislike.

The red eyes briefly widened. It was a name that inspired fear throughout Chicago. "Of course. Forgive me for not recognizing you, sir. You . . . ah . . . " He swallowed heavily. "You have the cash upon you?"

With a motion too swift for most eyes, Viper had reached beneath his cloak and tossed a large packet onto the stairs leading to the stage.

"I do."

With a flourish, Evor banged the gavel on the podium. "Sold."

There was a low hiss from the Shalott, but before Viper could give her the proper attention, there was the sound of low cursing and a small, wiry human was pushing his way through the crowd.

"Wait. The bidding is not yet closed," the stranger charged.

Viper narrowed his gaze. He might have laughed at

the absurdity of the scrawny man attempting to bully his way through towering demons, but he didn't miss the scent of sour desperation that clouded about him, or the blackness that darkened his soul.

This was a man who had been touched by evil.

The troll, Evor, frowned as he regarded the man, clearly unimpressed by the cheap, baggy suit and secondhand shoes. "You wish to continue?"

"Yes."

"You have the cash upon you?"

The man swiped a hand over the sweat clinging to his bald head. "Not upon me, but I can easily have it to you—"

"Cash and carry only," Evor growled, his gavel once again hitting the podium.

"No. I will get you the money."

"The bidding is over."

"Wait. You must wait. I—"

"Get out before I have you thrown out."

"No." Without warning the man was racing up the stairs with a knife in his hand. "The demon is mine."

As quick as the man was, Viper had already moved to place himself between the stranger and his Shalott. The man gave a low growl before turning and stalking toward the troll. Easier prey than a determined vampire. But then again, most things were.

"Now, now. There is no need to become unreasonable." Evor hastily gestured toward the hulking bodyguards at the edge of the stage. "You knew the rules when you came."

With lumbering motions the mountain trolls moved forward, their hulking size and skin as thick as tree bark making them nearly impossible to kill.

Viper folded his arms over his chest. His attention

remained on the demented human, but he couldn't deny that he was disturbingly aware of the Shalott behind him.

It was in the sweet scent of her blood. The warmth of her skin. And the shimmering energy that swirled about her.

His entire body reacted to her proximity. It was as if he had stepped close to a smoldering fire that offered a promise of heat he had long forgotten.

Unfortunately, his attention was forced to remain on the seeming madman waving the knife in a threatening motion. There was something decidedly strange in the human's determination. A stark panic that was out of place.

He would be an idiot to underestimate the danger of the sudden standoff.

"Stay back," the small man squeaked.

The trolls continued forward until Viper lifted a slender hand. "I would not come close to the knife. It is hexed."

"Hexed?" Evor's face hardened with fury. "Magical artifacts are forbidden. The punishment is death."

"You think a pathetic troll and his goons can frighten me?" The intruder lifted his knife to point it directly at Evor's face. "I came here for the Shalott and I'm not leaving without her. I'll kill you all if I have to."

"You may try," Viper drawled.

The man spun about to confront him. "I have no fight with you, vampire."

"You are attempting to steal my demon."

"I'll pay you. Whatever you want."

"Whatever?" Viper flicked a brow upward. "A generous if rather foolhardy bargain."

"What is your price?"

Viper pretended to consider a moment. "Nothing you could offer."

That sour desperation thickened in the air. "How do you know? My employer is very rich . . . very powerful."

Ah. Now they were getting somewhere.

"Employer. So you are merely an envoy?"

The man nodded, his eyes burning like coals in their sunken sockets. "Yes."

"And your employer will no doubt be quite disappointed to learn you have failed in your task to gain the Shalott?"

The pale skin became a sickly grey. Viper suspected that the sense of darkness he could detect was directly related to the mysterious employer.

"He will kill me."

"Then you are in quite a quandary, my friend, because I have no intention of allowing you to leave the room with my prize."

"What do you care?"

Viper's smile was cold. "Surely you must know that Shalott blood is an aphrodisiac for vampires? It is a most rare treat that has been denied us for too long."

"You intend to drain her?"

"That is none of your concern. She is mine. Bought and paid for."

He heard a strangled curse from behind him, along with the rattle of chains. His beauty was clearly unhappy with his response and anxious to prove her displeasure by ripping him limb from limb.

A tiny flicker of excitement raced through him.

Blood of the saints, but he liked his women dangerous.